Agatha Christie

Five Little Pigs

HARPER

HARPER

An imprint of HarperCollins*Publishers*
77–85 Fulham Palace Road,
Hammersmith, London W6 8JB
www.harpercollins.co.uk

This *Agatha Christie Signature Edition* published 2007
1

First published in Great Britain by
Collins 1943

ISBN 13: 978 0 00 793694 6

Typeset by Palimpsest Book Production Limited,
Grangemouth, Stirlingshire

Printed and bound in Great Britain by
Clays Ltd, St Ives plc

Five Little Pigs

Agatha Christie is known throughout the world as the Queen of Crime. Her books have sold over a billion copies in English with another billion in 100 foreign languages. She is the most widely published author of all time and in any language, outsold only by the Bible and Shakespeare. She is the author of 80 crime novels and short story collections, 19 plays, and six novels written under the name of Mary Westmacott.

Agatha Christie's first novel, *The Mysterious Affair at Styles*, was written towards the end of the First World War, in which she served as a VAD. In it she created Hercule Poirot, the little Belgian detective who was destined to become the most popular detective in crime fiction since Sherlock Holmes. It was eventually published by The Bodley Head in 1920.

In 1926, after averaging a book a year, Agatha Christie wrote her masterpiece. *The Murder of Roger Ackroyd* was the first of her books to be published by Collins and marked the beginning of an author-publisher relationship which lasted for 50 years and well over 70 books. *The Murder of Roger Ackroyd* was also the first of Agatha Christie's books to be dramatised – under the name *Alibi* – and to have a successful run in London's West End. *The Mousetrap*, her most famous play of all, opened in 1952 and is the longest-running play in history.

Agatha Christie was made a Dame in 1971. She died in 1976, since when a number of books have been published posthumously: the bestselling novel *Sleeping Murder* appeared later that year, followed by her autobiography and the short story collections *Miss Marple's Final Cases*, *Problem at Pollensa Bay* and *While the Light Lasts*. In 1998 *Black Coffee* was the first of her plays to be novelised by another author, Charles Osborne.

The Agatha Christie Collection

The Man In The Brown Suit
The Secret of Chimneys
The Seven Dials Mystery
The Mysterious Mr Quin
The Sittaford Mystery
The Hound of Death
The Listerdale Mystery
Why Didn't They Ask Evans?
Parker Pyne Investigates
Murder Is Easy
And Then There Were None
Towards Zero
Death Comes as the End
Sparkling Cyanide
Crooked House
They Came to Baghdad
Destination Unknown
Spider's Web *
The Unexpected Guest *
Ordeal by Innocence
The Pale Horse
Endless Night
Passenger To Frankfurt
Problem at Pollensa Bay
While the Light Lasts

Poirot

The Mysterious Affair at Styles
The Murder on the Links
Poirot Investigates
The Murder of Roger Ackroyd
The Big Four
The Mystery of the Blue Train
Black Coffee *
Peril at End House
Lord Edgware Dies
Murder on the Orient Express
Three-Act Tragedy
Death in the Clouds
The ABC Murders
Murder in Mesopotamia
Cards on the Table
Murder in the Mews
Dumb Witness
Death on the Nile
Appointment With Death
Hercule Poirot's Christmas
Sad Cypress
One, Two, Buckle My Shoe
Evil Under the Sun
Five Little Pigs

* novelised by Charles Osborne

The Hollow
The Labours of Hercules
Taken at the Flood
Mrs McGinty's Dead
After the Funeral
Hickory Dickory Dock
Dead Man's Folly
Cat Among the Pigeons
The Adventure of the Christmas Pudding
The Clocks
Third Girl
Hallowe'en Party
Elephants Can Remember
Poirot's Early Cases
Curtain: Poirot's Last Case

Marple

The Murder at the Vicarage
The Thirteen Problems
The Body in the Library
The Moving Finger
A Murder is Announced
They Do It With Mirrors
A Pocket Full of Rye
The 4.50 from Paddington
The Mirror Crack'd from Side to Side
A Caribbean Mystery
At Bertram's Hotel
Nemesis
Sleeping Murder
Miss Marple's Final Cases

Tommy & Tuppence

The Secret Adversary
Partners in Crime
N or M?
By the Pricking of My Thumbs
Postern of Fate

Published as Mary Westmacott

Giant's Bread
Unfinished Portrait
Absent in the Spring
The Rose and the Yew Tree
A Daughter's a Daughter
The Burden

Memoirs

An Autobiography
Come, Tell Me How You Live

Play Collections

The Mousetrap and Selected Plays
Witness for the Prosecution and
  Selected Plays

To Stephen Glanville

Contents

Book II

Book III

Introduction

Carla Lemarchant

Hercule Poirot looked with interest and appreciation at the young woman who was being ushered into the room.

There had been nothing distinctive in the letter she had written. It had been a mere request for an appointment, with no hint of what lay behind that request. It had been brief and business-like. Only the firmness of the handwriting had indicated that Carla Lemarchant was a young woman.

And now here she was in the flesh – a tall, slender young woman in the early twenties. The kind of young woman that one definitely looked at twice. Her clothes were good, an expensive well-cut coat and skirt and luxurious furs. Her head was well poised on her shoulders, she had a square brow, a sensitively cut nose and a determined chin. She looked very much alive. It was her aliveness, more than her beauty, which struck the predominant note.

Agatha Christie

Before her entrance, Hercule Poirot had been feeling old – now he felt rejuvenated – alive – keen!

As he came forward to greet her, he was aware of her dark grey eyes studying him attentively. She was very earnest in that scrutiny.

She sat down and accepted the cigarette that he offered her. After it was lit she sat for a minute or two smoking, still looking at him with that earnest, thoughtful gaze.

Poirot said gently:

'Yes, it has to be decided, does it not?'

She started. 'I beg your pardon?'

Her voice was attractive, with a faint, agreeable huskiness in it.

'You are making up your mind, are you not, whether I am a mere mountebank, or the man you need?'

She smiled. She said:

'Well, yes – something of that kind. You see, M. Poirot, you – you don't look exactly the way I pictured you.'

'And I am old, am I not? Older than you imagined?'

'Yes, that too.' She hesitated. 'I'm being frank, you see. I want – I've got to have – the best.'

'Rest assured,' said Hercule Poirot. 'I *am* the best!'

Carla said: 'You're not modest . . . All the same, I'm inclined to take you at your word.'

Poirot said placidly:

'One does not, you know, employ merely the muscles. I do not need to bend and measure the footprints and pick up the cigarette ends and examine the bent blades of grass. It is enough for me to sit back in my chair and *think*. It is this' – he tapped his egg-shaped head – '*this* that functions!'

'I know,' said Carla Lemarchant. 'That's why I've come to you. I want you, you see, to do something fantastic!'

'That,' said Hercule Poirot, 'promises well!'

He looked at her in encouragement.

Carla Lemarchant drew a deep breath.

'My name,' she said, 'isn't Carla. It's Caroline. The same as my mother's. I was called after her.' She paused. 'And though I've always gone by the name of Lemarchant – my real name is Crale.'

Hercule Poirot's forehead creased a moment perplexedly. He murmured: 'Crale – I seem to remember . . .'

She said:

'My father was a painter – rather a well-known painter. Some people say he was a great painter. *I* think he was.'

Hercule Poirot said: 'Amyas Crale?'

'Yes.' She paused, then she went on: 'And my mother, Caroline Crale, was tried for murdering him!'

'Aha,' said Hercule Poirot. 'I remember now – but

only vaguely. I was abroad at the time. It was a long time ago.'

'Sixteen years,' said the girl.

Her face was very white now and her eyes two burning lights.

She said:

'Do you understand? *She was tried and convicted . . .* She wasn't hanged because they felt that there were extenuating circumstances – so the sentence was commuted to penal servitude for life. But she died only a year after the trial. You see? It's all over – done – finished with . . .'

Poirot said quietly: 'And so?'

The girl called Carla Lemarchant pressed her hands together. She spoke slowly and haltingly but with an odd, pointed emphasis.

She said:

'You've got to understand – exactly – where I come in. I was five years old at the time it – happened. Too young to know anything about it. I remember my mother and my father, of course, and I remember leaving home suddenly – being taken to the country. I remember the pigs and a nice fat farmer's wife – and everybody being very kind – and I remember, quite clearly, the funny way they used to look at me – everybody – a sort of furtive look. I knew, of course, children do, that there was something wrong – but I didn't know what.

'And then I went on a ship – it was exciting – it went on for days, and then I was in Canada and Uncle Simon met me, and I lived in Montreal with him and with Aunt Louise, and when I asked about Mummy and Daddy they said they'd be coming soon. And then – and then I think I forgot – only I sort of knew that they were dead without remembering any one actually telling me so. Because by that time, you see, I didn't think about them any more. I was very hapy, you know. Uncle Simon and Aunt Louise were sweet to me, and I went to school and had a lot of friends, and I'd quite forgotten that I'd ever had another name, not Lemarchant. Aunt Louise, you see, told me that that was my name in Canada and that seemed quite sensible to me at the time – it was just my Canadian name – but as I say I forgot in the end that I'd ever had any other.'

She flung up her defiant chin. She said:

'Look at me. You'd say – wouldn't you? if you met me: "There goes a girl who's got nothing to worry about!" I'm well off, I've got splendid health, I'm sufficiently good to look at, I can enjoy life. At twenty, there wasn't a girl anywhere I'd have changed places with.

'But already, you know, I'd begun to ask questions. About my own mother and father. Who they were and what they did? I'd have been bound to find out in the end –

'As it was, they told me the truth. When I was twenty-one. They had to then, because for one thing I came into my own money. And then, you see, there was the letter. The letter my mother left for me when she died.'

Her expression changed, dimmed. Her eyes were no longer two burning points, they were dark dim pools. She said:

'That's when I learnt the truth. That my mother had been convicted of murder. It was – rather horrible.'

She paused.

'There's something else I must tell you. I was engaged to be married. They said we must wait – that we couldn't be married until I was twenty-one. When I knew, I understood why.'

Poirot stirred and spoke for the first time. He said:

'And what was your fiancé's reaction?'

'John? John didn't care. He said it made no difference – not to him. He and I were John and Carla – and the past didn't matter.'

She leaned forward.

'We're still engaged. But all the same, you know, it *does* matter. It matters to me. And it matters to John too . . . It isn't the past that matters to us – it's the future.' She clenched her hands. 'We want children, you see. We both want children. And we don't want to watch our children growing up and be afraid.'

Poirot said:

'Do you not realize that amongst every one's ancestors there has been violence and evil?'

'You don't understand. That's so, of course. But then, one doesn't usually know about it. We do. It's very near to us. And sometimes – I've seen John just look at me. Such a quick glance – just a flash. Supposing we were married and we'd quarrelled – and I saw him look at me and – and *wonder*?'

Hercule Poirot said: 'How was your father killed?'

Carla's voice came clear and firm.

'He was poisoned.'

Hercule Poirot said: 'I see.'

There was a silence.

Then the girl said in a calm, matter-of-fact voice:

'Thank goodness you're sensible. You see that it does matter – and what it involves. You don't try and patch it up and trot out consoling phrases.'

'I understand very well,' said Poirot. 'What I do not understand is what you want of *me*?'

Carla Lemarchant said simply:

'I want to marry John! And I mean to marry John! And I want to have at least two girls and two boys. And you're going to make that possible!'

'You mean – you want me to talk to your fiancé? Ah

no, it is idiocy what I say there! It is something quite different that you are suggesting. Tell me what is in your mind.'

'Listen, M. Poirot. Get this – and get it clearly. I'm hiring you to investigate a case of murder.'

'Do you mean –?'

'Yes, I do mean. A case of murder is a case of murder whether it happened yesterday or sixteen years ago.'

'But my dear young lady –'

'Wait, M. Poirot. You haven't got it all yet. There's a very important point.'

'Yes?'

'My mother was innocent,' said Carla Lemarchant.

Hercule Poirot rubbed his nose. He murmured:

'Well, naturally – I comprehend that –'

'It isn't sentiment. There's her letter. She left it for me before she died. It was to be given to me when I was twenty-one. She left it for that one reason – that I should be quite sure. That's all that was in it. That she hadn't done it – that she was innocent – that I could be sure of that always.'

Hercule Poirot looked thoughtfully at the young vital face staring so earnestly at him. He said slowly:

'*Tout de même –*'

Carla smiled.

'No, mother wasn't like that! You're thinking that it might be a lie – a sentimental lie?' She leaned forward earnestly. 'Listen, M. Poirot, there are some things that children know quite well. I can remember my mother – a patchy remembrance, of course, but I remember quite well the *sort* of person she was. She didn't tell lies – kind lies. If a thing was going to hurt she always told you so. Dentists, or thorns in your finger – all that sort of thing. Truth was a – a natural impulse to her. I wasn't, I don't think, especially fond of her – but I trusted her. I *still* trust her! If she says she didn't kill my father then she didn't kill him! She wasn't the sort of person who would solemnly write down a lie when she knew she was dying.'

Slowly, almost reluctantly, Hercule Poirot bowed his head.

Carla went on.

'That's why it's all right for *me* marrying John. *I* know it's all right. *But he doesn't.* He feels that naturally I would think my mother was innocent. It's got to be cleared up, M. Poirot. And *you're* going to do it!'

Hercule Poirot said slowly:

'Granted that what you say is true, mademoiselle, sixteen years have gone by!'

Carla Lemarchant said: 'Oh! of course it's going to be *difficult*! Nobody but *you* could do it!'

Hercule Poirot's eyes twinkled slightly. He said:

'You give me the best butter – *hein?*'

17

Agatha Christie

Carla said:

'I've heard about you. The things you've done. The *way* you have done them. It's psychology that interests you, isn't it? Well, that doesn't change with time. The tangible things are gone – the cigarette-end and the footprints and the bent blades of grass. You can't look for those any more. But you can go over all the facts of the case, and perhaps talk to the people who were there at the time – they're all alive still – and then – and then, as you said just now, you can lie back in your chair and *think. And you'll know what really happened . . .*'

Hercule Poirot rose to his feet. One hand caressed his moustache. He said:

'Mademoiselle, I am honoured! I will justify your faith in me. I will investigate your case of murder. I will search back into the events of sixteen years ago and I will find out the truth.'

Carla got up. Her eyes were shining. But she only said:

'Good.'

Hercule Poirot shook an eloquent forefinger.

'One little moment. I have said I will find out the truth. I do not, you understand, have the bias. I do not accept your assurance of your mother's innocence. If she was guilty – *eh bien*, what then?'

Carla's proud head went back. She said:

'I'm her daughter. I want the *truth*!'

Hercule Poirot said:

'*En avant*, then. Though it is not that, that I should say. On the contrary. *En arrière* . . .'

Book I

Chapter 1

Counsel for the Defence

'Do I remember the Crale case?' asked Sir Montague Depleach. 'Certainly I do. Remember it very well. Most attractive woman. But unbalanced, of course. No self-control.'

He glanced sideways at Poirot.

'What makes you ask me about it?'

'I am interested.'

'Not really tactful of you, my dear man,' said Depleach, showing his teeth in his sudden famous 'wolf's smile', which had been reputed to have such a terrifying effect upon witnesses. 'Not one of my successes, you know. I didn't get her off.'

'I know that.'

Sir Montague shrugged his shoulders. He said:

'Of course I hadn't quite as much experience then as I have now. All the same I think I did all that could humanly be done. One can't do much without *co-operation*. We *did*

23

get it commuted to penal servitude. Provocation, you know. Lots of respectable wives and mothers got up a petition. There was a lot of sympathy for her.'

He leaned back stretching out his long legs. His face took on a judicial, appraising look.

'If she'd shot him, you know, or even knifed him – I'd have gone all out for manslaughter. But poison – no, you can't play tricks with that. It's tricky – very tricky.'

'What was the defence?' asked Hercule Poirot.

He knew because he had already read the newspaper files, but he saw no harm in playing the complete ignorant to Sir Montague.

'Oh, suicide. Only thing you *could* go for. But it didn't go down well. Crale simply wasn't that kind of man! You never met him, I suppose? No? Well, he was a great blustering, vivid sort of chap. Great womanizer, beer drinker – all the rest of it. Went in for the lusts of the flesh and enjoyed them. You can't persuade a jury that a man like that is going to sit down and quietly do away with himself. It just doesn't fit. No, I was afraid I was up against a losing proposition from the first. And she wouldn't play up! I knew we'd lost as soon as she went into the box. No fight in her at all. But there it is – if you *don't* put your client into the box, the jury draw their own conclusions.'

Poirot said:

'Is that what you meant when you said just now that one cannot do much without co-operation?'

'Absolutely, my dear fellow. We're not magicians, you know. Half the battle is the impression the accused makes on the jury. I've known juries time and again bring in verdicts dead against the judge's summing up. "'E did it, all right" – that's the point of view. Or "*He* never did a thing like that – don't tell me!" Caroline Crale didn't even *try* to put up a fight.'

'Why was that?'

Sir Montague shrugged his shoulders.

'Don't ask me. Of course, she was fond of the fellow. Broke her all up when she came to and realized what she'd done. Don't believe she ever rallied from the shock.'

'So in your opinion she was guilty?'

Depleach looked rather startled. He said:

'Er – well, I thought we were taking that for granted.'

'Did she ever admit to you that she was guilty?'

Depleach looked shocked.

'Of course not – of course not. We have our code, you know. Innocence is always – er – assumed. If you're so interested it's a pity you can't get hold of old Mayhew. Mayhews were the solicitors who briefed me. Old Mayhew could have told you more than I can. But there – he's joined the great majority. There's young George Mayhew, of course, but he was only a boy at the time. It's a long time ago, you know.'

'Yes, I know. It is fortunate for me that you remember so much. You have a remarkable memory.'

Depleach looked pleased. He murmured:

'Oh well, one remembers the main headings, you know. Especially when it's a capital charge. And, of course, the Crale case got a lot of publicity from the press. Lot of sex interest and all that. The girl in the case was pretty striking. Hard-boiled piece of goods, I thought.'

'You will forgive me if I seem too insistent,' said Poirot, 'but I repeat once more, you had no doubt of Caroline Crale's guilt?'

Depleach shrugged his shoulders. He said:

'Frankly – as man to man – I don't think there's much doubt about it. Oh yes, she did it all right.'

'What was the evidence against her?'

'Very damning indeed. First of all there was motive. She and Crale had led a kind of cat and dog life for years – interminable rows. He was always getting mixed up with some woman or other. Couldn't help it. He was that kind of man. She stood it pretty well on the whole. Made allowances for him on the score of temperament – and the man really was a first-class painter, you know. His stuff's gone up enormously in price – enormously. Don't care for that style of painting myself – ugly forceful stuff, but it's *good* – no doubt of that.

'Well, as I say, there had been trouble about women from time to time. Mrs Crale wasn't the meek kind who suffers in silence. There were rows all right. But he always came back to her in the end. These affairs of his blew over. But this final affair was rather different. It was a girl, you see – and quite a young girl. She was only twenty.

'Elsa Greer, that was her name. She was the only daughter of some Yorkshire manufacturer. She'd got money and determination, and she knew what she wanted. What she wanted was Amyas Crale. She got him to paint her – he didn't paint regular Society portraits, "Mrs Blinkety Blank in satin and pearls", but he painted figures. I don't know that most women would have cared to be painted by him – he didn't spare them! But he painted the Greer girl, and he ended by falling for her good and proper. He was getting on for forty, you know, and he'd been married a good many years. He was just ripe for making a fool of himself over some chit of a girl. Elsa Greer was the girl. He was crazy about her, and his idea was to get a divorce from his wife and marry Elsa.

'Caroline Crale wasn't standing for that. She threatened him. She was overheard by two people to say that if he didn't give the girl up she'd kill him. And she meant it all right! The day before it happened, they'd been having tea with a neighbour. He was by way of dabbling in herbs and home-brewed medicines. Amongst his patent brews was one of coniine – spotted hemlock. There was some talk about it and its deadly properties.

'The next day he noticed that half the contents of the bottle had gone. Got the wind up about it. They found an almost empty bottle of it in Mrs Crale's room, hidden away at the bottom of a drawer.'

Hercule Poirot moved uncomfortably. He said:

'Somebody else might have put it there.'

'Oh! She admitted to the police she'd taken it. Very unwise, of course, but she didn't have a solicitor to advise her at that stage. When they asked her about it, she admitted quite frankly that she had taken it.'

'For what reason?'

'She made out that she'd taken it with the idea of doing herself in. She couldn't explain how the bottle came to be empty – nor how it was that there were only her fingerprints on it. That part of it was pretty damaging. She contended, you see, that Amyas Crale had committed suicide. But if he'd taken the coniine from the bottle she'd hidden in her room, *his* fingerprints would have been on the bottle as well as hers.'

'It was given him in beer, was it not?'

'Yes. She got out the bottle from the refrigerator and took it down herself to where he was painting in the garden. She poured it out and gave it to him and watched him drink it. Every one went up to lunch and left him – he often didn't come in to meals. Afterwards she and the governess found him there dead. Her story was that the beer *she* gave him was all right. Our theory was that he suddenly felt so worried and remorseful that he slipped the poison in himself. All poppycock – he wasn't that kind of man! And the fingerprint evidence was the most damning of all.'

'They found her fingerprints on the bottle?'

'No, they didn't – they found only *his* – and they were phoney ones. She was alone with the body, you see, while the governess went to call up a doctor. And what she must have done was to wipe the bottle and glass and then press his fingers on them. She wanted to pretend, you see, that she'd never even handled the stuff. Well, that didn't work. Old Rudolph, who was prosecuting, had a lot of fun with that – proved quite definitely by demonstration in court that a man *couldn't* hold a bottle with his fingers in that position! Of course *we* did our best to prove that he *could* – that his hands would take up a contorted attitude when he was dying – but frankly our stuff wasn't very convincing.'

Hercule Poirot said:

29

'The coniine in the bottle must have been put there before she took it down to the garden.'

'There was no coniine in the bottle at all. Only in the glass.'

He paused – his large handsome face suddenly altered – he turned his head sharply. 'Hallo,' he said. 'Now then, Poirot, *what are you driving at?*'

Poirot said:

'*If* Caroline Crale was innocent, how did that coniine get into the beer? The defence said at the time that Amyas Crale himself put it there. But you say to me that that was in the highest degree unlikely – and for my part I agree with you. He was not that kind of man. Then, if Caroline Crale did not do it, *someone else did.*'

Depleach said with almost a splutter:

'Oh, damn it all, man, you can't flog a dead horse. It's all over and done with years ago. Of course she did it. You'd know that well enough if you'd seen her at the time. It was written all over her! I even fancy that the verdict was a relief to her. She wasn't frightened. No nerves at all. Just wanted to get through the trial and have it over. A very brave woman, really . . .'

'And yet,' said Hercule Poirot, 'when she died she left a letter to be given to her daughter in which she swore solemnly that she was innocent.'

'I dare say she did,' said Sir Montague Depleach. 'You or I would have done the same in her place.'

'Her daughter says she was not that kind of woman.'

'The daughter says – pah! What does *she* know about it? My dear Poirot, the daughter was a mere infant at the time of the trial. What was she – four – five? They changed her name and sent her out of England somewhere to some relatives. What can *she* know or remember?'

'Children know people very well sometimes.'

'Maybe they do. But that doesn't follow in this case. Naturally the girl wants to believe her mother didn't do it. Let her believe it. It doesn't do any harm.'

'But unfortunately she demands proof.'

'Proof that Caroline Crale didn't kill her husband?'

'Yes.'

'Well,' said Depleach. 'She won't get it.'

'You think not?'

The famous K.C. looked thoughtfully at his companion.

'I've always thought you were an honest man, Poirot. What are you doing? Trying to make money by playing on a girl's natural affections?'

'You do not know the girl. She is an unusual girl. A girl of great force of character.'

'Yes, I should imagine the daughter of Amyas and Caroline Crale might be that. What does she want?'

'She wants the truth.'

Agatha Christie

'Hm – I'm afraid she'll find the truth unpalatable. Honestly, Poirot, I don't think there's any doubt about it. She killed him.'

'You will forgive me, my friend, but I must satisfy myself on that point.'

'Well, I don't know what more you can do. You can read up the newspaper accounts of the trial. Humphrey Rudolph appeared for the Crown. He's dead – let me see, who was his junior? Young Fogg, I think. Yes, Fogg. You can have a chat with him. And then there are the people who were there at the time. Don't suppose they'll enjoy your butting in and raking the whole thing up, but I dare say you'll get what you want out of them. You're a plausible devil.'

'Ah yes, the people concerned. That is very important. You remember, perhaps, who they were?'

Depleach considered.

'Let me see – it's a long time ago. There were only five people who were really in it, so to speak – I'm not counting the servants – a couple of faithful old things, scared-looking creatures – they didn't know anything about anything. No one could suspect them.'

'There are five people, you say. Tell me about them.'

'Well, there was Philip Blake. He was Crale's greatest friend – had known him all his life. He was staying in the house at the time. *He's* alive. I see him now and again on the links. Lives at St George's Hill. Stockbroker. Plays the markets and gets away with it. Successful man, running to fat a bit.'

'Yes. And who next?'

'Then there was Blake's elder brother. Country squire – stay at home sort of chap.'

A jingle ran through Poirot's head. He repressed it. He must *not* always be thinking of nursery rhymes. It seemed an obsession with him lately. And yet the jingle persisted.

'*This little pig went to market, this little pig stayed at home . . .*'

He murmured:

'He stayed at home – yes?'

'He's the fellow I was telling you about – messed about with drugs – and herbs – bit of a chemist. His hobby. What was his name now? Literary sort of name – I've got it. Meredith. Meredith Blake. Don't know whether he's alive or not.'

'And who next?'

'Next? Well, there's the cause of all the trouble. The girl in the case. Elsa Greer.'

'*This little pig ate roast beef,*' murmured Poirot.

Depleach stared at him.

'They've fed her meat all right,' he said. 'She's been a go-getter. She's had three husbands since then. In and out of the divorce court as easy as you please. And every time she makes a change, it's for the better. Lady Dittisham – that's who she is now. Open any *Tatler* and you're sure to find her.'

'And the other two?'

'There was the governess woman. I don't remember her name. Nice capable woman. Thompson – Jones – something like that. And there was the child. Caroline Crale's half-sister. She must have been about fifteen. She's made rather a name for herself. Digs up things and goes trekking to the back of beyond. Warren – that's her name. Angela Warren. Rather an alarming young woman nowadays. I met her the other day.'

'She is not, then, the little pig who cried Wee Wee Wee . . . ?'

Sir Montague Depleach looked at him rather oddly. He said drily:

'She's had something to cry Wee-Wee about in her life! She's disfigured, you know. Got a bad scar down one side of her face. She – Oh well, you'll hear all about it, I dare say.'

Poirot stood up. He said:

'I thank you. You have been very kind. If Mrs Crale did *not* kill her husband –'

Depleach interrupted him:

'But she did, old boy, she did. Take my word for it.'

Poirot continued without taking any notice of the interruption.

'Then it seems logical to suppose that one of these five people must have done so.'

'One of them *could* have done it, I suppose,' said Depleach, doubtfully. 'But I don't see why any of them *should*. No reason at all! In fact, I'm quite sure none of them *did* do it. Do get this bee out of your bonnet, old boy!'

But Hercule Poirot only smiled and shook his head.

Chapter 2

Counsel for the Prosecution

'Guilty as Hell,' said Mr Fogg succinctly.

Hercule Poirot looked meditatively at the thin clear-cut face of the barrister.

Quentin Fogg, K.C. was a very different type from Montague Depleach. Depleach had force, magnetism, an over-bearing and slightly bullying personality. He got his effects by a rapid and dramatic change of manner. Handsome, urbane, charming one minute – then an almost magical transformation, lips back, snarling smile – out for your blood.

Quentin Fogg was thin, pale, singularly lacking in what is called personality. His questions were quiet and unemotional – but steadily persistent. If Depleach was like a rapier, Fogg was like an auger. He bored steadily. He had never reached spectacular fame, but he was known as a first-class man on law. He usually won his cases.

Hercule Poirot eyed him meditatively.

'So that,' he said, 'was how it struck you?'

Fogg nodded. He said:

'You should have seen her in the box. Old Humpie Rudolph (he was leading, you know) simply made mincemeat of her. Mincemeat!'

He paused and then said unexpectedly:

'On the whole, you know, it was rather too much of a good thing.'

'I am not sure,' said Hercule Poirot, 'that I quite understand you?'

Fogg drew his delicately marked brows together. His sensitive hand stroked his bare upper lip. He said:

'How shall I put it? It's a very English point of view. "Shooting the sitting bird" describes it best. Is that intelligible to you?'

'It is, as you say, a very English point of view, but I think I understand you. In the Central Criminal Court, as on the playing fields of Eton, and in the hunting country, the Englishman likes the victim to have a sporting chance.'

'That's it, exactly. Well, in this case, the accused *didn't* have a chance. Humpie Rudolph did as he liked with her. It started with her examination by Depleach. She stood up there, you know – as docile as a little girl at a party, answering Depleach's questions with the answers she'd learnt off by heart. Quite docile, word perfect – and absolutely unconvincing! She'd been told what to say and she said it. It wasn't Depleach's fault. That old mountebank played his part perfectly – but in any scene that needs two actors, one alone can't carry it. She didn't play up to him. It made the worst possible effect on the jury. And then old Humpie got up. I expect you've seen him? He's a great loss. Hitching his gown up, swaying back on his feet – and then – straight off the mark!

'As I tell you, he made mincemeat of her! Led up to this and that – and she fell into the pitfall every time. He got her to admit the absurdities of her own statements, he got her to contradict herself, she floundered in deeper and deeper. And then he wound up with his usual stuff. Very compelling – very convinced: "I suggest to you, Mrs Crale, that this story of yours about stealing coniine in order to commit suicide is a tissue of falsehood. I suggest that you took it in order to administer it to your husband who was about to leave you for another woman, and that you *did* deliberately administer it to him." And she looked at him – such a pretty creature – graceful, delicate – and she said: "Oh, no – no, I didn't." It was the flattest thing you ever heard – the most unconvincing. I saw old Depleach squirm in his seat. He knew it was all up them.'

Fogg paused a minute – then he went on:

'And yet – I don't know. In some ways it was

the cleverest thing she could have done! It appealed to chivalry – to that queer chivalry closely allied to blood sports which makes most foreigners think us such almighty humbugs! The jury felt – the whole court felt – that she hadn't got a chance. She couldn't even fight for herself. She certainly couldn't put up any kind of a show against a great big clever brute like old Humpie. That weak, unconvincing: "*Oh no – no, I didn't,*" it was pathetic – simply pathetic. She was done for!

'Yes, in a way, it was the best thing she could have done. The jury were only out just over half an hour. They brought her in: Guilty with a recommendation to mercy.

'Actually, you know, she made a good contrast to the other woman in the case. The girl. The jury were unsympathetic to *her* from the start. She never turned a hair. Very good looking, hard-boiled, modern. To the women in the court she stood for a type – type of the home-breaker. Homes weren't safe when girls like that were wandering abroad. Girls damn full of sex and contemptuous of the rights of wives and mothers. She didn't spare herself, I will say. She was honest. Admirably honest. She'd fallen in love with Amyas Crale and he with her, and she'd no scruples at all about taking him away from his wife and child.

'I admired her in a way. She had guts. Depleach put

in some nasty stuff in cross-examination and she stood up well to it. But the court was unsympathetic. And the judge didn't like her. Old Avis, it was. Been a bit of a rip himself when young – but he's very hot on morality when he's presiding in his robes. His summing up against Caroline Crale was mildness itself. He couldn't deny the facts but he threw out pretty strong hints as to provocation and all that.'

Hercule Poirot asked:

'He did not support the suicide theory of the defence?'

Fogg shook his head.

'*That* never really had a leg to stand upon. Mind you, I don't say Depleach didn't do his best with it. He was magnificent. He painted a most moving picture of a great-hearted, pleasure-loving, temperamental man, suddenly overtaken by a passion for a lovely young girl, conscience stricken, yet unable to resist. Then his recoil, his disgust with himself, his remorse for the way he was treating his wife and child and his sudden decision to end it all! The honourable way out. I can tell you, it was a most moving performance; Depleach's voice brought tears to your eyes. You saw the poor wretch torn by his passions and his essential decency. The effect was terrific. Only – when it was all over – and the spell was broken, you couldn't quite square that mythical figure with Amyas Crale. Everybody knew too much about Crale. He wasn't at all that kind of man. And Depleach hadn't been able to get hold of any evidence to show that he was. I should say Crale came as near as possible to being a man without even a rudimentary conscience. He was a ruthless, selfish, good-tempered happy egoist. Any ethics he had would have applied to painting. He wouldn't, I'm convinced, have painted a sloppy, bad picture – no matter what the inducement. But for the rest, he was a full-blooded man and he loved life – he had a zest for it. Suicide? Not he!'

'Not, perhaps, a very good defence to have chosen?'

Fogg shrugged his thin shoulders. He said:

'What else was there? Couldn't sit back and plead that there was no case for the jury – that the prosecution had got to prove their case against the accused. There was a great deal too much proof. She'd handled the poison – admitted pinching it, in fact. There was means, motive, opportunity – everything.'

'One might have attempted to show that these things were artificially arranged?'

Fog said bluntly:

'She admitted most of them. And, in any case, it's too far-fetched. You're implying, I presume, that somebody else murdered him and fixed it up to look as though she had done it.'

'You think that quite untenable?'

Fogg said slowly:

'I'm afraid I do. You're suggesting the mysterious X. Where do we look for him?'

Poirot said:

'Obviously in a close circle. There were five people, were there not, who *could* have been concerned?'

'Five? Let me see. There was the old duffer who messed about with his herb brewing. A dangerous hobby – but an amiable creature. Vague sort of person. Don't see him as X. There was the girl – she might have polished off Caroline, but certainly not Amyas. Then there was the stockbroker – Crale's best friend. That's popular in detective stories, but I don't believe in it in real life. There's no one else – oh yes, the kid sister, but one doesn't seriously consider her. That's four.'

Hercule Poirot said:

'You forget the governess.'

'Yes, that's true. Wretched people, governesses, one never does remember them. I do recall her dimly though. Middle-aged, plain, competent. I suppose a psychologist would say that she had a guilty passion for Crale and therefore killed him. The repressed spinster! It's no good – I just don't believe it. As far as my dim remembrance goes she wasn't the neurotic type.'

'It is a long time ago.'

'Fifteen or sixteen years, I suppose. Yes, quite that. You can't expect my memories of the case to be very acute.'

Hercule Poirot said:

'But on the contrary, you remember it amazingly well. That astounds me. You can see it, can you not? When you talk the picture is there before your eyes.'

Fogg said slowly:

'Yes, you're right – I do see it – quite plainly.'

Poirot said:

'It would interest me, my friend, very much, if you would tell me *why*?'

'Why?' Fogg considered the question. His thin intellectual face was alert – interested. 'Yes, now *why*?'

Poirot asked:

'*What* do you see so plainly? The witnesses? The counsel? The judge? The accused standing in the dock?'

Fogg said quietly:

'That's the reason, of course! You've put your finger on it. I shall always see *her* . . . Funny thing, romance. She had the quality of it. I don't know if she was really beautiful . . . She wasn't very young – tired looking – circles under her eyes. But it all centered round her. The interest – the drama. And yet, half the time, *she wasn't there*. She'd gone away somewhere, quite far away – just left her body there, quiescent, attentive, with the little polite smile on her lips. She was all half tones, you know, lights and shades. And yet, with it all, she was more alive than the other – that girl with the perfect body, and the beautiful face, and the crude young strength. I admired Elsa Greer because she had guts, because she could fight, because she stood up to her tormentors and never quailed! But I admired Caroline Crale because she didn't fight, because she retreated into her world of half lights and shadows. She was never defeated because she never gave battle.'

He paused:

'I'm only sure of one thing. She loved the man she killed. Loved him so much that half of her died with him . . .'

Mr Fogg, K.C., paused and polished his glasses.

'Dear me,' he said. 'I seem to be saying some very strange things! I was quite a young man at the time, you know. Just an ambitious youngster. These things make an impression. But all the same I'm sure that Caroline Crale was a very remarkable woman. I shall never forget her. No – I shall never forget her . . .'

Chapter 3

The Young Solicitor

George Mayhew was cautious and non-committal.

He remembered the case, of course, but not at all clearly. His father had been in charge – he himself had been only nineteen at the time.

Yes, the case had made a great stir. Because of Crale being such a well-known man. His pictures were very fine – very fine indeed. Two of them were in the Tate. Not that that meant anything.

M. Poirot would excuse him, but he didn't see quite what M. Poirot's interest was in the matter. Oh, the *daughter*! Really? Indeed? Canada? He had always heard it was New Zealand.

George Mayhew became less rigid. He unbent.

A shocking thing in a girl's life. He had the deepest sympathy for her. Really it would have been better if she had never learned the truth. Still, it was no use saying that *now*.

She wanted to know? Yes, but what *was* there to know? There were the reports of the trial, of course. He himself didn't really know anything.

No, he was afraid there wasn't much doubt as to Mrs Crale's being guilty. There was a certain amount of excuse for her. These artists – difficult people to live with. With Crale, he understood, it had always been some woman or other.

And she herself had probably been the possessive type of woman. Unable to accept facts. Nowadays she'd simply have divorced him and got over it. He added cautiously:

'Let me see – er – Lady Dittisham, I believe, was the girl in the case.'

Poirot said that he believed that that was so.

'The newspapers bring it up from time to time,' said Mayhew. 'She's been in the divorce court a good deal. She's a very rich woman, as I expect you know. She was married to that explorer fellow before Dittisham. She's always more or less in the public eye. The kind of woman who likes notoriety, I should imagine.'

'Or possibly a hero worshipper,' suggested Poirot.

The idea was upsetting to George Mayhew. He accepted it dubiously.

'Well, possibly – yes, I suppose that might be so.'

He seemed to be turning the idea over in his mind.

Poirot said:

'Had your firm acted for Mrs Crale for a long period of years?'

George Mayhew shook his head.

'On the contrary. Jonathan and Jonathan were the Crale solicitors. Under the circumstances, however, Mr Jonathan felt that he could not very well act for Mrs Crale, and he arranged with us – with my father – to take over her case. You would do well, I think, M. Poirot, to arrange a meeting with old Mr Jonathan. He has retired from active work – he is over seventy – but he knew the Crale family intimately, and he could tell you far more than I can. Indeed, I myself can tell you nothing at all. I was a boy at the time. I don't think I was even in court.'

Poirot rose and George Mayhew, rising too, added:

'You might like to have a word with Edmunds, our managing clerk. He was with the firm then and took a great interest in the case.'

Edmunds was a man of slow speech. His eyes gleamed with legal caution. He took his time in sizing up Poirot before he let himself be betrayed into speech. He said:

'Ay, I mind the Crale case.'

He added severely: 'It was a disgraceful business.'

His shrewd eyes rested appraisingly on Hercule Poirot.

He said:

'It's a long time since to be raking things up again.'

'A court verdict is not always an ending.'

Edmunds's square head nodded slowly.

'I'd not say that you weren't in the right of it there.'

Hercule Poirot went on: 'Mrs Crale left a daughter.'

'Ay, I mind there was a child. Sent abroad to relatives, was she not?'

Poirot went on:

'That daughter believes firmly in her mother's innocence.'

The huge bushy eyebrows of Mr Edmunds rose.

'That's the way of it, is it?'

Poirot asked:

'Is there anything you can tell me to support that belief?'

Edmunds reflected. Then, slowly, he shook his head.

'I could not conscientiously say there was. I admired Mrs Crale. Whatever else she was, she was a lady! Not like the other. A hussy – no more, no less. Bold as brass! Jumped-up trash – that's what *she* was – and showed it! Mrs Crale was quality.'

'But none the less a murderess?'

Edmunds frowned. He said, with more spontaneity than he had yet shown:

'That's what I used to ask myself, day after day.

Sitting there in the dock so calm and gentle. "I'll not believe it," I used to say to myself. But, if you take my meaning, Mr Poirot, there wasn't anything else to believe. That hemlock didn't get into Mr Crale's beer by accident. It was put there. And if Mrs Crale didn't put it there, who did?'

'That is the question,' said Poirot. 'Who did?'

Again those shrewd old eyes searched his face.

'So that's your idea?' said Mr Edmunds.

'What do you think yourself?'

There was a pause before the officer answered. Then he said:

'There was nothing that pointed that way – nothing at all.'

Poirot said:

'You were in court during the hearing of the case?'

'Every day.'

'You heard the witnesses give evidence?'

'I did.'

'Did anything strike you about them – any abnormality, any insincerity?'

Edmunds said bluntly:

'Was one of them lying, do you mean? Had one of them a reason to wish Mr Crale dead? If you'll excuse me, Mr Poirot, that's a very *melodramatic* idea.'

'At least consider it,' Poirot urged.

He watched the shrewd face, the screwed-up,

thoughtful eyes. Slowly, regretfully, Edmunds shook his head.

'That Miss Greer,' he said, 'she was bitter enough, *and* vindictive! I'd say she overstepped the mark in a good deal she said, but it was Mr Crale alive she wanted. He was no use to her dead. She wanted Mrs Crale hanged all right – but that was because death had snatched her man away from her. Like a baulked tigress she was! But, as I say, it was Mr Crale alive she'd wanted. Mr Philip Blake, *he* was against Mrs Crale too. Prejudiced. Got his knife into her whenever he could. But I'd say he was honest according to his lights. He'd been Mr Crale's great friend. His brother, Mr Meredith Blake – a bad witness he was – vague, hesitating – never seemed sure of his answers. I've seen many witnesses like that. Look as though they're lying when all the time they're telling the truth. Didn't want to say anything more than he could help, Mr Meredith Blake didn't. Counsel got all the more out of him on that account. One of these quiet gentlemen who get easily flustered. The governess now, she stood up well to them. Didn't waste words and answered pat and to the point. You couldn't have told, listening to her, which side she was on. Got all her wits about her, she had. The brisk kind.' He paused. 'Knew a lot more than she ever let on about the whole thing, I shouldn't wonder.'

'I, too, should not wonder,' said Hercule Poirot.

He looked sharply at the wrinkled, shrewd face of Mr Alfred Edmunds. It was quite bland and impassive. But Hercule Poirot wondered if he had been vouchsafed a hint.

Chapter 4

The Old Solicitor

Mr Caleb Jonathan lived in Essex. After a courteous exchange of letters, Poirot received an invitation, almost royal in its character, to dine and sleep. The old gentleman was decidedly a character. After the insipidity of young George Mayhew, Mr Jonathan was like a glass of his own vintage port.

He had his own methods of approach to a subject, and it was not until well on towards midnight, when sipping a glass of fragrant old brandy, that Mr Jonathan really unbent. In oriental fashion he had appreciated Hercule Poirot's courteous refusal to rush him in any way. Now, in his own good time, he was willing to elaborate the theme of the Crale family.

'Our firm, of course, has known many generations of the Crales. I knew Amyas Crale and his father, Richard Crale, and I can remember Enoch Crale – the grandfather. Country squires, all of them, thought more of horses than human beings. They rode straight, liked women, and had no truck with ideas. They distrusted ideas. But Richard Crale's wife was cram full of ideas – more ideas than sense. She was poetical and musical – she played the harp, you know. She enjoyed poor health and looked very picturesque on her sofa. She was an admirer of Kingsley. That's why she called her son Amyas. His father scoffed at the name – but he gave in.

'Amyas Crale profited by his mixed inheritance. He got his artistic trend from his weakly mother, and his driving power and ruthless egoism from his father. All the Crales were egoists. They never by any chance saw any point of view but their own.'

Tapping with a delicate finger on the arm of his chair, the old man shot a shrewd glance at Poirot.

'Correct me if I am wrong, M. Poirot, but I think you are interested in – character, shall we say?'

Poirot replied.

'That, to me, is the principal interest of all my cases.'

'I can conceive of it. To get under the skin, as it were, of your criminal. How interesting. How absorbing. Our firm, of course, have never had a criminal practice. We should not have been competent to act for Mrs Crale, even if taste had allowed. Mayhews, however, were a very adequate firm. They briefed Depleach – they didn't perhaps show much imagination there – still, he was very expensive and, of course, exceedingly dramatic! What they hadn't the wits to see was that Caroline would never play up in the way he wanted her to. She wasn't a dramatic woman.'

'What was she?' asked Poirot. 'It is that that I am chiefly anxious to know.'

'Yes, yes – of course. How did she come to do what she did? That is the really vital question. I knew her, you know, before she married. Caroline Spalding, she was. A turbulent unhappy creature. Very alive. Her mother was left a widow early in life and Caroline was devoted to her mother. Then the mother married again – there was another child. Yes – yes, very sad, very painful. These young, ardent, adolescent jealousies.'

'She was jealous?'

'Passionately so. There was a regrettable incident. Poor child, she blamed herself bitterly afterwards. But you know, M. Poirot, these things happen. There is an inability to put on the brakes. It comes – it comes with maturity.'

Poirot said:

'What happened?'

'She struck the child – the baby – flung a paperweight at her. The child lost the sight of one eye and was permanently disfigured.'

Mr Jonathan sighed. He said:

'You can imagine the effect a simple question on that point had at the trial.'

He shook his head:

'It gave the impression that Caroline Crale was a woman of ungovernable temper. That was not true. No, that was not true.'

He paused and then resumed:

'Caroline Spalding came often to stay at Alderbury. She rode well, and was keen. Richard Crale was fond of her. She waited on Mrs Crale and was deft and gentle – Mrs Crale also liked her. The girl was not happy at home. She was happy at Alderbury. Diana Crale, Amyas's sister, and she were by way of being friends. Philip and Meredith Blake, boys from the adjoining estate, were frequently at Alderbury. Philip was always a nasty, money-grubbing little brute. I must confess I have always had a distaste for him. But I am told that he tells a very good story and that he has the reputation of being a staunch friend. Meredith was what my contemporaries used to call Namby Pamby. Liked botany and butterflies and observing birds and beasts. Nature study they call it nowadays. Ah, dear – all the young people were a disappointment to their parents. None of them ran true to type – huntin', shootin', fishin'. Meredith preferred watching birds and animals to shooting or hunting them, Philip definitely preferred town to country and went into the business of money-making. Diana married a fellow who wasn't a gentleman – one of the temporary officers in the war. And Amyas, strong, handsome, virile Amyas, blossomed into being a painter, of all things in the world. It's my opinion that Richard Crale died of the shock.

'And in due course Amyas married Caroline Spalding. They'd always fought and sparred, but it was a love match all right. They were both crazy about each other. And they continued to care. But Amyas was like all the Crales, a ruthless egoist. He loved Caroline but he never once considered her in any way. He did as he pleased. It's my opinion that he was as fond of her as he could be of anybody – but she came a long way behind his art. That came first. And I should say at no time did his art give place to a woman. He had affairs with women – they stimulated him – but he left them high and dry when he'd finished with them. He wasn't a sentimental man, nor a romantic one. And he wasn't entirely a sensualist either. The only woman he cared a button for was his own wife. And because she knew that she put up with a lot. He was a very fine painter, you know. She realized that, and respected it. He chased off in his amorous pursuits and came back again – usually with a picture to show for it.

'It might have gone on like that if it hadn't come to Elsa Greer. Elsa Greer –'

Mr Jonathan shook his head.

Poirot said: 'What of Elsa Greer?'

Mr Jonathan said unexpectedly:

'Poor child. Poor child.'

Poirot said: 'So you feel like that about her?'

Jonathan said:

'Maybe it is because I am an old man, but I find, M. Poirot, that there is something about the defencelessness of youth that moves me to tears. Youth is so vulnerable. It is so ruthless – so sure. So generous and so demanding.'

Getting up, he crossed to the bookcase. Taking out a volume he opened it, turned the pages, and then read out:

> *'"If that thy bent of love be honourable,*
> *The purpose marriage, send me word tomorrow*
> *By one that I'll procure to come to thee,*
> *Where and what time thou wilt perform the rite,*
> *And all my fortunes at thy foot I'll lay,*
> *And follow thee my lord throughout the world."'*

'There speaks love allied to youth, in Juliet's words. No reticence, no holding back, no so-called maiden modesty. It is the courage, the insistence, the ruthless force of youth. Shakespeare knew youth. Juliet singles out Romeo. Desdemona claims Othello. They have no doubts, the young, no fear, no pride.'

Poirot said thoughtfully:

'So to you Elsa Greer spoke in the words of Juliet?'

'Yes. She was a spoiled child of fortune – young, lovely, rich. She found her mate and claimed him – no young Romeo, a married, middle-aged painter. Elsa Greer had no code to restrain her, she had the code of modernity. "*Take what you want – we shall only live once!*'

He sighed, leaned back, and again tapped gently on the arm of his chair.

'A predatory Juliet. Young, ruthless, but horribly vulnerable! Staking everything on the one audacious throw. And seemingly she won . . . and then – at the last moment – death steps in – and the living, ardent, joyous Elsa died also. There was left only a vindictive, cold, hard woman, hating with all her soul the woman whose hand had done this thing.'

His voice changed:

'Dear, dear. Pray forgive this little lapse into melodrama. A crude young woman – with a crude outlook on life. Not, I think, an interesting character. *Rose white youth, passionate, pale*, etc. Take that away and what remains? Only a somewhat mediocre young woman seeking for another life-sized hero to put on an empty pedestal.'

Poirot said:

'If Amyas Crale had not been a famous painter –'

Mr Jonathan agreed quickly. He said:

'Quite – quite. You have taken the point admirably. The Elsas of this world are hero-worshippers. A man must have *done* something, must be somebody . . . Caroline Crale, now, could have recognized quality in a bank clerk or an insurance agent! Caroline loved Amyas Crale the man, not Amyas Crale the painter. Caroline Crale was not crude – Elsa Greer was.'

He added:

'But she was young and beautiful and to my mind infinitely pathetic.'

Hercule Poirot went to bed thoughtful. He was fascinated by the problem of personality.

To Edmunds, the clerk, Elsa Greer was a hussy, no more, no less.

To old Mr Jonathan she was the eternal Juliet.

And Caroline Crale?

Each person had seen her differently. Montague Depleach had despised her as a defeatist – a quitter. To young Fogg she had represented Romance. Edmunds saw her simply as a 'lady'. Mr Jonathan had called her a stormy, turbulent creature.

How would he, Hercule Poirot, have seen her?

On the answer to that question depended, he felt, the success of his quest.

So far, not one of the people he had seen had doubted that whatever else she was, Caroline Crale was also a murderess.

Chapter 5

The Police Superintendent

Ex-Superintendent Hale pulled thoughtfully at his pipe.

He said:

'This is a funny fancy of yours, M. Poirot.'

'It is, perhaps, a little unusual,' Poirot agreed cautiously.

'You see,' said Hale, 'it's all such a long time ago.'

Hercule Poirot foresaw that he was going to get a little tired of that particular phrase. He said mildly:

'That adds to the difficulty, of course.'

'Raking up the past,' mused the other. 'If there were an *object* in it, now . . .'

'There is an object.'

'What is it?'

'One can enjoy the pursuit of truth for its own sake. I do. And you must not forget the young lady.'

Hale nodded.

Agatha Christie

'Yes, I see *her* side of it. But – you'll excuse me, M. Poirot – you're an ingenious man. You could cook her up a tale.'

Poirot replied:

'You do not know the young lady.'

'Oh, come now – a man of your experience!'

Poirot drew himself up.

'I may be, *mon cher*, an artistic and competent liar – you seem to think so. But it is not my idea of ethical conduct. I have my standards.'

'Sorry, M. Poirot. I didn't mean to hurt your feelings. But it would be all in a good cause, so to speak.'

'Oh I wonder, would it really?'

Hale said slowly:

'It's tough luck on a happy innocent girl who's just going to get married to find that her mother was a murderess. If I were you I'd go to her and say that, after all, suicide was what it was. Say the case was mishandled by Depleach. Say that there's no doubt in *your* mind that Crale poisoned himself!'

'But there is every doubt in my mind! I do not believe for one minute that Crale poisoned himself. Do you consider it even reasonably possible yourself?'

Slowly Hale shook his head.

'You see? No, it is the truth I must have – not a plausible – or not very plausible – lie.'

Hale turned and looked at Poirot. His square rather

red face grew a little redder and even appeared to get a little squarer. He said:

'You talk about the *truth*. I'd like to make it plain to you that we think we *got* the truth in the Crale case.'

Poirot said quickly:

'That pronouncement from you means a great deal. I know you for what you are, an honest and capable man. Now tell me this, was there no doubt at any time in your mind as to the guilt of Mrs Crale?'

The Superintendent's answer came promptly.

'No doubt at all, M. Poirot. The circumstances pointed to her straight away, and every single fact that we uncovered supported that view.'

'You can give me an outline of the evidence against her?'

'I can. When I received your letter I looked up the case.' He picked up a small notebook. 'I've jotted down all the salient facts here.'

'Thank you, my friend. I am all eagerness to hear.'

Hale cleared his throat. A slight official intonation made itself heard in his voice.

He said:

'At two forty-five on the afternoon of September 18th, Inspector Conway was rung up by Dr Andrew Faussett. Dr Faussett stated that Mr Amyas Crale of Alderbury had died suddenly and that in consequence

Agatha Christie

of the circumstances of that death and also of a statement made to him by a Mr Blake, a guest staying in the house, he considered that it was a case for the police.

'Inspector Conway, in company with a sergeant and the police surgeon, came over to Alderbury straight away. Dr Faussett was there and took him to where the body of Mr Crale had not been disturbed.

'Mr Crale had been painting in a small enclosed garden, known as the Battery garden, from the fact that it overlooked the sea, and had some miniature cannon placed in embattlements. It was situated at about four minutes' walk from the house. Mr Crale had not come up to the house for lunch as he wanted to get certain effects of light on the stone – and the sun would have been wrong for this later. He had, therefore, remained alone in the Battery garden, painting. This was stated not to be an unusual occurrence. Mr Crale took very little notice of meal times. Sometimes a sandwich would be sent down to him, but more often he preferred to remain undisturbed. The last people to see him alive were Miss Elsa Greer (staying in the house) and Mr Meredith Blake (a near neighbour). These two went up together to the house and went with the rest of the household in to lunch. After lunch, coffee was served on the terrace. Mrs Crale finished drinking her coffee and then observed that she would "go down and see how Amyas was getting on." Miss Cecilia Williams, governess, got up and accompanied her. She was looking for a pullover belonging to her pupil, Miss Angela Warren, sister of Mrs Crale, which the latter had mislaid and she thought it possible it might have been left down on the beach.

'These two started off together. The path led downwards, through some woods, until it emerged at the door leading into the Battery garden. You could either go into the Battery garden or you could continue on the same path, which led down to the seashore.

'Miss Williams continued on down and Mrs Crale went into the Battery garden. Almost at once, however, Mrs Crale screamed and Miss Williams hurried back. Mr Crale was reclining on a seat and he was dead.

'At Mrs Crale's urgent request Miss Williams left the Battery garden and hurried up to the house to telephone for a doctor. On her way, however, she met Mr Meredith Blake and entrusted her errand to him, herself returning to Mrs Crale whom she felt might be in need of someone. Dr Faussett arrived on the scene a quarter of an hour later. He saw at once that Mr Crale had been dead for some time – he placed the probable time of death at between one and two o'clock. There was nothing to show what had caused death. There was no sign of any wound and Mr Crale's attitude was a perfectly natural one. Nevertheless Dr Faussett, who was well acquainted with Mr Crale's state of health, and who knew positively that there was no disease or weakness of any kind, was inclined to take a grave view of the situation. It was at this point that Mr Philip Blake made a certain statement to Dr Faussett.'

Superintendent Hale paused, drew a deep breath and passed, as it were, to Chapter Two.

'Subsequently Mr Blake repeated this statement to Inspector Conway. It was to this effect. He had that morning received a telephone message from his brother, Mr Meredith Blake (who lived at Handcross Manor, a mile and a half away). Mr Meredith Blake was an amateur chemist – or perhaps herbalist would describe it best. On entering his laboratory that morning, Mr Meredith Blake had been startled to note that a bottle containing a preparation of hemlock, which had been quite full the day before, was now nearly empty. Worried and alarmed by this fact he had rung up his brother to ask his advice as to what he should do about it. Mr Philip Blake had urged his brother to come over to Alderbury at once and they would talk the matter over. He himself walked part way to meet his brother and they had come up to the house together. They had come to no decision as to what course to adopt and had left the matter in order to consult again after lunch.

'As a result of further inquiries, Inspector Conway ascertained the following facts: On the preceding after-noon five people had walked over from Alderbury to tea at Handcross Manor. There were Mr and Mrs Crale, Miss Angela Warren, Miss Elsa Greer and Mr Philip Blake. During the time spent there, Mr Meredith Blake had given quite a dissertation on his hobby and had taken the party into his little laboratory and "shown them round". In the course of this tour, he had mentioned certain specific drugs – one of which was coniine, the active principle of the spotted hemlock. He had explained its properties, had lamented the fact that it had now disappeared from the Pharmacopœia and boasted that he had known small doses of it to be very efficacious in whooping cough and asthma. Later he had mentioned its lethal properties and had actually read to his guests some passage from a Greek author describing its effects.'

Superintendent Hale paused, refilled his pipe and passed on to Chapter Three.

'Colonel Frere, the Chief Constable, put the case into my hands. The result of the autopsy put the matter beyond any doubt. Coniine, I understand, leaves no definite post-mortem appearances, but the doctors knew what to look for, and an ample amount of the drug was recovered. The doctor was of the opinion that it had been administered two or three hours before death. In front of Mr Crale, on the table, there had been an empty glass and an empty beer bottle. The dregs of both were analysed. There was no coniine in the bottle, but there was in the glass. I made inquiries and learned that although a case of beer and glasses were kept in a small summerhouse in the Battery garden in case Mr Crale should feel thirsty when painting, on this particular morning Mrs Crale had brought down from the house a bottle of freshly iced beer. Mr Crale was busy painting when she arrived and Miss Greer was posing for him, sitting on one of the battlements.

'Mrs Crale opened the beer, poured it out and put the glass into her husband's hand as he was standing before the easel. He tossed it off in one draught – a habit of his, I learned. Then he made a grimace, set down the glass on the table, and said: "Everything tastes foul to me today!" Miss Greer upon that laughed and said, "Liver!" Mr Crale said: "Well, at any rate it was *cold*."'

Hale paused. Poirot said:

'At what time did this take place?'

'At about a quarter-past eleven. Mr Crale continued to paint. According to Miss Greer, he later complained of stiffness in the limbs and grumbled that he must have got a touch of rheumatism. But he was the type of man who hates to admit to illness of any kind, and he undoubtedly tried not to admit that he was feeling ill. His irritable demand that he should be left alone and the others go up to lunch was quite characteristic of the man, I should say.'

Poirot nodded.

Hale continued.

'So Crale was left alone in the Battery garden. No doubt he dropped down on the seat and relaxed as soon as he was alone. Muscular paralysis would then set in. No help was at hand, and death supervened.'

Again Poirot nodded.

Hale said:

'Well, I proceeded according to routine. There wasn't much difficulty in getting down to the facts. On the preceding day there had been a set-to between Mrs Crale and Miss Greer. The latter had pretty insolently described some change in the arrangement of the furniture "when I am living here." Mrs Crale took her up, and said, "What do you mean? When *you* are living here." Miss Greer replied: "Don't pretend you don't know what I mean, Caroline. You're just like an ostrich that buries its head in the sand. You know perfectly well that Amyas and I care for each other and are going to be married." Mrs Crale said: "I know nothing of the kind." Miss Greer then said: "Well, you know it now." Whereupon, it seems, Mrs Crale turned to her husband who had just come into the room and said: "Is it true, Amyas, that you are going to marry Elsa?"'

Poirot said with interest:

'And what did Mr Crale say to that?'

71

'Apparently he turned on Miss Greer and shouted at her: "What the devil do you mean by blurting that out? Haven't you got the sense to hold your tongue?"'

'Miss Greer said: "I think Caroline ought to recognize the truth."'

'Mrs Crale said to her husband: "Is it true, Amyas?"'

'He wouldn't look at her, it seems, turned his face away and mumbled something.

'She said: "Speak out. I've got to know." Whereupon he said:

'"Oh, it's true enough – but I don't want to discuss it now."

'Then he flounced out of the room again and Miss Greer said:

'"You see!" and went on – with something about its being no good for Mrs Crale to adopt a dog-in-the-manger attitude about it. They must all behave like rational people. She herself hoped that Caroline and Amyas would always remain good friends.'

'And what did Mrs Crale say to that?' asked Poirot curiously.

'According to the witnesses she laughed. She said: "Over my dead body, Elsa." She went to the door and Miss Greer called after her: "What do you mean?" Mrs Crale looked back and said: "I'll kill Amyas before I give him up to *you*."'

Hale paused.

'Pretty damning – eh?'

'Yes.' Poirot seemed thoughtful. 'Who overheard this scene?'

'Miss Williams was in the room and Philip Blake. Very awkward for them.'

'Their accounts of the scene agree?'

'Near enough – you never got two witnesses to remember a thing exactly alike. *You* know that just as well as I do, M. Poirot.'

Poirot nodded. He said thoughtfully:

'Yes, it will be interesting to see –' He stopped with the sentence unfinished.

Hale went on: 'I instituted a search of the house. In Mrs Crale's bedroom I found in a bottom drawer, tucked away underneath some winter stockings, a small bottle labelled jasmine scent. It was empty. I finger-printed it. The only prints on it were those of Mrs Crale. On analysis it was found to contain faint traces of oil of jasmine, and a strong solution of coniine hydrobromide.

'I cautioned Mrs Crale and showed her the bottle. She replied readily. She had, she said, been in a very unhappy state of mind. After listening to Mr Meredith Blake's description of the drug she had slipped back to the laboratory, had emptied out a bottle of jasmine scent which was in her bag and had filled the bottle up with coniine solution. I asked her why she had done this

73

and she said: "I don't want to speak of certain things more than I can help, but I had received a bad shock. My husband was proposing to leave me for another woman. If that was so, I didn't want to live. That is why I took it."'

Hale paused.

Poirot said: 'After all – it is likely enough.'

'Perhaps, M. Poirot. But it doesn't square with what she was overheard to say. And then there was a further scene on the following morning. Mr Philip Blake overheard a portion of it. Miss Greer overheard a different portion of it. It took place in the library between Mr and Mrs Crale. Mr Blake was in the hall and caught a fragment or two. Miss Greer was sitting outside near the open library window and heard a good deal more.'

'And what did they hear?'

'Mr Blake heard Mrs Crale say: "You and your women. I'd like to kill you. Some day I will kill you."'

'No mention of suicide?'

'Exactly. None at all. No words like "If you do this thing, I'll kill *myself*." Miss Greer's evidence was much the same. According to her, Mr Crale said: "Do try and be reasonable about this, Caroline. I'm fond of you and will always wish you well – you and the child. But I'm going to marry Elsa. We've always agreed to leave each other free." Mrs Crale answered to that: "Very well, don't say I haven't warned you." He said: "What do you mean?" And she said: "I mean that I love you and I'm not going to lose you. I'd rather kill you than let you go to that girl."'

Poirot made a slight gesture.

'It occurs to me,' he murmured, 'that Miss Greer was singularly unwise to raise this issue? Mrs Crale could easily have refused her husband a divorce.'

'We had some evidence bearing on that point,' said Hale. 'Mrs Crale, it seems, confided partly in Mr Meredith Blake. He was an old and trusted friend. He was very distressed and managed to get a word with Mr Crale about it. This, I may say, was on the preceding afternoon. Mr Blake remonstrated delicately with his friend, said how distressed he would be if the marriage between Mr and Mrs Crale was to break up so disastrously. He also stressed the point that Miss Greer was a very young girl and that it was a very serious thing to drag a young girl through the divorce court. To this Mr Crale replied, with a chuckle (callous sort of brute he must have been): "That isn't Elsa's idea at all. *She* isn't going to appear. We shall fix it up in the usual way."'

Poirot said: 'Therefore even more imprudent of Miss Greer to have broken out the way she did.'

Superintendent Hale said:

'Oh, you know what women are! Have to get at each

other's throats. It must have been a difficult situation anyhow. I can't understand Mr Crale allowing it to happen. According to Mr Meredith Blake he wanted to finish his picture. Does that make sense to you?'

'Yes, my friend, I think it does.'

'It doesn't to me. The man was asking for trouble!'

'He was probaby seriously annoyed with his young woman for breaking out the way she did.'

'Oh, he was. Meredith Blake said so. If he had to finish the picture I don't see why he couldn't have taken some photographs and worked from them. I know a chap – does watercolours of places – *he* does that.'

Poirot shook his head.

'No – I can understand Crale the artist. You must realize, my friend, that at that moment, probably, his picture was all that mattered to Crale. However much he wanted to marry the girl, the picture came first. That's why he hoped to get through her visit without its coming to an open issue. The girl, of course, didn't see it that way. With women, love always comes first.'

'Don't I know it?' said Superintendent Hale with feeling.

'Men,' continued Poirot, 'and especially artists – are different.'

'Art!' said the Superintendent with scorn. 'All this talk about *Art*! I never *have* understood it and I never shall! You should have seen that picture Crale was painting. All lopsided. He'd made the girl look as though she'd got toothache, and the battlements were all cock-eyed. Unpleasant looking, the whole thing. I couldn't get it out of my mind for a long time afterwards. I even dreamt about it. And what's more it affected my eyesight – I began to see battlements and walls and things all out of drawing. Yes, and women too!'

Poirot smiled. He said:

'Although you do not know it, you are paying a tribute to the greatness of Amyas Crale's art.'

'Nonsense. Why can't a painter paint something nice and cheerful to look at? Why go out of your way to look for ugliness?'

'Some of us, *mon cher*, see beauty in curious places.'

'The girl was a good looker, all right,' said Hale. 'Lots of make-up and next to no clothes on. It isn't decent the way these girls go about. And that was sixteen years ago, mind you. Nowadays one wouldn't think anything of it. But then – well, it shocked me. Trousers and one of those canvas shirts, open at the neck – and not another thing, I should say!'

'You seem to remember these points very well,' murmured Poirot slyly.

Superintendent Hale blushed. 'I'm just passing on the impression I got,' he said austerely.

'Quite – quite,' said Poirot soothingly. He went on:

'So it would seem that the principal witnesses against Mrs Crale were Philip Blake and Elsa Greer?'

'Yes. Vehement, they were, both of them. But the governess was called by the prosecution too, and what she said carried more weight than the other two. She was on Mrs Crale's side entirely, you see. Up in arms for her. But she was an honest woman and gave her evidence truthfully without trying to minimize it in any way.'

'And Meredith Blake?'

'He was very distressed by the whole thing, poor gentleman. As well he might be! Blamed himself for his drug brewing – and the coroner blamed him for it too. Coniine and AE Salts comes under Schedule I of the Poisons Acts. He came in for some pretty sharp censure. He was a friend of both parties, and it hit him very hard – besides being the kind of county gentleman who shrinks from notoriety and being in the public eye.'

'Did not Mrs Crale's young sister give evidence?'

'No. It wasn't necessary. She wasn't there when Mrs Crale threatened her husband, and there was nothing she could tell us that we couldn't get from someone else equally well. She saw Mrs Crale go to the refrigerator and get the iced beer out and, of course, the Defence could have subpœnaed her to say that Mrs Crale took it straight down without tampering with it in any way. But that point wasn't relevant because we never claimed that the coniine was in the beer bottle.'

'How did she manage to put it in the glass with those two looking on?'

'Well, first of all, they weren't looking on. That is to say, Mr Crale was painting – looking at his canvas and at the sitter. And Miss Greer was posed, sitting with her back almost to where Mrs Crale was standing, and her eyes looking over Mr Crale's shoulder.'

Poirot nodded.

'As I say neither of the two was looking at Mrs Crale. She had the stuff in one of those pipette things – one used to fill fountain pens with them. We found it crushed to splinters on the path up to the house.'

Poirot murmured:

'You have an answer to everything.'

'Well, come now, M. Poirot! Without prejudice. *She* threatens to kill him. *She* takes the stuff from the laboratory. The empty bottle is found in *her* room and *nobody has handled it but her*. She deliberately takes down iced beer to him – a funny thing, anyway, when you realize that they weren't on speaking terms –'

'A very curious thing. I had already remarked on it.'

'Yes. Bit of a give away. *Why* was she so amiable all of a sudden? He complains of the taste of the stuff – and coniine *has* a nasty taste. She arranges to find the body and she sends the other woman off to telephone. Why? So that she can wipe that bottle and glass and then press *his* fingers on it. After that she can pipe up and say that it was remorse and that he committed suicide. A likely story.'

'It was certainly not very well imagined.'

'No. If you ask me she didn't take the trouble to *think*. She was so eaten up with hate and jealousy. All she thought of was doing him in. And then, when it's over, when she sees him there dead – well, *then*, I should say, she suddenly comes to herself and realizes that what she's done is murder – and that you get hanged for murder. And desperately she goes bald-headed for the only thing she can think of – which is suicide.'

Poirot said:

'It is very sound what you say there – yes. Her mind might work that way.'

'In a way it was a premeditated crime and in a way it wasn't,' said Hale. 'I don't believe she really thought it out, you know. Just went on with it blindly.'

Poirot murmured:

'I wonder . . .'

Hale looked at him curiously. He said:

'Have I convinced you, M. Poirot, that it was a straightforward case?'

'Almost. Not quite. There are one or two peculiar points . . . !'

'Can you suggest an alternative solution – that will hold water?'

Poirot said:

'What were the movements of the other people on that morning?'

'We went into them, I can assure you. We checked up on everybody. Nobody had what you could call an alibi – you can't have with poisoning. Why, there's nothing to prevent a would-be murderer from handing his victim some poison in a capsule the day before, telling him it's a specific cure for indigestion and he must take it before lunch – and then going away to the other end of England.'

'But you don't think that happened in this case?'

'Mr Crale didn't suffer from indigestion. And in any case I can't see that kind of thing happening. It's true that Mr Meredith Blake was given to recommending quack nostrums of his own concocting, but I don't see Mr Crale trying any of them. And if he did he'd probably talk and joke about it. Besides, why *should* Mr Meredith Blake want to kill Mr Crale? Everything goes to show that he was on very good terms with him. They all were. Mr Philip Blake was his best friend. Miss Greer was in love with him. Miss Williams disapproved of him, I imagine, very strongly – but moral disapprobation doesn't lead to poisoning. Little Miss Warren scrapped with him a lot, she was at a tiresome age – just off to school, I believe, but he was quite fond of her and she of him. She was treated, you know, with particular tenderness and consideration in that house. You may have heard why. She was badly injured when she was a child – injured by Mrs Crale in a kind of maniacal fit of rage. That rather shows, doesn't it, that she was a pretty uncontrolled sort of person? To go for a child – and maim her for life!'

'It might show,' said Poirot thoughtfully, 'that Angela Warren had good reason to bear a grudge against Caroline Crale.'

'Perhaps – but not against Amyas Crale. And anyway Mrs Crale was devoted to her young sister – gave her a home when her parents died, and, as I say, treated her with special affection – spoiled her badly, so they say. The girl was obviously fond of Mrs Crale. She was kept away from the trial and sheltered from it all as far as possible – Mrs Crale was very insistent about that, I believe. But the girl was terribly upset and longed to be taken to see her sister in prison. Caroline Crale wouldn't agree. She said that sort of thing might injure a girl's mentality for life. She arranged for her to go to school abroad.'

He added:

'Miss Warren's turned out a very distinguished woman. Traveller to weird places. Lectures at the Royal Geographical – all that sort of thing.'

'And no one remembers the trial?'

'Well, it's a different name for one thing. They hadn't even the same maiden name. They had the same mother but different fathers. Mrs Crale's name was Spalding.'

'This Miss Williams, was she the child's governess, or Angela Warren's?'

'Angela's. There was a nurse for the child – but she used to do a few little lessons with Miss Williams every day, I believe.'

'Where was the child at the time?'

'She'd gone with the nurse to pay a visit to her grandmother. A Lady Tressillian. A widow lady who'd lost her own two little girls and who was devoted to this kid.'

Poirot nodded. 'I see.'

Hale continued:

'As to the movements of the other people on the day of the murder, I can give them to you.

'Miss Greer sat on the terrace near the library window after breakfast. There, as I say, she overheard the quarrel between Crale and his wife. After that she accompanied Crale down to the Battery and sat for him until lunch time with a couple of breaks to ease her muscles.

'Philip Blake was in the house after breakfast, and overheard part of the quarrel. After Crale and Miss

Greer went off, he read the paper until his brother telephoned him. Thereupon he went down to the shore to meet his brother. They walked together up the path again past the Battery garden. Miss Greer had just gone up to the house to fetch a pullover as she felt chilly and Mrs Crale was with her husband discussing arrangements for Angela's departure to school.'

'Ah, an amicable interview.'

'Well, no, not amicable. Crale was fairly shouting at her, I understand. Annoyed at being bothered with domestic details. I suppose she wanted to get things straightened up if there *was* going to be a break.'

Poirot nodded.

Hale went on:

'The two brothers exchanged a few words with Amyas Crale. Then Miss Greer reappeared and took up her position, and Crale picked up his brush again, obviously wanting to get rid of them. They took the hint and went up to the house. It was when they were at the Battery, by the way, that Amyas Crale complained all the beer down there was hot and his wife promised to send him down some iced beer.'

'Aha!'

'Exactly – Aha! Sweet as sugar she was about it. They went up to the house and sat on the terrace outside. Mrs Crale and Angela Warren brought them out beer there.

'Later, Angela Warren went down to bathe and Philip Blake went with her.

'Meredith Blake went down to a clearing with a seat just above the Battery garden. He could just see Miss Greer as she posed on the battlements and could hear her voice and Crale's as they talked. He sat there and thought over the coniine business. He was still very worried about it and didn't know quite what to do. Elsa Greer saw him and waved her hand to him. When the bell went for lunch he came down to the Battery and Elsa Greer and he went back to the house together. He noticed then that Crale was looking, as he put it, very queer, but he didn't really think anything of it at the time. Crale was the kind of man who is never ill – and so one didn't imagine he would be. On the other hand, he *did* have moods of fury and despondency according as to whether his painting was not going as he liked it. On those occasions one left him alone and said as little as possible to him. That's what these two did on this occasion.

'As to the others, the servants were busy with housework and cooking lunch. Miss Williams was in the schoolroom part of the morning correcting some exercise books. Afterwards she took some household mending to the terrace. Angela Warren spent most of the morning wandering about the garden, climbing trees and eating things – you know what a girl of fifteen

Agatha Christie

is! Plums, sour apples, hard pears, etc. After she came back to the house and, as I say, went down with Philip Blake to the beach and had a bathe before lunch.'

Superintendent Hale paused:

'Now then,' he said belligerently, 'do you find anything phoney about that?'

Poirot said: 'Nothing at all.'

'Well, then!'

The two words expressed volumes.

'But all the same,' said Hercule Poirot. 'I am going to satisfy myself. I –'

'What are you going to do?'

'I am going to visit these five people – and from each one I am going to get his or her own story.'

Superintendent Hale sighed with a deep melancholy.

He said:

'Man, you're nuts! None of their stories are going to agree! Don't you grasp that elementary fact? No two people remember a thing in the same order anyway. And after all this time! Why, you'll hear five accounts of five separate murders!'

'That,' said Poirot, 'is what I am counting upon. It will be very instructive.'

Chapter 6

This Little Pig Went to Market . . .

Philip Blake was recognizably like the description given of him by Montague Depleach. A prosperous, shrewd, jovial-looking man – slightly running to fat.

Hercule Poirot had timed his appointment for half-past six on a Saturday afternoon. Philip Blake had just finished his eighteen holes, and he had been on his game – winning a fiver from his opponent. He was in the mood to be friendly and expansive.

Hercule Poirot explained himself and his errand. On this occasion at least he showed no undue passion for unsullied truth. It was a question, Blake gathered, of a series of books dealing with famous crimes.

Philip Blake frowned. He said:

'Good Lord, why make up these things?'

Hercule Poirot shrugged his shoulders. He was at his most foreign today. He was out to be despised but patronized.

He murmured:

'It is the public. They eat it up – yes, eat it up.'

'Ghouls,' said Philip Blake.

But he said it good-humouredly – not with the fastidiousness and the distaste that a more sensitive man might have displayed.

Hercule Poirot said with a shrug of the shoulders:

'It is human nature. You and I, Mr Blake, who know the world, have no illusions about our fellow human beings. Not bad people, most of them, but certainly not to be idealized.'

Blake said heartily:

'I've parted with my illusions long ago.'

'Instead, you tell a very good story, so I have been told.'

'Ah!' Blake's eyes twinkled. 'Heard this one?'

Poirot's laugh came at the right place. It was not an edifying story, but it was funny.

Philip Blake lay back in his chair, his muscles relaxed, his eyes creased with good humour.

Hercule Poirot thought suddenly that he looked rather like a contented pig.

A pig. *This little pig went to market . . .*

What was he like, this man, this Philip Blake? A man, it would seem, without cares. Prosperous, contented. No remorseful thoughts, no uneasy twinges of conscience from the past, no haunting memories here. No, a well-fed pig who had gone to market – and fetched the full market price . . .

But once, perhaps, there had been more to Philip Blake. He must have been, when young, a handsome man. Eyes always a shade too small, a fraction too near together, perhaps – but otherwise a well made, well set up young man. How old was he now? At a guess between fifty and sixty. Nearing forty, then, at the time of Crale's death. Less stultified, then, less sunk in the gratifications of the minute. Asking more of life, perhaps, and receiving less . . .

Poirot murmured as a mere catch-phrase:

'You comprehend my position.'

'No, really, you know, I'm hanged if I do.' The stockbroker sat upright again, his glance was once more shrewd. 'Why *you*? You're not a writer?'

'Not precisely – no. Actually I am a detective.'

The modesty of this remark had probably not been equalled before in Poirot's conversation.

'Of course you are. We all know that. The famous Hercule Poirot!'

But his tone held a subtly mocking note. Intrinsically, Philip Blake was too much of an Englishman to take the pretensions of a foreigner seriously.

To his cronies he would have said:

'Quaint little mountebank. Oh well, I expect his stuff goes down with the women all right.'

And although that derisive patronizing attitude was exactly the one which Hercule Poirot had aimed at inducing, nevertheless he found himself annoyed by it.

This man, this successful man of affairs, was unimpressed by Hercule Poirot! It was a scandal.

'I am gratified,' said Poirot untruly, 'that I am so well known to you. My success, let me tell you, has been founded on the psychology – the eternal *why*? of human behaviour. That, M. Blake, is what interests the world in crime today. It used to be romance. Famous crimes were retold from one angle only – the love-story connected with them. Nowadays it is very different. People read with interest that Dr Crippen murdered his wife because she was a big bouncing woman and he was little and insignificant and therefore she made him feel inferior. They read of some famous woman criminal that she killed because she'd been snubbed by her father when she was three years old. It is, as I say, the *why* of crime that interests nowadays.'

Philip Blake said, with a slight yawn:

'The why of most crimes is obvious enough, I should say. Usually money.'

Poirot cried:

'Ah, but my dear sir, the why must never be obvious. That is the whole point!'

'And that's where *you* come in?'

'And that, as you say, is where I come in! It is proposed to rewrite the stories of certain bygone crimes – from the psychological angle. Psychology in crime, it is my speciality. I have accepted the commission.'

Philip Blake grinned.

'Pretty lucrative, I suppose?'

'I hope so – I certainly hope so.'

'Congratulations. Now, perhaps, you'll tell me where *I* come in?'

'Most certainly. The Crale case, Monsieur.'

Phillip Blake did not look startled. But he looked thoughtful. He said:

'Yes, of course, the Crale case . . .'

Hercule Poirot said anxiously:

'It is not displeasing to you, Mr Blake?'

'Oh, as to that.' Philip Blake shrugged his shoulders. 'It's no use resenting a thing that you've no power to stop. The trial of Caroline Crale is public property. Any one can go ahead and write it up. It's no use *my* objecting. In a way – I don't mind telling you – I do dislike it a good deal. Amyas Crale was one of my best friends. I'm sorry the whole unsavoury business has to be raked up again. But these things happen.'

'You are a philosopher, Mr Blake.'

'No, no. I just know enough not to start kicking against the pricks. I dare say you'll do it less offensively than many others.'

'I hope, at least, to write with delicacy and good taste,' said Poirot.

Philip Blake gave a loud guffaw but without any real amusement. 'Makes me chuckle to hear you say that.'

'I assure you, Mr Blake, I am really interested. It is not just a matter of money with me. I genuinely want to recreate the past, to feel and see the events that took place, to see behind the obvious and to visualize the thoughts and feelings of the actors in the drama.'

Philip Blake said:

'I don't know that there was much subtlety about it. It was a pretty obvious business. Crude female jealousy, that was all there was to it.'

'It would interest me enormously, Mr Blake, if I could have your own reactions to the affair.'

Philip Blake said with sudden heat, his face deepening in colour.

'Reactions! Reactions! Don't speak so pedantically. I didn't just stand there and react! You don't seem to understand that my friend – *my friend*, I tell you, had been killed – poisoned! And that if I'd acted quicker I could have saved him.'

'How do you make that out, Mr Blake?'

'Like this. I take it that you've already read up the facts of the case?' Poirot nodded. 'Very well. Now on that morning my brother Meredith called me up. He was in a pretty good stew. One of his Hell brews was missing – and it was a fairly deadly Hell brew. What did I do? I told him to come along and we'd talk it over. Decide what was best to be done. "Decide what was best." It beats me now how I could have been such a hesitating fool! I ought to have realized that there was no time to lose. I ought to have gone to Amyas straight away and warned him. I ought to have said: "Caroline's pinched one of Meredith's patent poisons, and you and Elsa had better look out for yourselves."'

Blake got up. He strode up and down in his excitement.

'Good God, man. Do you suppose I haven't gone over it in my mind again and again? I *knew*. I had the chance to save him – and I dallied about – waiting for Meredith! Why hadn't I the sense to realize that Caroline wasn't going to have any qualms or hesitancies. She'd taken that stuff to use – and, by God, she'd used it at the very first opportunity. She wouldn't wait till Meredith discovered his loss. I knew – of course I knew – that Amyas was in deadly danger – and I did nothing!'

'I think you reproach yourself unduly, Monsieur. You had not much time –'

The other interrupted him:

'Time? I had plenty of time. Any amount of courses open to me. I could have gone to Amyas, as I say – but there was the chance, of course, that he wouldn't believe me. Amyas wasn't the sort of man who'd believe easily in his own danger. He'd have scoffed at the notion. And he never thoroughly understood the sort of devil Caroline was. But I could have gone to her. I could have said: "I know what you're up to. I know what you're planning to do. But if Amyas or Elsa die of coniine poisoning, you'll be hanged by your neck!" That would have stopped her. Or I might have rung up the police. Oh! there were things that could have been done – and instead, I let myself be influenced by Meredith's slow, cautious methods. "We must be sure – talk it over – make quite certain who could have taken it . . ." Damned old fool – never made a quick decision in his life! A good thing for him he was the eldest son and has an estate to live on. If he'd ever tried to *make* money he'd have lost every penny he had.'

Poirot asked:

'You had no doubt yourself who had taken the poison?'

'Of course not. I knew at once it must be Caroline. You see, I knew Caroline very well.'

Poirot said:

'That is very interesting. I want to know, Mr Blake, what kind of a woman Caroline Crale was?'

Philip Blake said sharply:

'She wasn't the injured innocent people thought she was at the time of the trial!'

'What was she, then?'

Blake sat down again. He said seriously:

'Would you really like to know?'

'I would like to know very much indeed.'

'Caroline was a rotter. She was a rotter through and through. Mind you, she had charm. She had that kind of sweetness of manner that deceives people utterly. She had a frail, helpless look about her that appealed to people's chivalry. Sometimes, when I've read a bit of history, I think Mary Queen of Scots must have been a bit like her. Always sweet and unfortunate and magnetic – and actually a cold calculating woman, a scheming woman who planned the murder of Darnley and got away with it. Caroline was like that – a cold, calculating planner. And she had a wicked temper.

'I don't know whether they've told you – it isn't a vital point of the trial, but it shows her up – what she did to her baby sister? She was jealous, you know. Her mother had married again, and all the notice and affection went to little Angela. Caroline couldn't stand that. She tried to kill the baby with a crowbar – smash its head in. Luckily the blow wasn't fatal. But it was a pretty ghastly thing to do.'

'Yes, indeed.'

'Well, that was the real Caroline. She had to be first. That was the thing she simply could not stand – not being first. And there was a cold, egotistical devil in her that was capable of being stirred to murderous lengths.

'She appeared impulsive, you know, but she was really calculating. When she stayed at Alderbury as a girl, she gave us all the once over and made her plans. She'd no money of her own. I was never in the running – a younger son with his way to make. (Funny, that, I could probably buy up Meredith and Crale, if he'd lived, nowadays!) She considered Meredith for a bit, but she finally fixed on Amyas. Amyas would have Alderbury, and though he wouldn't have much money with it, she realized that his talent as a painter was something quite out of the way. She gambled on his being not only a genius but a financial success as well.

'And she won. Recognition came to Amyas early. He wasn't a fashionable painter exactly – but his genius was recognized and his pictures were bought. Have you seen any of his paintings? There's one here. Come and look at it.'

He led the way into the dining-room and pointed to the left-hand wall.

'There you are. That's Amyas.'

Poirot looked in silence. It came to him with fresh amazement that a man could so imbue a conventional subject with his own particular magic. A vase of roses on a polished mahogany table. That hoary old set-piece. How then did Amyas Crale contrive to make his roses flame and burn with a riotous almost obscene life. The polished wood of the table trembled and took on sentient life. How explain the excitement the picture roused? For it was exciting. The proportions of the table would have distressed Superintendent Hale, he would have complained that no known roses were precisely of that shape or colour. And afterwards he would have gone about wondering vaguely why the roses he saw were unsatisfactory, and round mahogany tables would have annoyed him for no known reason.

Poirot gave a little sigh.

He murmured:

'Yes – it is all there.'

Blake led the way back. He mumbled:

'Never have understood anything about art myself. Don't know why I like looking at that thing so much, but I do. It's – oh, damn it all, it's *good*.'

Poirot nodded emphatically.

Blake offered his guest a cigarette and lit one himself. He said:

'And that's the man – the man who painted those roses – the man who painted the "Woman with a Cocktail Shaker" – the man who painted that amazing painful "Nativity", *that's* the man who was cut short in his prime, deprived of his vivid forceful life all because of a vindictive mean-natured woman!'

He paused:

'You'll say that I'm bitter – that I'm unduly prejudiced against Caroline. She *had* charm – I've felt it. But I knew – I always knew – the real woman behind. And that woman, M. Poirot, was evil. She was cruel and malignant and a grabber!'

'And yet it has been told me that Mrs Crale put up with many hard things in her married life?'

'Yes, and didn't she let everybody know about it! Always the martyr! Poor old Amyas. His married life was one long hell – or rather it would have been if it hadn't been for his exceptional quality. His art, you see – he always had that. It was an escape. When he was painting he didn't care, he shook off Caroline and her nagging and all the ceaseless rows and quarrels. They were endless, you know. Not a week passed without a thundering row over one thing or another. *She* enjoyed it. Having rows stimulated her, I believe. It was an outlet. She could say all the hard bitter stinging things she wanted to say. She'd positively purr after one of those set-tos – go off looking as sleek and well-fed as a cat. But it took it out of *him*. *He* wanted peace – rest – a quiet life. Of course a man like that ought never to marry – he isn't out for domesticity. A man like Crale should have affairs but no binding ties. They're bound to chafe him.'

'He confided in you?'

'Well – he knew that I was a pretty devoted pal. He

let me see things. He didn't complain. He wasn't that kind of man. Sometimes he'd say, "Damn all women." Or he'd say, "Never get married, old boy. Wait for hell till after this life."'

'You knew about his attachment to Miss Greer?'

'Oh yes – at least I saw it coming on. He told me he'd met a marvellous girl. She was different, he said, from anything or any one he'd ever met before. Not that I paid much attention to that. Amyas was always meeting one woman or other who was "different". Usually a month later he'd stare at you if you mentioned them, and wonder who you were talking about! But this Elsa Greer really was different. I realized that when I came down to Alderbury to stay. She'd got him, you know, hooked him good and proper. The poor mutt fairly ate out of her hand.'

'You did not like Elsa Greer either?'

'No, I didn't like her. She was definitely a predatory creature. She, too, wanted to own Crale body and soul. But I think, all the same, that she'd have been better for him than Caroline. She might conceivably have let him alone once she was sure of him. Or she might have got tired of him and moved on to someone else. The best thing for Amyas would have been to be quite free of female entanglements.'

'But that, it would seem, was not to his taste?'

Philip Blake said with a sigh:

'The damned fool was always getting himself involved with some woman or other. And yet, in a way, women really meant very little to him. The only two women who really made any impression on him at all in his life were Caroline and Elsa.'

Poirot said:

'Was he fond of the child?'

'Angela? Oh! we all liked Angela. She was such a sport. She was always game for anything. What a life she led that wretched governess of hers. Yes, Amyas liked Angela all right – but sometimes she went too far and then he used to get really mad with her – and then Caroline would step in – Caro was always on Angela's side and that would finish Amyas altogether. He hated it when Caro sided with Angela against him. There was a bit of jealousy all round, you know. Amyas was jealous of the way Caro always put Angela first and would do anything for her. And Angela was jealous of Amyas and rebelled against his overbearing ways. It was his decision that she should go to school that autumn, and she was furious about it. Not, I think, because she didn't like the idea of school, she really rather wanted to go, I believe – but it was Amyas's high-handed way of settling it all offhand that infuriated her. She played all sorts of tricks on him in revenge. Once she put ten slugs in his bed. On the whole, I think Amyas was right. It was time she got some discipline. Miss Williams was very efficient, but even she confessed that Angela was getting too much for her.'

He paused. Poirot said:

'When I asked if Amyas was fond of the child – I referred to his own child, his daughter?'

'Oh, you mean little Carla? Yes, she was a great pet. He enjoyed playing with her when he was in the mood. But his affection for her wouldn't have deterred him from marrying Elsa, if that's what you mean. He hadn't *that* kind of feeling for her.'

'Was Caroline Crale very devoted to the child?'

A kind of spasm contorted Philip's face. He said:

'I can't say that she wasn't a good mother. No, I can't say that. It's the one thing –'

'Yes, Mr Blake?'

Philip said slowly and painfully:

'It's the one thing I really – regret – in this affair. The thought of that child. Such a tragic background to her young life. They sent her abroad to Amyas's cousin and her husband. I hope – I sincerely hope – they managed to keep the truth from her.'

Poirot shook his head. He said:

'The truth, Mr Blake, has a habit of making itself known. Even after many years.'

The stockbroker murmured: 'I wonder.'

Poirot went on:

'In the interests of truth, Mr Blake, I am going to ask you to do something.'

'What is it?'

'I am going to beg that you will write me out an exact account of what happened on those days at Alderbury. That is to say, I am going to ask you to write me out a full account of the murder and its attendant circumstances.'

'But, my dear fellow, after all this time? I should be hopelessly inaccurate.'

'Not necessarily.'

'Surely.'

'No, for one thing, with the passage of time, the mind retains a hold on essentials and rejects superficial matters.'

'Ho! You mean a mere broad outline?'

'Not at all. I mean a detailed conscientious account of each event as it occurred, and every conversation you can remember.'

'And supposing I remember them wrong?'

'You can give the wording at least to the best of your reflection. There may be gaps, but that cannot be helped.'

Blake looked at him curiously.

'But what's the idea? The police files will give you the whole thing far more accurately.'

'No, Mr Blake. We are speaking now from the

psychological point of view. I do not want bare *facts. I want your own selections of facts.* Time and your memory are responsible for that selection. There may have been things done, words spoken, that I should seek for in vain in the police files. Things and words that you never mentioned because, maybe, you judged them irrelevant, or because you preferred not to repeat them.'

Blake said sharply:

'Is this account of mine for publication?'

'Certainly not. It is for my eye only. To assist me to draw my own deductions.'

'And you won't quote from it without my consent?'

'Certainly not.'

'Hm,' said Philip Blake. 'I'm a very busy man, M. Poirot.'

'I appreciate that there will be time and trouble involved. I should be happy to agree to a – reasonable fee.'

There was a moment's pause. Then Philip Blake said suddenly:

'No, if I do it – I'll do it for nothing.'

'And you will do it?'

Philip said warningly:

'Remember, I can't vouch for the accuracy of my memory.'

'That is perfectly understood.'

'Then I think,' said Philip Blake, 'that I should *like* to do it. I feel I owe it – in a way – to Amyas Crale.'

Chapter 7

This Little Pig Stayed at Home

Hercule Poirot was not a man to neglect details.

His advance towards Meredith Blake was carefully thought out. Meredith Blake was, he already felt sure, a very different proposition from Philip Blake. Rush tactics would not succeed here. The assault must be leisurely.

Hercule Poirot knew that there was only one way to penetrate the stronghold. He must approach Meredith Blake with the proper credentials. Those credentials must be social, not professional. Fortunately, in the course of his career, Hercule Poirot had made friends in many counties. Devonshire was no exception. He sat down to review what resources he had in Devonshire. As a result he discovered two people who were acquaintances or friends of Mr Meredith Blake. He descended upon him therefore armed with two letters, one from Lady Mary Lytton-Gore, a gentle widow

Agatha Christie

lady of restricted means, the most retiring of creatures; and the other from a retired Admiral, whose family had been settled in the county for four generations.

Meredith Blake received Poirot in a state of some perplexity.

As he had often felt lately, things were not what they used to be. Dash it all, private detectives used to be private detectives – fellows you got to guard wedding presents at country receptions, fellows you went to – rather shame-facedly – when there was some dirty business afoot and you'd got to get the hang of it.

But here was Lady Mary Lytton-Gore writing: 'Hercule Poirot is a very old and valued friend of mine. Please do all you can to help him, won't you?' And Mary Lytton-Gore wasn't – no, decidedly she wasn't – the sort of woman you associate with private detectives and all that they stand for. And Admiral Cronshaw wrote: 'Very good chap – absolutely sound. Grateful if you will do what you can for him. Most entertaining fellow, can tell you lots of good stories.'

And now here was the man himself. Really a most impossible person – the wrong clothes – button boots! – an incredible moustache! Not his – Meredith Blake's – kind of fellow at all. Didn't look as though he'd ever hunted or shot – or even played a decent game. A foreigner.

Slightly amused, Hercule Poirot read accurately these thoughts passing through the other's head.

He had felt his own interest rising considerably as the train brought him into the West Country. He would see now, with his own eyes, the actual place where these long past events happened.

It was here, at Handcross Manor, that two young brothers had lived and gone over to Alderbury and joked and played tennis and fraternized with a young Amyas Crale and a girl called Caroline. It was from here that Meredith had started out to Alderbury on that fatal morning. That had been sixteen years ago. Hercule Poirot looked with interest at the man who was confronting him with somewhat uneasy politeness.

Very much what he had expected. Meredith Blake resembled superficially every other English country gentleman of straitened means and outdoor tastes.

A shabby old coat of Harris tweed, a weather-beaten, pleasant, middle-aged face with somewhat faded blue eyes, a weak mouth, half hidden by a rather straggly moustache. Poirot found Meredith Blake a great contrast to his brother. He had a hesitating manner, his mental processes were obviously leisurely. It was as though his tempo had slowed down with the years just as his brother's had been accelerated.

As Poirot had already guessed, he was a man whom

you could not hurry. The leisurely life of the English countryside was in his bones.

He looked, the detective thought, a good deal older than his brother, though, from what Mr Jonathan had said, it would seem that only a couple of years separated them.

Hercule Poirot prided himself on knowing how to handle an 'old school tie'. It was no moment for trying to seem English. No, one must be a foreigner – frankly a foreigner – and be magnanimously forgiven for the fact. 'Of course, these foreigners don't quite know the ropes. *Will* shake hands at breakfast. Still, a decent fellow really . . .'

Poirot set about creating this impression of himself. The two men talked, cautiously, of Lady Mary Lytton-Gore and of Admiral Cronshaw. Other names were mentioned. Fortunately Poirot knew someone's cousin and had met somebody else's sister-in-law. He could see a kind of warmth dawning in the Squire's eye. The fellow seemed to know the right people.

Gracefully, insidiously, Poirot slid into the purpose of his visit. He was quick to counteract the inevitable recoil. This book was, alas! going to be written. Miss Crale – Miss Lemarchant, as she was now called – was anxious for him to exercise a judicious editorship. The facts, unfortunately, were public property. But much could be done in their presentation to avoid wounding susceptibilities. Poirot murmured that before now he had been able to use discreet influence to avoid certain purple passages in a book of memoirs.

Meredith Blake flushed angrily. His hand shook a little as he filled a pipe. He said, a slight stammer in his voice:

'It's – it's g-ghoulish the way they dig these things up. S-sixteen years ago. Why can't they let it be?'

Poirot shrugged his shoulders. He said:

'I agree with you. But what will you? There is a demand for such things. And any one is at liberty to reconstruct a proved crime and to comment on it.'

'Seems disgraceful to me.'

Poirot murmured:

'Alas – we do not live in a delicate age . . . You would be surprised, Mr Blake, if you knew the unpleasant publications I had succeeded in – shall we say – softening. I am anxious to do all I can to save Miss Crale's feeling in the matter.'

Meredith Blake murmured: 'Little Carla! That child! A grown-up woman. One can hardly believe it.'

'I know. Time flies swiftly, does it not?'

Meredith Blake sighed. He said: 'Too quickly.'

Poirot said:

'As you will have seen in the letter I handed you from Miss Crale, she is very anxious to know everything possible about the sad events of the past.'

Meredith Blake said with a touch of irritation:

'Why? Why rake up everything again? How much better to let it all be forgotten.'

'You say that, Mr Blake, because you know all the past too well. Miss Crale, remember, knows nothing. That is to say she knows only the story as she has learnt it from the official accounts.'

Meredith Blake winced. He said:

'Yes, I forgot. Poor child. What a detestable position for her. The shock of learning the truth. And then – those soulless, callous reports of the trial.'

'The truth,' said Hercule Poirot, 'can never be done justice to in a mere legal recital. It is the things that are left out that are the things that matter. The emotions, the feelings – the characters of the actors in the drama. The extenuating circumstances –'

He paused and the other man spoke eagerly like an actor who had received his cue.

'Extenuating circumstances! That's just it. If ever there were extenuating circumstances, there were in this case. Amyas Crale was an old friend – his family and mine had been friends for generations, but one has to admit that his conduct was, frankly, outrageous. He was an artist, of course, and presumably that explains it. But there it is – he allowed a most extraordinary set of affairs to arise. The position was one that no ordinary decent man could have contemplated for a moment.'

Hercule Poirot said:

'I am interested that you should say that. It had puzzled me, that situation. Not so does a well-bred man, a man of the world, go about his affairs.'

Blake's thin, hesitating face had lit up with animation. He said:

'Yes, but the whole point is that Amyas never was an ordinary man! He was a painter, you see, and with him painting came first – really sometimes in the most extraordinary way! I don't understand these so-called artistic people myself – never have. I understood Crale a little because, of course, I'd known him all my life. His people were the same sort as my people. And in many ways Crale ran true to type – it was only where art came in that he didn't conform to the usual standards. He wasn't, you see, an amateur in any way. He was first-class – really first-class. Some people say he's a genius. They may be right. But as a result, he was always what I should describe as unbalanced. When he was painting a picture – nothing else mattered, nothing could be allowed to get in the way. He was like a man in a dream. Completely obsessed by what he was doing. Not till the canvas was finished did he come out of this absorption and start to pick up the threads of ordinary life again.'

He looked questioningly at Poirot and the latter nodded.

'You understand, I see. Well, that explains, I think, why this particular situation arose. He was in love with this girl. He wanted to marry her. He was prepared to leave his wife and child for her. But he'd started painting her down here, and he wanted to finish that picture. Nothing else mattered to him. He didn't *see* anything else. And the fact that the situation was a perfectly impossible one for the two women concerned, doesn't seem to have occurred to him.'

'Did either of them understand his point of view?'

'Oh yes – in a way. Elsa did, I suppose. She was terrifically enthusiastic about his painting. But it was a difficult position for her – naturally. And as for Caroline –'

He stopped. Poirot said:

'For Caroline – yes, indeed.'

Meredith Blake said, speaking with a little difficulty:

'Caroline – I had always – well, I had always been very fond of Caroline. There was a time when – when I hoped to marry her. But that was soon nipped in the bud. Still, I remained, if I may say so, devoted to – to her service.'

Poirot nodded thoughtfully. That slightly old-fashioned phrase expressed, he felt, the man before him very typically. Meredith Blake was the kind of man who would devote himself readily to a romantic and honourable devotion. He would serve his lady faithfully and without hope of reward. Yes, it was all very much in character.

He said, carefully weighing the words:

'You must have resented this – attitude – on *her* behalf?'

'I did. Oh, I did. I – I actually remonstrated with Crale on the subject.'

'When was this?'

'Actually the day before – before it all happened. They came over to tea here, you know. I got Crale aside and I – I put it to him. I even said, I remember, that it wasn't fair on either of them.'

'Ah, you said that?'

'Yes. I didn't think – you see, that he *realized*.'

'Possibly not.'

'I said to him that it was putting Caroline in a perfectly unendurable position. If he meant to marry this girl, he ought not to have her staying in the house and – well – more or less flaunt her in Caroline's face. It was, I said, an unendurable insult.'

Poirot asked curiously: 'What did he answer?'

Meredith Blake replied with distaste:

'He said: "Caroline must lump it."'

Hercule Poirot's eyebrows rose.

'Not,' he said, 'a very sympathetic reply.'

'I thought it abominable. I lost my temper. I said that no doubt, not caring for his wife, he didn't mind how much he made her suffer, but what, I said, about the girl? Hadn't he realized it was a pretty rotten position for *her*? His reply to that was that Elsa must lump it too!

'Then he went on: "You don't seem to understand, Meredith, that this thing I'm painting is the best thing I've done. It's *good*, I tell you. And a couple of jealous quarrelling women aren't going to upset it – no, by hell, they're not."

'It was hopeless talking to him. I said he seemed to have taken leave of all ordinary decency. Painting, I said, wasn't everything. He interrupted there. He said: "Ah, but it is to *me*."

'I was still very angry. I said it was perfectly disgraceful the way he had always treated Caroline. She had had a miserable life with him. He said he knew that and he was sorry about it. Sorry! He said: "I know, Merry, you don't believe that – but it's the truth. I've given Caroline the hell of a life and she's been a saint about it. But she did know, I think, what she might be letting herself in for. I told her candidly the sort of damnable egoistic, loose-living kind of chap I was."

'I put it to him then very strongly that he ought not to break up his married life. There was the child to be considered and everything. I said that I could understand that a girl like Elsa could bowl a man over, but that even for her sake he ought to break off the whole thing. She was very young. She was going into this bald-headed, but she might regret it bitterly afterwards. I said couldn't he pull himself together, make a clean break and go back to his wife?'

'And what did he say?'

Blake said: 'He just looked – embarrassed. He patted me on the shoulder and said: "You're a good chap, Merry. But you're too sentimental. You wait till the picture's finished and you'll admit that I was right."

'I said: "Damn your picture." And he grinned and said all the neurotic women in England couldn't do that. Then I said that it would have been more decent to have kept the whole thing from Caroline until after the picture was finished. He said that that wasn't *his* fault. It was Elsa who had insisted on spilling the beans. I said, Why? And he said that she had had some idea that it wasn't straight otherwise. She wanted everything to be clear and above board. Well, of course, in a way, one could understand that and respect the girl for it. However badly she was behaving, she did at least want to be honest.'

'A lot of additional pain and grief is caused by honesty,' remarked Hercule Poirot.

Meredith Blake looked at him doubtfully. He did not quite like the sentiment. He sighed:

'It was a – a most unhappy time for us all.'

'The only person who does not seem to have been affected by it was Amyas Crale,' said Poirot.

'And why? Because he was a rank egoist. I remember him now. Grinning at me as he went off saying: "Don't worry, Merry. Everything's going to pan out all right!"'

'The incurable optimist,' murmured Poirot.

Meredith Blake said:

'He was the kind of man who didn't take women seriously. *I* could have told him that Caroline was desperate.'

'Did she tell you so?'

'Not in so many words. But I shall always see her face as it was that afternoon. White and strained with a kind of desperate gaiety. She talked and laughed a lot. But her eyes – there was a kind of anguished grief in them that was the most moving thing I have ever known. Such a gentle creature, too.'

Hercule Poirot looked at him for a minute or two without speaking. Clearly the man in front of him felt no incongruity in speaking thus of a woman who on the day after had deliberately killed her husband.

Meredith Blake went on. He had by now quite overcome his first suspicious hostility. Hercule Poirot had the gift of listening. To men such as Meredith Blake, the reliving of the past has a definite attraction. He spoke now almost more to himself than to his guest.

'I ought to have suspected something, I suppose. It was Caroline who turned the conversation to – to my little hobby. It was, I must confess, an enthusiasm of mine. The old English herbalists, you know, are a very interesting study. There are so many plants that were formerly used in medicine and which have now disappeared from the official Pharmacopœia. And it's astonishing, really, how a simple decoction of something or other will really work wonders. No need for doctors half the time. The French understand these things – some of their *tisanes* are first rate.' He was well away now on his hobby.

'Dandelion tea, for instance; marvellous stuff. And a decoction of hips – I saw the other day somewhere that that's coming into fashion with the medical profession again. Oh yes, I must confess, I got a lot of pleasure out of my brews. Gathering the plants at the right time, drying them – macerating them – all the rest of it. I've even dropped to superstition sometimes and gathered my roots at the full of the moon or whatever it was the ancients advised. On that day I gave my guests, I remember, a special disquisition on the spotted hemlock. It flowers biennially. You gather the fruits when they're ripening, just before they turn yellow. Coniine, you know, is a drug that's dropped out – I don't believe there's any official preparation of it in the last Pharmacopœia – but I've proved the

117

usefulness of it in whooping cough – and in asthma too, for that matter –'

'You talked of all this in your laboratory?'

'Yes, I showed them round – explained the various drugs to them – valerian and the way it attracts cats – one sniff at that was enough for them! Then they asked about deadly nightshade and I told them about belladonna and atropine. They were very much interested.'

'They? What is comprised in that word?'

Meredith Blake looked faintly surprised as though he had forgotten that his listener had no first-hand knowledge of the scene.

'Oh, the whole party. Let me see, Philip was there and Amyas, and Caroline, of course. Angela. And Elsa Greer.'

'That was all?'

'Yes – I think so. Yes, I am sure of it,' Blake looked at him curiously. 'Who else should there be?'

'I thought perhaps the governess –'

'Oh, I see. No, she wasn't there that afternoon. I believe I've forgotten her name now. Nice women. Took her duties very seriously. Angela worried her a good deal I think.'

'Why was that?'

'Well, she was a nice kid, but she was inclined to run wild. Always up to something or other. Put a slug or something down Amyas's back one day when he was hard at work painting. He went up in smoke. Cursed her up and down dale. It was after that that he insisted on this school idea.'

'Sending her to school?'

'Yes. I don't mean he wasn't fond of her, but he found her a bit of a nuisance sometimes. And I think – I've always thought –'

'Yes?'

'That he was a bit jealous. Caroline, you see, was a slave to Angela. In a way, perhaps, Angela came first with her – and Amyas didn't like that. There was a reason for it of course. I won't go into that, but –'

Poirot interrupted.

'The reason being that Caroline Crale reproached herself for an action that had disfigured the girl?'

Blake exclaimed: 'Oh, you know that? I wasn't going to mention it. All over and done with. But yes, that was the cause of her attitude I think. She always seemed to feel that there was nothing too much she could do – to make up, as it were.'

Poirot nodded thoughtfully. He asked:

'And Angela? Did she bear a grudge against her half sister?'

'Oh no, don't run away with that idea. Angela was devoted to Caroline. She never gave that old business a thought, I'm sure. It was just Caroline who couldn't forgive herself.'

'Did Angela take kindly to the idea of boarding school?'

'No, she didn't. She was furious with Amyas. Caroline took her side, but Amyas had absolutely made his mind up about it. In spite of a hot temper, Amyas was an easy man in most respects, but when he really got his back up, everyone had to give in. Both Caroline and Angela knuckled under.'

'She was to go to school – when?'

'The autumn term – they were getting her kit together, I remember. I suppose, if it hadn't been for the tragedy, she would have gone off a few days later. There was some talk of her packing on the morning of that day.'

Poirot said: 'And the governess?'

'What do you mean – the governess?'

'How did she like the idea? It deprived her of a job, did it not?'

'Yes – well, I suppose it did in a way. Little Carla used to do a few lessons, but of course she was only – what? Six or thereabouts. She had a nurse. They wouldn't have kept Miss Williams on for her. Yes, that's the name – Williams. Funny how things come back to you when you talk them over.'

'Yes, indeed. You are back now, are you not, in the

past? You relive the scenes – the words that people said, their gestures – the expressions on their faces?'

Meredith Blake said slowly:

'In a way – yes . . . But there are gaps, you know . . . Great chunks missed out. I remember, for instance, the shock it was to me when I first learned that Amyas was going to leave Caroline – but I can't remember whether it was he who told me or Elsa. I do remember arguing with Elsa on the subject – trying to show her, I mean, that it was a pretty rotten thing to do. And she only laughed at me in that cool way of hers and said I was old fashioned. Well, I dare say I *am* old fashioned, but I still think I was right. Amyas had a wife and child – he ought to have stuck to them.'

'But Miss Greer thought that point of view out of date?'

'Yes. Mind you, sixteen years ago, divorce wasn't looked on quite so much as a matter of course as it is now. But Elsa was the kind of girl who went in for being modern. Her point of view was that when two people weren't happy together it was better to make a break. She said that Amyas and Caroline never stopped having rows and that it was far better for the child that she shouldn't be brought up in an atmosphere of disharmony.'

'And her argument did not impress you?'

Meredith Blake said slowly:

'I felt, all the time, that she didn't really know what she was talking about. She was rattling these things off – things she'd read in books or heard from her friends – it was like a parrot. She was – it's a queer thing to say – pathetic somehow. So young and so self-confident.' He paused. 'There is something about youth, M. Poirot, that is – that can be – terribly moving.'

Hercule Poirot said, looking at him with some interest: 'I know what you mean . . .'

Blake went on, speaking more to himself than to Poirot.

'That's partly, I think, why I tackled Crale. He was nearly twenty years older than the girl. It didn't seem fair.'

Poirot murmured:

'Alas – how seldom one makes any effect. When a person has determined on a certain course – it is not easy to turn them from it.'

Meredith Blake said:

'That is true enough.' His tone was a shade bitter. 'I certainly did no good by my interference. But then, I am not a very convincing person. I never have been.'

Poirot threw him a quick glance. He read into that slight acerbity of tone the dissatisfaction of a sensitive man with his own lack of personality. And he acknowledged to himself the truth of what Blake had just said.

Meredith Blake was not the man to persuade any one into or out of any course. His well-meaning attempts would always be set aside – indulgently usually, without anger, but definitely set aside. They would not carry weight. He was essentially an ineffective man.

Poirot said, with an appearance of changing a painful subject: 'You still have your laboratory of medicines and cordials, yes?'

'No.'

The word came sharply – with an almost anguished rapidity Meridith Blake said, his face flushing:

'I abandoned the whole thing – dismantled it. I couldn't go on with it – how could I? – after what had happened. The whole thing, you see, might have been said to be *my* fault.'

'No, no, Mr Blake, you are too sensitive.'

'But don't you see? If I hadn't collected those damned drugs? If I hadn't laid stress on them – boasted about them – forced them on those people's notice that afternoon? But I never thought – I never dreamed – how could I –'

'How indeed.'

'But I went bumbling on about them. Pleased with my little bit of knowledge. Blind, conceited fool. I pointed out that damned coniine. I even, fool that I was, took them back into the library and read them out that passage from the Phaedo describing Socrates' death. A

123

beautiful piece of writing – I've always admired it. But it's haunted me ever since.'

Poirot said:

'Did they find any fingerprints on the coniine bottle?'

'Hers.'

'Caroline Crale's?'

'Yes.'

'Not yours?'

'No. I didn't handle the bottle, you see. Only pointed to it.'

'But at the same time, surely, you had handled it?'

'Oh, of course, but I gave the bottles a periodic dusting from time to time – I never allowed the servants in there, of course – and I had done that about four or five days previously.'

'You kept the room locked up?'

'Invariably.'

'When did Caroline Crale take the coniine from the bottle?'

Meredith Blake replied reluctantly:

'She was the last to leave the room. I called her, I remember, and she came hurrying out. Her cheeks were just a little pink – and her eyes wide and excited. Oh, God, I can see her now.'

Poirot said: 'Did you have any conversation with her at all that afternoon? I mean by that, did you discuss the situation as between her and her husband at all?'

Blake said slowly in a low voice:

'Not directly. She was looking as I've told you – very upset. I said to her at a moment when we were more or less by ourselves: "Is anything the matter, my dear?" she said: "Everything's the matter . . ." I wish you could have heard the desperation in her voice. Those words were the absolute literal truth. There's no getting away from it – Amyas Crale was Caroline's whole world. She said, "Everything's gone – finished. I'm finished, Meredith." And then she laughed and turned to the others and was suddenly wildly and very unnaturally gay.'

Hercule Poirot nodded his head slowly. He looked very like a china mandarin. He said:

'Yes – I see – it was like that . . .'

Meredith Blake pounded suddenly with his fist. His voice rose. It was almost a shout.

'And I'll tell you this M. Poirot – when Caroline Crale said at the trial that she took the stuff for herself, I'll swear she was speaking the truth! There was no thought in her mind of murder at that time. I swear there wasn't. That came later.'

Hercule Poirot asked:

'Are you sure that it *did* come later?'

Blake stared. He said:

'I beg your pardon? I don't quite understand –'

Poirot said:

Agatha Christie

'I ask you whether you are sure that the thought of murder ever did come? Are you perfectly convinced in your own mind that Caroline Crale did deliberately commit murder?'

Meredith Blake's breath came unevenly. He said: 'But if not – if not – are you suggesting an – well, accident of some kind?'

'Not necessarily.'

'That's a very extraordinary thing to say.'

'Is it? You have called Caroline Crale a gentle creature. Do gentle creatures commit murder?'

'She was a gentle creature – but all the same – well, there were very violent quarrels, you know.'

'Not such a gentle creature, then?'

'But she *was* – Oh, how difficult these things are to explain.'

'I am trying to understand.'

'Caroline had a quick tongue – a vehement way of speaking. She might say "I hate you. I wish you were dead." But it wouldn't mean – it wouldn't entail – *action*.'

'So in your opinion, it was highly uncharacteristic of Mrs Crale to commit murder?'

'You have the most extraordinary ways of putting things, M. Poirot. I can only say that – yes – it does seem to me uncharacteristic of her. I can only explain it by realizing that the provocation was extreme. She adored her husband. Under those circumstances a woman might – well – kill.'

Poirot nodded. 'Yes, I agree . . .'

'I was dumbfounded at first. I didn't feel it *could* be true. And it wasn't true – if you know what I mean – it wasn't the real Caroline who did that.'

'But you are quite sure that – in the legal sense – Caroline Crale did do it?'

Again Meredith Blake stared at him.

'My dear man – if she didn't –'

'Well, if she didn't?'

'I can't imagine any alternative solution. Accident? Surely impossible.'

'Quite impossible, I should say.'

'And I can't believe in the suicide theory. It had to be brought forward, but it was quite unconvincing to any one who knew Crale.'

'Quite.'

'So what remains?' asked Meredith Blake.

Poirot said coolly: 'There remains the possibility of Amyas Crale having been killed by somebody else.'

'But that's absurd!'

'You think so?'

'I'm sure of it. Who would have wanted to kill him? Who *could* have killed him?'

'You are more likely to know than I am.'

'But you don't seriously believe –'

Agatha Christie

'Perhaps not. It interests me to examine the possibility. Give it your serious consideration. Tell me what you think.'

Meredith stared at him for a minute or two. Then he lowered his eyes. After a minute or two he shook his head. He said:

'I can't imagine *any* possible alternative. I should like to do so. If there were any reason for suspecting anybody else I would readily believe Caroline innocent. I don't want to think she did it. I couldn't believe it at first. But who else is there? Who else was there. Philip? Crale's best friend. Elsa? Ridiculous. Myself? Do I look like a murderer? A respectable governess? A couple of old faithful servants? Perhaps you'd suggest that the child Angela did it? No, M. Poirot, there's *no* alternative. *Nobody* could have killed Amyas Crale but his wife. But he drove her to it. And so, in a way, it was suicide after all, I suppose.'

'Meaning that he died by the result of his own actions, though not by his own hand?'

'Yes, it's a fanciful point of view, perhaps. But – well – cause and effect, you know.'

Hercule Poirot said:

'Have you ever reflected, Mr Blake, that the reason for murder is nearly always to be found by a study of the person murdered?'

'I hadn't exactly – yes, I suppose I see what you mean.'

Poirot said:

'Until you know exactly *what sort of a person the victim was*, you cannot begin to see the circumstances of a crime clearly.'

He added:

'That is what I am seeking for – and what you and your brother have helped to give me – a reconstruction of the man Amyas Crale.'

Meredith Blake passed the main point of the remark over. His attention had been attracted by a single word. He said quickly:

'Philip?'

'Yes.'

'You have talked with him also?'

'Certainly.'

Meredith Blake said sharply:

'You should have come to me first.'

Smiling a little, Poirot made a courteous gesture.

'According to the laws of primogenitude, that is so,' he said. 'I am aware that you are the elder. But you comprehend that as your brother lives near London, it was easier to visit him first.'

Meredith Blake was still frowning. He pulled uneasily at his lip. He repeated:

'You should have come to me first.'

This time, Poirot did not answer. He waited. And presently Meredith Blake went on:

'Philip,' he said, 'is prejudiced.'

'Yes?'

'As a matter of fact he's a mass of prejudices – always has been.' He shot a quick uneasy glance at Poirot. 'He'll have tried to put you against Caroline.'

'Does that matter, so long – after?'

Meredith Blake gave a sharp sigh.

'I know. I forget that it's so long ago – that it's all over. Caroline is beyond being harmed. But all the same I shouldn't like you to get a false impression.'

'And you think your brother might give me a false impression?'

'Frankly, I do. You see, there was always a certain – how shall I put it? – antagonism between him and Caroline.'

'Why?'

The question seemed to irritate Blake. He said:

'Why? How should I know *why*? These things are so. Philip always crabbed her whenever he could. He was annoyed, I think, when Amyas married her. He never went near them for over a year. And yet Amyas was almost his best friend. That was the reason really, I suppose. He didn't feel that any woman was good enough. And he probably felt that Caroline's influence would spoil their friendship.'

'And did it?'

'No, of course it didn't. Amyas was always just as fond of Philip – right up to the end. Used to twit him with being a money grabber and with growing a corporation and being a Philistine generally. Philip didn't care. He just used to grin and say it was a good thing Amyas had one respectable friend.'

'How did your brother react to the Elsa Greer affair?'

'Do you know, I find it rather difficult to say. His attitude wasn't really easy to define. He was annoyed, I think, with Amyas for making a fool of himself over the girl. He said more than once that it wouldn't work and that Amyas would live to regret it. At the same time I have a feeling – yes, very definitely I have a feeling that he was just faintly pleased at seeing Caroline let down.'

Poirot's eyebrows rose. He said:

'He really felt like that?'

'Oh, don't misunderstand me. I wouldn't go further than to say that I believe that feeling was at the back of his mind. I don't know that he ever quite realized himself that that is what he felt. Philip and I have nothing much in common, but there is a link, you know, between people of the same blood. One brother often knows what the other brother is thinking.'

'And after the tragedy?'

Meredith Blake shook his head. A spasm of pain crossed his face. He said:

'Poor Phil. He was terribly cut up. Just broken up by it. He'd always been devoted to Amyas, you see. There was an element of hero worship about it, I think. Amyas Crale and I are the same age. Philip was two years younger. And he looked up to Amyas always. Yes – it was a great blow to him. He was – he was terribly bitter against Caroline.'

'He, at least, had no doubts, then?'

Meredith Blake said:

'None of us had any doubts . . .'

There was a silence. Then Blake said with the irritable plaintiveness of a weak man:

'It was all over – forgotten – and now *you* come – raking it all up . . .'

'Not I. Caroline Crale.'

Meredith stared at him: '*Caroline?* What do you mean?'

Poirot said, watching him:

'Caroline Crale the second.'

Meredith's face relaxed.

'Ah yes, the child. Little Carla. I – I misunderstood you for a moment.'

'You thought I meant the original Caroline Crale? You thought that it was she who would not – how shall I say it – rest easy in her grave?'

Meredith Blake shivered.

'Don't, man.'

'You know that she wrote to her daughter – the last words she ever wrote – that she was innocent?'

Meredith stared at him. He said – and his voice sounded utterly incredulous:

'Caroline wrote *that*?'

'Yes.'

Poirot paused and said:

'It surprises you?'

'It would surprise you if you'd seen her in court. Poor, hunted, defenceless creature. Not even struggling.'

'A defeatist?'

'No, no. She wasn't that. It was, I think, the knowledge that she'd killed the man she loved – or I thought it was that.'

'You are not so sure now?'

'To write a thing like that – solemnly – when she was dying.'

Poirot suggested:

'A pious lie, perhaps.'

'Perhaps.' But Meredith was dubious. 'That's not – that's not like Caroline . . .'

Hercule Poirot nodded. Carla Lemarchant had said that. Carla had only a child's obstinate memory. But Meredith Blake had known Caroline well. It was the first confirmation Poirot had got that Carla's belief was to be depended upon.

Meredith Blake looked up at him. He said slowly:

'If – *if* Caroline was innocent – why, the whole thing's madness! I don't see – any other possible solution . . .'

He turned sharply on Poirot.

'And you? What do you think?'

There was a silence.

'As yet,' said Poirot at last, 'I think nothing. I collect only the impressions. What Caroline Crale was like. What Amyas Crale was like. What the other people who were there at the time were like. What happened exactly on those two days. *That* is what I need. To go over the facts laboriously one by one. Your brother is going to help me there. He is sending me an account of the events as he remembers them.'

Meredith Blake said sharply:

'You won't get much from that. Philip's a busy man. Things slip his memory once they're past and done with. Probably he'll remember things all wrong.'

'There will be gaps, of course. I realize that.'

'I tell you what –' Meredith paused abruptly, then went on, reddening a little as he spoke. 'If you like, I – I could do the same. I mean, it would be a kind of check, wouldn't it?'

Hercule Poirot said warmly:

'It would be most valuable. An idea of the first excellence!'

'Right. I will. I've got some old diaries somewhere. Mind you,' he laughed awkwardly. 'I'm not much of a hand at literary language. Even my spelling's not too good. You – you won't expect too much?'

'Ah, it is not the style I demand. Just a plain recital of everything you can remember. What every one said, how they looked – just what happened. Never mind if it doesn't seem relevant. It all helps with the atmosphere, so to speak.'

'Yes, I can see that. It must be difficult visualizing people and places you have never seen.'

Poirot nodded.

'There is another thing I wanted to ask you. Alderbury is the adjoining property to this, is it not? Would it be possible to go there – to see with my own eyes where the tragedy occurred?'

Meredith Blake said slowly:

'I can take you over there right away. But, of course, it is a good deal changed.'

'It has not been built over?'

'No, thank goodness – not quite so bad as that. But it's a kind of hostel now – it was bought by some society. Hordes of young people come down to it in the summer, and of course all the rooms have been cut up and partitioned into cubicles, and the grounds have been altered a good deal.'

'You must reconstruct it for me by your explanations.'

'I'll do my best. I wish you could have seen it in the old days. It was one of the loveliest properties I know.'

He led the way out through the window and began walking down a slope of lawn.

'Who was responsible for selling it?'

'The executors on behalf of the child. Everything Crale had came to her. He hadn't made a will, so I imagine that it would be divided automatically between his wife and the child. Caroline's will left what she had to the child also.'

'Nothing to her half-sister?'

'Angela had a certain amount of money of her own left her by her father.'

Poirot nodded. 'I see.'

Then he uttered an exclamation:

'But where is it that you take me? This is the seashore ahead of us!'

'Ah, I must explain our geography to you. You'll see for yourself in a minute. There's a creek, you see, Camel Creek, they call it, runs inland – looks almost like a river mouth, but it isn't – it's just sea. To get to Alderbury by land you have to go right inland and round the creek, but the shortest way from one house to the other is to row across this narrow bit of the creek. Alderbury is just opposite – there, you can see the house through the trees.'

They had come out on a little beach. Opposite them was a wooded headland and a white house could just be distinguished high up amongst the trees.

Two boats were drawn up on the beach. Meredith Blake, with Poirot's somewhat awkward assistance, dragged one of them down to the water and presently they were rowing across to the other side.

'We always went this way in the old days,' Meredith explained. 'Unless, of course, there was a storm or it was raining, and then we'd take the car. But it's nearly three miles if you go round that way.'

He ran the boat neatly alongside a stone quay on the other side. He cast a disparaging eye on a collection of wooden huts and some concrete terraces.

'All new, this. Used to be a boathouse – tumbledown old place – and nothing else. And one walked along the shore and bathed off those rocks over there.'

He assisted his guest to alight, made fast the boat, and led the way up a steep path.

'Don't suppose we'll meet any one,' he said over his shoulder. 'Nobody here in April – except for Easter. Doesn't matter if we do. I'm on good terms with my neighbours. Sun's glorious today. Might be summer.

137

It was a wonderful day then. More like July than September. Brilliant sun – but a chilly little wind.'

The path came out of the trees and skirted an outcrop of rock. Meredith pointed up with his hand.

'That's what they called the Battery. We're more or less underneath it now – skirting round it.'

They plunged into trees again and then the path took another sharp turn and they emerged by a door set in a high wall. The path itself continued to zigzag upwards, but Meredith opened the door and the two men passed through it.

For a moment Poirot was dazzled coming in from the shade outside. The Battery was an artificially cleared plateau with battlements set with cannon. It gave one the impression of overhanging the sea. There were trees above it and behind it, but on the sea side there was nothing but the dazzling blue water below.

'Attractive spot,' said Meredith. He nodded contemptuously towards a kind of pavilion set back against the back wall. 'That wasn't there, of course – only an old tumbledown shed where Amyas kept his painting muck and some bottled beer and a few deck chairs. It wasn't concreted then, either. There used to be a bench and a table – painted iron ones. That was all. Still – it hasn't changed much.'

His voice held an unsteady note.

Poirot said: 'And it was here that it happened?'

Meredith nodded.

'The bench was there – up against the shed. He was sprawled on that. He used to sprawl there sometimes when he was painting – just fling himself down and stare and stare – and then suddenly up he'd jump and start laying the paint on the canvas like mad.'

He paused.

'That's why, you know, he looked – almost natural. As though he might be asleep – just have dropped off. But his eyes were open – and he'd – just stiffened up. Stuff sort of paralyses you, you know. There isn't any pain . . . I've – I've always been glad of that . . .'

Poirot asked a thing that he already knew.

'Who found him?'

'She did. Caroline. After lunch. I and Elsa, I suppose, were the last ones to see him alive. It must have been coming on then. He – looked queer. I'd rather not talk about it. I'll write it to you. Easier that way.'

He turned abruptly and went out of the Battery. Poirot followed him without speaking.

The two men went on up the zigzag path. At a higher level than the Battery there was another small plateau. It was over-shadowed with trees and there was a bench there and a table.

Meredith said:

'They haven't changed this much. But the bench used not to be Ye Olde Rustic. It was just a painted

139

iron business. A bit hard for sitting, but a lovely view.'

Poirot agreed. Through a framework of trees one looked down over the Battery to the creek mouth.

'I sat up here part of the morning,' Meredith explained. 'Trees weren't quite so overgrown then. One could see the battlements of the Battery quite plainly. That's where Elsa was posing, you know. Sitting on one with her head twisted round.'

He gave a slight twitch of his shoulders.

'Trees grow faster than one thinks,' he muttered. 'Oh well, suppose I'm getting old. Come on up to the house.'

They continued to follow the path till it emerged near the house. It had been a fine old house, Georgian in style. It had been added to and on a green lawn near it were set some fifty little wooden bathing hutches.

'Young men sleep there, girls in the house,' Meredith explained. 'I don't suppose there's anything you want to see here. All the rooms have been cut about. Used to be a little conservatory tacked on here. These people have built a loggia. Oh well – I suppose they enjoy their holidays. Can't keep everything as it used to be – more's the pity.'

He turned away abruptly.

'We'll go down another way. It – it all comes back to me, you know. Ghosts. Ghosts everywhere.'

They returned to the quay by a somewhat longer and more rambling route. Neither of them spoke. Poirot respected his companion's mood.

When they reached Handcross Manor once more, Meredith Blake said abruptly:

'I bought that picture, you know. The one that Amyas was painting. I just couldn't stand the idea of its being sold for – well – publicity value – a lot of dirty-minded brutes gaping at it. It was a fine piece of work. Amyas said it was the best thing he'd ever done. I shouldn't be surprised if he was right. It was practically finished. He only wanted to work on it another day or so. Would – would you care to see it?'

Hercule Poirot said quickly: 'Yes, indeed.'

Blake led the way across the hall and took a key from his pocket. He unlocked a door and they went into a fair-sized, dusty smelling room. It was closely shuttered. Blake went across to the windows and opened the wooden shutters. Then, with a little difficulty, he flung up a window and a breath of fragrant spring air came wafting into the room.

Meredith said: 'That's better.'

He stood by the window inhaling the air and Poirot joined him. There was no need to ask what the room had been. The shelves were empty but there were marks upon them where bottles had stood. Against

141

one wall was some derelict chemical apparatus and a sink. The room was thick in dust.

Meredith Blake was looking out of the window. He said:

'How easily it all comes back. Standing here, smelling the jasmine – and talking – talking – like the damned fool I was – about my precious potions and distillations!'

Absently, Poirot stretched a hand through the window. He pulled off a spray of jasmine leaves just breaking from their woody stem.

Meredith Blake moved resolutely across the floor. On the wall was a picture covered with a dust sheet. He jerked the dust sheet away.

Poirot caught his breath. He had seen so far, four pictures of Amyas Crale's: two at the Tate, one at a London dealer's, one, the still life of roses. But now he was looking at what the artist himself had called his best picture, and Poirot realized at once what a superb artist the man had been.

The painting had an old superficial smoothness. At first sight it might have been a poster, so seemingly crude were its contrasts. A girl, a girl in a canary-yellow shirt and dark-blue slacks, sitting on a grey wall in full sunlight against a background of violent blue sea. Just the kind of subject for a poster.

But the first appearance was deceptive; there was a

subtle distortion – an amazing brilliance and clarity in the light. And the girl –

Yes, here was life. All there was, all there could be of life, of youth, of sheer blazing vitality. The face was alive and the eyes . . .

So much life! Such passionate youth! That, then, was what Amyas Crale had seen in Elsa Greer, which had made him blind and deaf to the gentle creature, his wife. Elsa *was* life. Elsa was youth.

A superb, slim, straight creature, arrogant, her head turned, her eyes insolent with triumph. Looking at you, watching you – waiting . . .

Hercule Poirot spread out his hands. He said:

'It is a great – yes, it is great –'

Meredith Blake said, a catch in his voice:

'She was so young –'

Poirot nodded. He thought to himself.

'What do most people mean when they say that? *So young*. Something innocent, something appealing, something helpless. But youth is not that! Youth is crude, youth is strong, youth is powerful – yes, and cruel! And one thing more – youth is vulnerable.'

He followed his host to the door. His interest was quickened now in Elsa Greer whom he was to visit next. What would the years have done to that passionate, triumphant crude child?

He looked back at the picture.

Those eyes. Watching him . . . watching him . . . Telling him something . . .

Supposing he couldn't understand what they were telling him? Would the real woman be able to tell him? Or were those eyes saying something that the real woman did not know?

Such arrogance, such triumphant anticipation.

And then Death had stepped in and taken the prey out of those eager, clutching young hands . . .

And the light had gone out of those passionately anticipating eyes. What were the eyes of Elsa Greer like now?

He went out of the room with one last look.

He thought: 'She was too much alive.'

He felt – a little – frightened . . .

Chapter 8

This Little Pig Had Roast Beef

The house in Brook Street had Darwin tulips in the window boxes. Inside the hall a great vase of white lilac sent eddies of perfume towards the open front door.

A middle-aged butler relieved Poirot of his hat and stick. A footman appeared to take them and the butler murmured deferentially:

'Will you come this way, sir?'

Poirot followed him along the hall and down three steps. A door was opened, the butler pronounced his name with every syllable correct.

Then the door closed behind him and a tall thin man got up from a chair by the fire and came towards him.

Lord Dittisham was a man just under forty. He was not only a Peer of the Realm, he was a poet. Two of his fantastical poetic dramas had been staged at vast expense and had had a *succès d'estime*. His forehead was rather prominent, his chin was eager, and his eyes and his mouth unexpectedly beautiful.

He said:

'Sit down, M. Poirot.'

Poirot sat down and accepted a cigarette from his host. Lord Dittisham shut the box, struck a match and held it for Poirot to light his cigarette, then he himself sat down and looked thoughtfully at his visitor.

Then he said:

'It is my wife you have come to see, I know.'

Poirot answered:

'Lady Dittisham was so kind as to give me an appointment.'

'Yes.'

There was a pause. Poirot hazarded:

'You do not, I hope, object, Lord Dittisham?'

The thin dreamy face was transformed by a sudden quick smile.

'The objections of husbands, M. Poirot, are never taken seriously in these days.'

'Then you do object?'

'No. I cannot say that. But I am, I must confess it, a little fearful of the effect upon my wife. Let me be quite frank. A great many years ago, when my wife was only a young girl, she passed through a terrible ordeal. She has, I hope, recovered from the shock. I have come to believe that she has forgotten it. Now you appear and necessarily your questions will reawaken these old memories.'

'It is regrettable,' said Hercule Poirot politely.

'I do not know quite what the result will be.'

'I can only assure you, Lord Dittisham, that I shall be as discreet as possible, and do all I can not to distress Lady Dittisham. She is, no doubt, of a delicate and nervous temperament.'

Then, suddenly and surprisingly, the other laughed. He said:

'Elsa? Elsa's as strong as a horse!'

'Then –' Poirot paused diplomatically. The situation intrigued him.

Lord Dittisham said:

'My wife is equal to any amount of shocks. I wonder if you know her reason for seeing you?'

Poirot replied placidly: 'Curiosity?'

A kind of respect showed in the other man's eyes.

'Ah, you realize that?'

Poirot said:

'It is inevitable. Women will *always* see a private detective! Men will tell him to go to the devil.'

'Some women might tell him to go to the devil too.'

'After they have seen him – not before.'

'Perhaps.' Lord Dittisham paused. 'What is the idea behind this book?'

Hercule Poirot shrugged his shoulders.

'One resurrects the old tunes, the old stage turns, the old costumes. One resurrects, too, the old murders.'

'Faugh!' said Lord Dittisham.

'Faugh! If you like. But you will not alter human nature by saying Faugh. Murder is a drama. The desire for drama is very strong in the human race.'

Lord Dittisham murmured:

'I know – I know . . .'

'So you see,' said Poirot, 'the book will be written. It is my part to make sure that there shall be no gross mis-statements, no tampering with the known facts.'

'The facts are public property I should have thought.'

'Yes. But not the interpretation of them.'

Dittisham said sharply:

'Just what do you mean by that, M. Poirot?'

'My dear Lord Dittisham, there are many ways of regarding, for instance, a historical fact. Take an example: many books have been written on your Mary Queen of Scots, representing her as a martyr, as an unprincipled and wanton woman, as a rather simple-minded saint, as a murderess and an intriguer, or again as a victim of circumstance and fate! One can take one's choice.'

'And in this case? Crale was killed by his wife – that is, of course, undisputed. At the trial my wife came in for some, in my opinion, undeserved calumny. She had to be smuggled out of court afterwards. Public opinion was very hostile to her.'

'The English,' said Poirot, 'are a very moral people.'

Lord Dittisham said: 'Confound them, they are!'

He added – looking at Poirot: 'And you?'

'Me,' said Poirot. 'I lead a very moral life. That is not quite the same thing as having moral ideas.'

Lord Dittisham said:

'I've wondered sometimes what this Mrs Crale was really like. All this injured wife business – I've a feeling there was something *behind* that.'

'Your wife might know,' agreed Poirot.

'My wife,' said Lord Dittisham, 'has never mentioned the case once.'

Poirot looked at him with quickened interest. He said:

'Ah, I begin to see –'

The other said sharply:

'What do you see?'

Poirot replied with a bow:

'The creative imagination of the poet . . .'

Lord Dittisham rose and rang the bell. He said brusquely:

'My wife will be waiting for you.'

The door opened.

'You rang, my lord?'

'Take M. Poirot up to her ladyship.'

Up two flights of stairs, feet sinking into soft pile carpets. Subdued flood lighting. Money, money everywhere. Of taste, not so much. There had been a sombre austerity in Lord Dittisham's room. But here, in the house, there was only a solid lavishness. The best. Not necessarily the showiest, or the most startling. Merely 'expense no object', allied to a lack of imagination.

Poirot said to himself: 'Roast beef? Yes, roast beef!'

It was not a large room into which he was shown. The big drawing-room was on the first floor. This was the personal sitting-room of the mistress of the house and the mistress of the house was standing against the mantelpiece as Poirot was announced and shown in.

A phrase leapt into his startled mind and refused to be driven out.

She died young . . .

That was his thought as he looked at Elsa Dittisham who had been Elsa Greer.

He would never have recognized her from the picture Meredith Blake had shown him. That had been, above all, a picture of youth, a picture of vitality. Here there was no youth – there might never have been youth. And yet he realized, as he had not realized from Crale's picture, that Elsa was beautiful. Yes, it was a very beautiful woman who came forward to meet him. And certainly not old. After all, what was she? Not more than thirty-six now if she had been twenty at the time of the tragedy. Her black hair was perfectly arranged round her shapely head, her features were almost classic, her make-up was exquisite.

He felt a strange pang. It was, perhaps, the fault of old Mr Jonathan, speaking of Juliet . . . No Juliet here – unless perhaps one could imagine Juliet a survivor – living on, deprived of Romeo . . . Was it not an essential part of Juliet's make-up that she should die young?

Elsa Greer had been left alive . . .

She was greeting him in a level rather monotonous voice.

'I am so interested, M. Poirot. Sit down and tell me what you want me to do?'

He thought:

'But she isn't interested. Nothing interests her.'

Big grey eyes – like dead lakes.

Poirot became, as was his way, a little obviously foreign.

He exclaimed:

'I am confused, madame, veritably I am confused.'

'Oh no, why?'

'Because I realize that this – this reconstruction of a past drama must be excessively painful to you!'

She looked amused. Yes, it was amusement. Quite genuine amusement.

She said:

'I suppose my husband put that idea into your head?

Agatha Christie

He saw you when you arrived. Of course he doesn't understand in the least. He never has. I'm not at all the sensitive sort of person he imagines I am.'

The amusement was still in her voice. She said:

'My father, you know, was a mill hand. He worked his way up and made a fortune. You don't do that if you're thin-skinned. I'm the same.'

Poirot thought to himself: Yes, that is true. A thin-skinned person would not have come to stay in Caroline Crale's house.

Lady Dittisham said:

'What is it you want me to do?'

'You are sure, madame, that to go over the past would not be painful to you?'

She considered a minute, and it struck Poirot suddenly that Lady Dittisham was a very frank woman. She might lie from necessity but never from choice.

Elsa Dittisham said slowly:

'No, not *painful*. In a way, I wish it were.'

'Why?'

She said impatiently:

'It's so stupid never to feel anything . . .'

And Hercule Poirot thought:

'Yes, Elsa Greer is dead . . .'

Aloud he said:

'At all events, Lady Dittisham, it makes my task very much easier.'

She said cheerfully:

'What do you want to know?'

'Have you a good memory, madame?'

'Reasonably good, I think.'

'And you are sure it will not pain you to go over those days in detail?'

'It won't pain me at all. Things can only pain you when they are happening.'

'It is so with some people, I know.'

Lady Dittisham said:

'That's what Edward – my husband – can't understand. He thinks the trial and all that was a terrible ordeal for me.'

'Was it not?'

Elsa Dittisham said:

'No, I enjoyed it.' There was a reflective satisfied quality in her voice. She went on: 'God, how that old brute Depleach went for me. He's a devil, if you like. I enjoyed fighting him. He didn't get me down.'

She looked at Poirot with a smile.

'I hope I'm not upsetting your illusions. A girl of twenty, I ought to have been prostrated, I suppose – agonized with shame or something. I wasn't. I didn't care what they said to me. I only wanted one thing.'

'What?'

'To get her hanged, of course,' said Elsa Dittisham.

He noticed her hands – beautiful hands but with long curving nails. Predatory hands.

She said:

'You're thinking me vindictive? So I am vindictive – to any one who has injured me. That woman was to my mind the lowest kind of woman there is. She knew that Amyas cared for me – that he was going to leave her and she killed him so that *I* shouldn't have him.'

She looked across at Poirot.

'Don't you think that's pretty mean?'

'You do not understand or sympathize with jealousy?'

'No, I don't think I do. If you've lost, you've lost. If you can't keep your husband, let him go with a good grace. It's possessiveness I don't understand.'

'You might have understood it if you had ever married him.'

'I don't think so. We weren't –' She smiled suddenly at Poirot. Her smile was, he felt, a little frightening. It was so far removed from any real feeling. 'I'd like you to get this right,' she said. 'Don't think that Amyas Crale seduced an innocent young girl. It wasn't like that at all! Of the two of us, *I* was responsible. I met him at a party and I fell for him – I knew I'd got to have him –'

A travesty – a grotesque travesty but –

And all my fortunes at thy foot I'll lay
And follow thee, my lord, throughout the world . . .

'Although he was married?'

'Trespassers will be prosecuted? It takes more than a printed notice to keep you from reality. If he was unhappy with his wife and could be happy with me, then why not? We've only one life to live.'

'But it has been said he was happy with his wife.'

Elsa shook her head.

'No. They quarrelled like cat and dog. She nagged at him. She was – oh, she was a horrible woman!'

She got up and lit a cigarette. She said with a little smile:

'Probably I'm unfair to her. But I really *do* think she was rather hateful.'

Poirot said slowly: 'It was a great tragedy.'

'Yes, it was a great tragedy.' She turned on him suddenly, into the dead monotonous weariness of her face something came quiveringly alive.

'It killed *me*, do you understand? It killed me. Ever since there's been nothing – nothing at all.' Her voice dropped. 'Emptiness!' She waved her hands impatiently. 'Like a stuffed fish in a glass case!'

'Did Amyas Crale mean so much to you?'

She nodded. It was a queer confiding little nod – oddly pathetic. She said:

'I think I've always had a single-track mind.' She mused sombrely. 'I suppose – really – one ought to put a knife into oneself – like Juliet. But – but to do that is to acknowledge that you're done for – that life's beaten you.'

'And instead?'

'There ought to be everything – just the same – once one has got over it. I *did* get over it. It didn't mean anything to me any more. I thought I'd go on to the next thing.'

Yes, the next thing. Poirot saw her plainly trying so hard to fulfil that crude determination. Saw her beautiful and rich, seductive to men, seeking with greedy predatory hands to fill up a life that was empty. Hero worship – a marriage to a famous aviator – then an explorer, that big giant of a man, Arnold Stevenson – possibly not unlike Amyas Crale physically – a reversion to the creative arts: Dittisham!

Elsa Dittisham said:

'I've never been a hypocrite! There's a Spanish proverb I've always liked. *Take what you want and pay for it, says God.* Well, I've done that. I've taken what I wanted – but I've always been willing to pay the price.'

Hercule Poirot said:

'What you do not understand is that there are things that cannot be bought.'

She stared at him. She said:

'I don't mean just money.'

Poirot said:

'No, no, I understand what you mean. But it is not everything in life that has its ticket, so much. There are things that are *not for sale*.'

'Nonsense!'

He smiled very faintly. In her voice was the arrogance of the successful mill hand who had risen to riches.

Hercule Poirot felt a sudden wave of pity. He looked at the ageless, smooth face, the weary eyes, and he remembered the girl whom Amyas Crale had painted . . .

Elsa Dittisham said:

'Tell me all about this book. What is the purpose of it? Whose idea is it?'

'Oh! my dear lady, what other purpose is there but to serve up yesterday's sensation with today's sauce.'

'But *you're* not a writer?'

'No, I am an expert on crime.'

'You mean they consult you on crime books?'

'Not always. In this case, I have a commission.'

'From whom?'

'I am – what do you say – vetting this publication on behalf of an interested party.'

'What party?'

'Miss Carla Lemarchant.'

'Who is she?'

'She is the daughter of Amyas and Caroline Crale.'

Elsa stared for a minute. Then she said:

'Oh, of course, there *was* a child. I remember. I suppose she's grown up now?'

'Yes, she is twenty-one.'

'What is she like?'

'She is tall and dark and, I think, beautiful. And she has courage and personality.'

Elsa said thoughtfully:

'I should like to see her.'

'She might not care to see you.'

Elsa looked surprised.

'Why? Oh, I see. But what nonsense! She can't possibly remember anything about it. She can't have been more than six.'

'She knows that her mother was tried for her father's murder.'

'And she thinks it's my fault?'

'It is a possible interpretation.'

Elsa shrugged her shoulders. She said:

'How stupid! If Caroline had behaved like a reasonable human being –'

'So you take no responsibility?'

'Why should I? *I've* nothing to be ashamed of. I loved him. I would have made him happy.' She looked across at Poirot. Her face broke up – suddenly, incredibly, he saw the girl of the picture. She said: 'If I could make you see. If you could see it from my side. If you knew –'

Poirot leaned forward.

'But that is what I want. See, Mr Philip Blake who was there at the time, he is writing me a meticulous account of everything that happened. Mr Meredith Blake the same. Now if you –'

Elsa Dittisham took a deep breath. She said contemptuously:

'Those two! Philip was always stupid. Meredith used to trot round after Caroline – but he was quite a dear. But you won't have *any* real idea from *their* accounts.'

He watched her, saw the animation rising in her eyes, saw a living woman take shape from a dead one. She said quickly and almost fiercely:

'Would you like the *truth*? Oh, not for publication. But just for yourself –'

'I will undertake not to publish without your consent.'

'I'd like to write down the truth . . .' She was silent a minute or two, thinking. He saw the smooth hardness of her cheeks falter and take on a younger curve, he saw life ebbing into her as the past claimed her again.

'To go back – to write it all down . . . To show you what she was –'

Her eyes flashed. Her breast heaved passionately.

Agatha Christie

'She killed him. She killed Amyas. Amyas who wanted to live – who enjoyed living. Hate oughtn't to be stronger than love – but her hate was. And my hate for her is – I hate her – I hate her – I hate her . . .'

She came across to him. She stooped, her hand clutched at his sleeve. She said urgently:

'You must understand – you *must* – how we felt about each other. Amyas and I, I mean. There's something – I'll show you.'

She whirled across the room. She was unlocking a little desk, pulling out a drawer concealed inside a pigeon hole.

Then she was back. In her hand was a creased letter, the ink faded. She thrust it on him and Poirot had a sudden poignant memory of a child he had known who had thrust on him one of her treasures – a special shell picked up on the seashore and zealously guarded. Just so had that child stood back and watched him. Proud, afraid, keenly critical of his reception of her treasure.

He unfolded the faded sheets.

Elsa – you wonderful child! There never was anything as beautiful. And yet I'm afraid – I'm too old – a middle-aged, ugly tempered devil with no stability in me. Don't trust me, don't believe in me – I'm no good – apart from my work.

The best of me is in that. There, don't say you haven't been warned.

Hell, my lovely – I'm going to have you all the same. I'd go to the devil for you and you know it. And I'll paint a picture of you that will make the fat-headed world hold its sides and gasp! I'm crazy about you – I can't sleep – I can't eat. Elsa – Elsa – Elsa – I'm yours for ever – yours till death. Amyas.

Sixteen years ago. Faded ink, crumbling paper. But the words still alive – still vibrating . . .

He looked across at the woman to whom they had been written.

But it was no longer a woman at whom he looked.

It was a young girl in love.

He thought again of Juliet . . .

Chapter 9

This Little Pig Had None

'May I ask why, M. Poirot?'

Hercule Poirot considered his answer to the question. He was aware of a pair of very shrewd grey eyes watching him out of the small wizened face.

He had climbed to the top floor of the bare building and knocked on the door of No. 584 Gillespie Buildings, which had come into existence to provide what were called 'flatlets' for working women.

Here, in a small cubic space, existed Miss Cecilia Williams, in a room that was bedroom, sitting-room, dining-room, and, by judicious use of the gas ring, kitchen – a kind of cubby hole attached to it contined a quarter-length bath and the usual offices.

Meagre though these surroundings might be, Miss Williams had contrived to impress upon them her stamp of personality.

The walls were distempered an ascetic pale grey, and

various reproductions hung upon them. Dante meeting Beatrice on a bridge – and that picture once described by a child as a 'blind girl sitting on an orange and called, I don't know why, "Hope".' There were also two water colours of Venice and a sepia copy of Botticelli's 'Primavera'. On the top of the low chest of drawers were a large quantity of faded photographs, mostly, by their style of hairdressing, dating from twenty to thirty years ago.

The square of carpet was threadbare, the furniture battered and of poor quality. It was clear to Hercule Poirot that Cecilia Williams lived very near the bone. There was no roast beef here. This was the little pig that had none.

Clear, incisive and insistent, the voice of Miss Williams repeated its demand.

'You want my recollections of the Crale case? May I ask why?'

It had been said of Hercule Poirot by some of his friends and associates, at moments when he has maddened them most, that he prefers lies to truth and will go out of his way to gain his ends by means of elaborate false statements, rather than trust to the simple truth.

But in this case his decision was quickly made. Hercule Poirot did not come of that class of Belgian or French children who have had an English governess, but he reacted as simply and inevitably as various small boys who had been asked in their time: 'Did you brush your teeth this morning, Harold (or Richard or Anthony)?' They considered fleetingly the possibility of a lie and instantly rejected it, replying miserably, 'No, Miss Williams.'

For Miss Williams had what every successful child educator must have, that mysterious quality – authority! When Miss Williams said 'Go up and wash your hands, Joan,' or 'I expect you to read this chapter on the Elizabethan poets and be able to answer my questions on it,' she was invariably obeyed. It had never entered Miss Williams' head that she would not be obeyed.

So in this case Hercule Poirot proffered no specious explanation of a book to be written on bygone crimes. Instead he narrated simply the circumstances in which Carla Lemarchant had sought him out.

The small, elderly lady in the neat shabby dress listened attentively.

She said:

'It interests me very much to have news of that child – to know how she has turned out.'

'She is a very charming and attractive young woman, with plenty of courage and a mind of her own.'

'Good,' said Miss Williams briefly.

'And she is, I may say, a very persistent person. She is not a person whom it is easy to refuse or put off.'

The ex-governess nodded thoughtfully. She asked:

'Is she artistic?'

'I think not.'

Miss Williams said drily:

'That's one thing to be thankful for!'

The tone of the remark left Miss Williams' views as to artists in no doubt whatever.

She added:

'From your account of her I should imagine that she takes after her mother rather than after her father.'

'Very possibly. That you can tell me when you have seen her. You would like to see her?'

'I should like to see her very much indeed. It is always interesting to see how a child you have known has developed.'

'She was, I suppose, very young when you last saw her?'

'She was five and a half. A very charming child – a little over-quiet, perhaps. Thoughtful. Given to playing her own little games and not inviting outside co-operation. Natural and unspoilt.'

Poirot said:

'It was fortunate she was so young.'

'Yes, indeed. Had she been older the shock of the tragedy might have had a very bad effect.'

'Nevertheless,' said Poirot, 'one feels that there *was* a handicap – however little the child understood or was allowed to know, there would have been an atmosphere of mystery and evasion and an abrupt uprooting. These things are not good for a child.'

Miss Williams replied thoughtfully:

'They may have been less harmful than you think.'

Poirot said:

'Before we leave the subject of Carla Lemarchant – little Carla Crale that was, there is something I would like to ask you. If any one can explain it, I think you can.'

'Yes?'

Her voice was inquiring, non-commital.

Poirot waved his hands in an effort to express his meaning.

'There is a something – a *nuance* I cannot define – but it seems to me always that the child, when I mention her, is not given her full representational value. When I mention her, the response comes always with a vague surprise, as though the person to whom I speak had forgotten altogether that there *was* a child. Now surely, Mademoiselle, that is not natural? A child, under these circumstances, is a person of importance, not in herself, but as a pivotal point. Amyas Crale may have had reasons for abandoning his wife – or for not abandoning her. But in the usual break-up of a marriage the child forms a very important point. But here the child seems to count for very little. That seems to me – strange.'

Miss Williams said quickly:

'You have put your finger on a vital point, M. Poirot. You are quite right. And that is partly why I said what I did just now – that Carla's transportation to different surroundings might have been in some respects a good thing for her. When she was older, you see, she might have suffered from a certain lack in her home life.'

She leaned forward and spoke slowly and carefully.

'Naturally, in the course of my work, I have seen a good many aspects of the parent and child problem. Many children, *most* children, I should say, suffer from over-attention on the part of their parents. There is too much love, too much watching over the child. It is uneasily conscious of this brooding, and seeks to free itself, to get away and be unobserved. With an only child that is particularly the case, and of course mothers are the worst offenders. The result on the marriage is often unfortunate. The husband resents coming second, seeks consolation – or rather flattery and attention – elsewhere, and a divorce results sooner or later. The best thing for a child, I am convinced, is to have what I should term healthy neglect on the part of both its parents. This happens naturally enough in the case of a large family of children and very little money. They are overlooked because the mother has literally no time to occupy herself with them. They realize quite well that she is fond of them, but they are not worried by too many manifestations of the fact.

'But there is another aspect. One does occasionally find a husband and wife who are so all-sufficient to each other, so wrapped up in each other, that the child of the marriage hardly seems very real to either of them. And in those circumstances I think a child comes to resent that fact, to feel defrauded and left out in the cold. You understand that I am not speaking of *neglect* in any way. Mrs Crale, for instance, was what is termed an excellent mother, always careful of Carla's welfare, of her health – playing with her at the right times and always kind and gay. But for all that, Mrs Crale was really completely wrapped up in her husband. She existed, one might say, only in him and for him.' Miss Williams paused a minute and then said quietly: 'That, I think, is the justification for what she eventually did.'

Hercule Poirot said:

'You mean that they were more like lovers than like husband and wife?'

Miss Williams, with a slight frown of distaste for foreign phraseology, said:

'You could certainly put it that way.'

'He was devoted to her as she was to him?'

'They were a devoted couple. But he, of course, was a man.'

Miss Williams contrived to put into that last word a wholly Victorian significance.

'Men –' said Miss Williams, and stopped.

As a rich property owner says 'Bolsheviks' – as an earnest Communist says 'Capitalists!' – as a good housewife says 'Blackbeetles' – so did Miss Williams say 'Men!'

From her spinster's, governess's life, there rose up a blast of fierce feminism. Nobody hearing her speak could doubt that to Miss Williams Men were the Enemy!

Poirot said: 'You hold no brief for men?'

She answered drily:

'Men have the best of this world. I hope that it will not always be so.'

Hercule Poirot eyed her speculatively. He could quite easily visualize Miss Williams methodically and efficiently padlocking herself to a railing, and later hunger-striking with resolute endurance. Leaving the general for the particular, he said:

'You did not like Amyas Crale?'

'I certainly did not like Mr Crale. Nor did I approve of him. If I were his wife I should have left him. There are things that no woman should put up with.'

'But Mrs Crale did put up with them?'

'Yes.'

'You thought she was wrong?'

'Yes, I do. A woman should have a certain respect for herself and not submit to humiliation.'

'Did you ever say anything of that kind to Mrs Crale?'

'Certainly not. It was not my place to do so. I was engaged to educate Angela, not to offer unasked advice to Mrs Crale. To do so would have been most impertinent.'

'You liked Mrs Crale?'

'I was very fond of Mrs Crale.' The efficient voice softened, held warmth and feeling. 'Very fond of her and very sorry for her.'

'And your pupil – Angela Warren?'

'She was a most interesting girl – one of the most interesting pupils I have had. A really good brain. Undisciplined, quick-tempered, most difficult to manage in many ways, but really a very fine character.'

She paused and then went on:

'I always hoped that she would accomplish something worth while. And she has! You have read her book – on the Sahara? And she excavated those very interesting tombs in the Fayum! Yes, I am proud of Angela. I was not at Alderbury very long – two years and a half – but I always cherish the belief that I helped to stimulate her mind and encourage her taste for archæology.'

Poirot murmured: 'I understand that it was decided to continue her education by sending her to school. You must have resented that decision.'

Agatha Christie

'Not at all, M. Poirot. I thoroughly concurred with it.'

She paused and went:

'Let me make the matter clear to you. Angela was a dear girl – really a very dear girl – warm-hearted and impulsive – but she was also what I call a difficult girl. That is, she was at a difficult age. There is always a moment where a girl feels unsure of herself – neither child nor woman. At one minute Angela would be sensible and mature – quite grown up, in fact – but a minute later she would relapse into being a hoydenish child – playing mischievous tricks and being rude and losing her temper. Girls, you know, *feel* difficult at that age – they are terribly sensitive. Everything that is said to them they resent. They are annoyed at being treated like a child and then they suddenly feel shy at being treated like adults. Angela was in that state. She had fits of temper, would suddenly resent teasing and flare out – and then she would be sulky for days at a time, sitting about and frowning – then again she would be in wild spirits, climbing trees, rushing about with the garden boys, refusing to submit to any kind of authority.'

Miss Williams paused and went on:

'When a girl gets to that stage, school is very helpful. She needs the stimulation of other minds – that, and the wholesome discipline of a community, help her to become a reasonable member of society. Angela's home conditions were not what I would have called ideal. Mrs Crale spoiled her, for one thing. Angela had only to appeal to her and Mrs Crale always backed her up. The result was that Angela considered she had first claim upon her sister's time and attention, and it was in these moods of hers that she used to clash with Mr Crale. Mr Crale naturally thought that *he* should come first – and intended to do so. He was really very fond of the girl – they were good companions and used to spar together quite amiably, but there were times when Mr Crale used suddenly to resent Mrs Crale's preoccupation with Angela. Like all men, he was a spoilt child; he expected everybody to make a fuss of *him*. Then he and Angela used to have a real set-to – and very often Mrs Crale would take Angela's side. Then he would be furious. On the other hand, if *she* supported *him*, Angela would be furious. It was on these occasions that Angela used to revert to childish ways and play some spiteful trick on him. He had a habit of tossing off his drinks and she once put a lot of salt into his drink. The whole thing, of course, acted as an emetic, and he was inarticulate with fury. But what really brought things to a head was when she put a lot of slugs into his bed. He had a queer aversion for slugs. He lost his temper completely and said that the girl had got to be sent away to school. He wasn't going to put up with all this petty nonsense any more. Angela was terribly upset – though

173

actually she had once or twice expressed a wish herself to go to a boarding school – but she chose to make a huge grievance of it. Mrs Crale didn't want her to go but allowed herself to be persuaded – largely owing, I think, to what I said to her on the subject. I pointed out to her that it would be greatly to Angela's advantage, and that I thought it would really be a great benefit to the girl. So it was settled that she should go to Helston – a very fine school on the south coast – in the autumn term. But Mrs Crale was still unhappy about it all those holidays. And Angela kept up a grudge against Mr Crale whenever she remembered. It wasn't really serious, you understand, M. Poirot, but it made a kind of undercurrent that summer to – well – to everything *else* that was going on.'

Poirot said: 'Meaning – Elsa Greer?'

Miss Williams said sharply:

'Exactly.' And shut her lips very tight after the word.

'What was your opinion of Elsa Greer?'

'I had no opinion of her at all. A thoroughly unprincipled young woman.'

'She was very young.'

'Old enough to know better. I can see no excuse for her – none at all.'

'She fell in love with him, I suppose –'

Miss Williams interrupted with a snort.

'Fell in love with him indeed. I should hope, M.

Poirot, that whatever our feelings, we can keep them in decent control. And we can certainly control our actions. That girl had absolutely no morals of any kind. It meant nothing to her that Mr Crale was a married man. She was absolutely shameless about it all – cool and determined. Possibly she may have been badly brought up – but that's the only excuse I can find for her.'

'Mr Crale's death must have been a terrible shock to her.'

'Oh, it was. And she herself was entirely to blame for it. I don't go as far as condoning murder, but all the same, M. Poirot, if ever a woman was driven to breaking point, that woman was Caroline Crale. I tell you frankly, there were moments when I would have liked to murder them both myself. Flaunting the girl in his wife's face, listening to her having to put up with the girl's insolence – and she *was* insolent, M. Poirot. Oh no, Amyas Crale deserved what he got. No man should treat his wife as he did and not be punished for it. His death was a just retribution.'

Hercule Poirot said: 'You feel strongly . . .'

The small woman looked at him with those indomitable grey eyes. She said:

'I feel *very strongly* about the marriage tie. Unless it is respected and upheld, a country degenerates. Mrs Crale was a devoted and faithful wife. Her husband deliberately flouted her and introduced his mistress into her home. As I say, he deserved what he got. He goaded her past endurance and I, for one, do not blame her for what she did.'

Poirot said slowly: 'He acted very badly – that I admit – but he was a great artist, remember.'

Miss Williams gave a terrific snort.

'Oh yes, I know. That's always the excuse nowadays. An artist! An excuse for every kind of loose living, for drunkenness, for brawling, for infidelity. And what kind of an artist was Mr Crale, when all is said and done? It may be the fashion to admire his pictures for a few years. But they won't last. Why, he couldn't even draw! His perspective was terrible! Even his anatomy was quite incorrect. I know something of what I am talking about, M. Poirot. I studied painting for a time, as a girl, in Florence, and to any one who knows and appreciates the great masters, these daubs of Mr Crale's are really ludicrous. Just splashing a few colours about on the canvas – no construction – no careful drawing. No,' she shook her head, 'don't ask me to admire Mr Crale's painting.'

'Two of them are in the Tate Gallery,' Poirot reminded her.

Miss Williams sniffed.

'Possibly. So is one of Mr Epstein's statues, I believe.'

Poirot perceived that, according to Miss Williams, the last word had been said. He abandoned the subject of art.

He said:

'You were with Mrs Crale when she found the body?'

'Yes. She and I went down from the house together after lunch. Angela had left her pullover on the beach after bathing, or else in the boat. She was always very careless about her things. I parted from Mrs Crale at the door of the Battery garden, but she called me back almost at once. I believe Mr Crale had been dead over an hour. He was sprawled on the bench near his easel.'

'Was she terribly upset at the discovery?'

'What exactly do you mean by that, M. Poirot?'

'I am asking you what your impressions were at the time.'

'Oh, I see. Yes, she seemed to me quite dazed. She sent me off to telephone for the doctor. After all, we couldn't be absolutely sure he was dead – it might have been a cataleptic seizure.'

'Did she suggest such a possibility?'

'I don't remember.'

'And you went and telephoned?'

Miss William's tone was dry and brusque.

'I had gone half up the path when I met Mr Meredith Blake. I entrusted my errand to him and returned to

Mrs Crale. I thought, you see, she might have collapsed – and men are no good in a matter of that kind.'

'And had she collapsed?'

Miss Williams said drily:

'Mrs Crale was quite in command of herself. She was quite different from Miss Greer, who made a hysterical and very unpleasant scene.'

'What kind of a scene?'

'She tried to attack Mrs Crale.'

'You mean she realized that Mrs Crale was responsible for Mr Crale's death?'

Miss Williams considered for a moment or two.

'No, she could hardly be sure of that. That – er – terrible suspicion had not yet arisen. Miss Greer just screamed out: "It's all your doing, Caroline. You killed him. It's all your fault." She did not actually say "You've poisoned him," but I think there is no doubt that she thought so.'

'And Mrs Crale?'

Miss Williams moved restlessly.

'Must we be hypocritical, M. Poirot? I cannot tell you what Mrs Crale really felt or thought at that moment. Whether it was horror at what she had done –'

'Did it seem like that?'

'N-no, n-no, I can't say it did. Stunned, yes – and, I think, frightened. Yes, I am sure, frightened. But that is natural enough.'

Hercule Poirot said in a dissatisfied tone:

'Yes, perhaps that is natural enough . . . What view did she adopt officially as to her husband's death?'

'Suicide. She said, very definitely from the first, that it must be suicide.'

'Did she say the same when she was talking to you privately, or did she put forward any other theory.'

'No. She – she – took pains to impress upon me that it must be suicide.'

Miss Williams sounded embarrassed.

'And what did you say to that?'

'Really, M. Poirot, does it matter *what* I said?'

'Yes, I think it does.'

'I don't see why –'

But as though his expectant silence hypnotized her, she said reluctantly:

'I think I said: "Certainly, Mrs Crale. It must have been suicide."'

'Did you believe your own words?'

Miss Williams raised her head. She said firmly:

'No, I did not. But please understand, M. Poirot, that I was entirely on Mrs Crale's side, if you like to put it that way. My sympathies were with her, not with the police.'

'You would have liked to have seen her acquitted?'

Miss Williams said defiantly:

'Yes, I would.'

Poirot said:

'Then you are in sympathy with her daughter's feelings?'

'I have every sympathy with Carla.'

'Would you have any objection to writing out for me a detailed account of the tragedy?'

'You mean for her to read?'

'Yes.'

Miss Williams said slowly:

'No, I have no objection. She is quite determined to go into the matter, is she?'

'Yes. I dare say it would have been preferable if the truth had been kept from her –'

Miss Williams interrupted him:

'No. It is always better to face the truth. It is no use evading unhappiness by tampering with facts. Carla has had a shock learning the truth – now she wants to know exactly how the tragedy came about. That seems to me the right attitude for a brave young woman to take. Once she knows all about it she will be able to forget it again and go on with the business of living her own life.'

'Perhaps you are right,' said Poirot.

'I'm quite sure I'm right.'

'But you see, there is more to it than that. She not only wants to know – she wants to prove her mother innocent.'

Miss Williams said: 'Poor child.'

'That is what you say, is it?'

Miss Williams said:

'I see now why you said that it might be better if she had never known. All the same, I think it is best as it is. To wish to find her mother innocent is a natural hope – and hard though the actual revelation may be, I think from what you say of her that Carla is brave enough to learn the truth and not flinch from it.'

'You are sure it *is* the truth?'

'I don't understand you?'

'You see no loophole for believing that Mrs Crale was innocent?'

'I don't think that possibility has ever been seriously considered.'

'And yet she herself clung to the theory of suicide?'

Miss Williams said drily:

'The poor woman had to say *something*.'

'Do you know that when Mrs Crale was dying she left a letter for her daughter in which she solemnly swears that she is innocent?'

Miss Williams stared.

'That was very wrong of her,' she said sharply.

'You think so?'

'Yes, I do. Oh, I dare say you are a sentimentalist like most men –'

Poirot interrupted indignantly:

'I am *not* a sentimentalist.'

'But there is such a thing as false sentiment. Why write that, a lie, at such a solemn moment? To spare your child pain? Yes, many women would do that. But I should not have thought it of Mrs Crale. She was a brave woman and a truthful woman. I should have thought it far more like her to have told her daughter not to judge.'

Poirot said with slight exasperation:

'You will not even consider then the possibility that what Caroline Crale wrote was the truth?'

'Certainly not!'

'And yet you profess to have loved her?'

'I did love her. I had a great affection and deep sympathy for her.'

'Well, then –'

Miss Williams looked at him in a very odd way.

'You don't understand, M. Poirot. It doesn't matter my saying this now – so long afterwards. You see, I happen to *know* that Caroline Crale was guilty!'

'*What?*'

'It's true. Whether I did right in withholding what I knew at the time I cannot be sure – but I *did* withhold it. But you must take it from me, quite definitely, that I *know* Caroline Crale was guilty . . .'

Chapter 10

This Little Pig Cried
'Wee Wee Wee'

Angela Warren's flat overlooked Regent's Park. Here, on this spring day, a soft air wafted in through the open window and one might have had the illusion that one was in the country if it had not been for the steady menacing roar of the traffic passing below.

Poirot turned from the window as the door opened and Angela Warren came into the room.

It was not the first time he had seen her. He had availed himself of the opportunity to attend a lecture she had given at the Royal Geographical. It had been, he considered, an excellent lecture. Dry, perhaps, from the view of popular appeal. Miss Warren had an excellent delivery, she neither paused nor hesitated for a word. She did not repeat herself. The tones of her voice were clear and not unmelodious. She made no concessions to romantic appeal or love of adventure. There was very little human interest in the lecture. It was an admirable recital of concise facts, adequately illustrated by excellent slides, and with intelligent deductions from the facts recited. Dry, precise, clear, lucid, highly technical.

The soul of Hercule Poirot approved. Here, he considered, was an orderly mind.

Now that he saw her at close quarters he realized that Angela Warren might easily have been a very handsome woman. Her features were regular, though severe. She had finely marked dark brows, clear intelligent brown eyes, a fine pale skin. She had very square shoulders and a slightly mannish walk.

There was certainly about her no suggestion of the little pig who cries 'Wee Wee.' But on the right cheek, disfiguring and puckering the skin, was that healed scar. The right eye was slightly distorted, the corner pulled downwards by it but no one would have realized that the sight of that eye was destroyed. It seemed to Hercule Poirot almost certain that she had lived with her disability so long that she was now completely unconscious of it. And it occurred to him that of the five people in whom he had become interested as a result of his investigations, those who might have been said to start with the fullest advantages were not those who had actually wrested the most success and happiness from life. Elsa, who might have been said to start with all advantages – youth, beauty, riches –

had done worst. She was like a flower overtaken by untimely frost – still in bud – but without life. Cecilia Williams, to outward appearances, had no assets of which to boast. Nevertheless, to Poirot's eye, there was no despondency there and no sense of failure. Miss Williams's life had been interesting to her – she was still interested in people and events. She had that enormous mental and moral advantage of a strict Victorian upbringing denied to us in these days – she had done her duty in that station of life to which it had pleased God to call her, and that assurance encased her in an armour impregnable to the slings and darts of envy, discontent and regret. She had her memories, her small pleasures, made possible by stringent economies, and sufficient health and vigour to enable her still to be interested in life.

Now, in Angela Warren – that young creature handicapped by disfigurement and its consequent humiliation, Poirot believed he saw a spirit strengthened by its necessary fight for confidence and assurance. The undisciplined schoolgirl had given place to a vital and forceful woman, a woman of considerable mental power and gifted with abundant energy to accomplish ambitious purposes. She was a woman, Poirot felt sure, both happy and successful. Her life was full and vivid and eminently enjoyable.

She was not, incidentally, the type of woman that

Poirot really liked. Though admiring the clear-cut precision of her mind, she had just a sufficient *nuance* of the *femme formidable* about her to alarm him as a mere man. His taste had always been for the flamboyant and extravagant.

With Angela Warren it was easy to come to the point of his visit. There was no subterfuge. He merely recounted Carla Lemarchant's interview with him.

Angela Warren's severe face lighted up appreciatively.

'Little Carla? She is over here? I would like to see her so much.'

'You have not kept in touch with her?'

'Hardly as much as I should have done. I was a schoolgirl at the time she went to Canada, and I realized, of course, that in a year or two she would have forgotten us. Of late years, an occasional present at Christmas has been the only link between us. I imagined that she would, by now, be completely immersed in the Canadian atmosphere and that her future would lie over there. Better so, in the circumstances.'

Poirot said: 'One might think so, certainly. A change of name – a change of scene. A new life. But it was not to be so easy as that.'

And he then told of Carla's engagement, the discovery she had made upon coming of age and her motives in coming to England.

Angela Warren listened quietly, her disfigured cheek resting on one hand. She betrayed no emotion during the recital, but as Poirot finished, she said quietly:

'Good for Carla.'

Poirot was startled. It was the first time that he had met with this reaction. He said:

'You approve, Miss Warren?'

'Certainly. I wish her every success. Anything I can do to help, I will. I feel guilty, you know, that I haven't attempted anything myself.'

'Then you think that there is a possibility that she is right in her views.'

Angela Warren said sharply:

'Of course she's right. Caroline didn't do it. I've always known that.'

Hercule Poirot murmured:

'You surprise me very much indeed, mademoiselle. Everybody else I have spoken to –'

She cut in sharply:

'You mustn't go by that. I've no doubt that the circumstantial evidence is overwhelming. My own conviction is based on knowledge – knowledge of my sister. I just know quite simply and definitely that Caro *couldn't* have killed any one.'

'Can one say that with certainty of any human creature?'

'Probably not in most cases. I agree that the human

animal is full of curious surprises. But in Caroline's case there were special reasons – reasons which I have a better chance of appreciating than any one else could.'

She touched her damaged cheek.

'You see this? You've probably heard about it?' Poirot nodded. 'Caroline did that. That's why I'm sure – I *know* – that she didn't do murder.'

'It would not be a convincing argument to most people.'

'No, it would be the opposite. It was actually used in that way, I believe. As evidence that Caroline had a violent and ungovernable temper! Because she had injured me as a baby, learned men argued that she would be equally capable of poisoning an unfaithful husband.'

Poirot said:

'I, at least, appreciated the difference. A sudden fit of ungovernable rage does not lead you to first abstract a poison and then use it deliberately on the following day.'

Angela Warren waved an impatient hand.

'That's not what I mean at all. I must try and make it plain to you. Supposing that you are a person normally affectionate and of kindly disposition – but that you are also liable to intense jealousy. And supposing that during the years of your life when control is most difficult, you do, in a fit of rage, come near to committing what is, in effect, murder. Think of the awful shock, the horror, the remorse that seizes upon you. To a sensitive person, like Caroline, that horror and remorse will never quite leave you. It never left her. I don't suppose I was consciously aware of it at the time, but looking back I recognize it perfectly. Caro was haunted, continually haunted, by the fact that she had injured me. That knowledge never left her in peace. It coloured all her actions. It explained her attitude to me. Nothing was too good for me. In her eyes, I must always come first. Half the quarrels she had with Amyas were on my account. I was inclined to be jealous of him and played all kinds of tricks on him. I pinched cat stuff to put in his drink, and once I put a hedgehog in his bed. But Caroline was always on my side.'

Miss Warren paused, then she went on:

'It was very bad for me, of course. I got horribly spoilt. But that's neither here nor there. We're discussing the effect on Caroline. The result of that impulse to violence was a life-long abhorrence of any further act of the same kind. Caro was always watching herself, always in fear that something of that kind might happen again. And she took her own ways of guarding against it. One of these ways was a great extravagance of language. She felt (and I think, psychologically quite truly) that if she were violent enough in speech she would have no temptation to violence in action. She found by experience that the method worked. That's why I've heard Caro say things like "I'd like to cut so and so in pieces and boil him slowly in oil." And she'd say to me, or to Amyas, "If you go on annoying me I shall murder you." In the same way she quarrelled easily and violently. She recognized, I think, the impulse to violence that there was in her nature, and she deliberately gave it an outlet that way. She and Amyas used to have the most fantastic and lurid quarrels.'

Hercule Poirot nodded.

'Yes, there was evidence of that. They quarrelled like cat and dog, it was said.'

Angela Warren said:

'Exactly. That's what is so stupid and misleading about evidence. Of course Caro and Amyas quarrelled! Of course they said bitter and outrageous and cruel things to each other! What nobody appreciates is that they *enjoyed* quarrelling. But they did! Amyas enjoyed it too. They were that kind of couple. They both of them liked drama and emotional scenes. Most men don't. They like peace. But Amyas was an artist. He liked shouting and threatening and generally being outrageous. It was like letting off steam to him. He was the kind of man who when he loses his collar stud bellows the house down. It sounds very odd, I know, but living that way with continual rows and makings-up was Amyas's and Caroline's idea of fun!'

She made an impatient gesture.

'If they'd only not hustled me away and let me give evidence, I'd have told them that.' Then she shrugged her shoulders. 'But I don't suppose they would have believed me. And anyway then it wouldn't have been as clear in my mind as it is now. It was the kind of thing I knew but hadn't thought about and certainly had never dreamed of putting into words.'

She looked across at Poirot.

'You do see what I mean?'

He nodded vigorously.

'I see perfectly – and I realize the absolute rightness of what you have said. There are people to whom agreement is monotony. They require the stimulant of dissension to create drama in their lives.'

'Exactly.'

'May I ask you, Miss Warren, what were your own feelings at the time?'

Angela Warren sighed.

'Mostly bewilderment and helplessness, I think. It seemed a fantastic nightmare. Caroline was arrested very soon – about three days afterwards, I think. I can still remember my indignation, my dumb fury – and, of course, my childish faith that it was just a silly mistake, that it would be all right. Caro was chiefly perturbed about *me* – she wanted me kept right away from it all as far as possible. She got Miss Williams to take me away to some relations almost at once. The police had no objection. And then, when it was decided that my evidence would not be needed, arrangements were made for me to go to school abroad.

'I hated going, of course. But it was explained to me that Caro had me terribly on her mind and that the only way I could help her was by going.'

She paused. Then she said:

'So I went to Munich. I was there when – when the verdict was given. They never let me go to see Caro. Caro wouldn't have it. That's the only time, I think, when she failed in understanding.'

'You cannot be sure of that, Miss Warren. To visit someone dearly loved in a prison might make a terrible impression on a young sensitive girl.'

'Possibly.'

Angela Warren got up. She said:

'After the verdict, when she had been condemned, my sister wrote me a letter. I have never shown it to any one. I think I ought to show it to you now. It may help you to understand the kind of person Caroline was. If you like you may take it to show to Carla also.'

She went to the door, then turning back she said:

'Come with me. There is a portrait of Caroline in my room.'

For a second time, Poirot stood gazing up at a portrait.

As a painting, Caroline Crale's portrait was mediocre. But Poirot looked at it with interest – it was not its artistic value that interested him.

He saw a long oval face, a gracious line of jaw and a sweet, slightly timid expression. It was a face uncertain of itself, emotional, with a withdrawn hidden beauty. It lacked the forcefulness and vitality of her daughter's face – that energy and joy of life Carla Lemarchant had doubtless inherited from her father. This was a less positive creature. Yet, looking at the painted face, Hercule Poirot understood why an imaginative man like Quentin Fogg had not been able to forget her.

Angela Warren stood at his side again – a letter in her hand.

She said quietly:

'Now that you have seen what she was like – read her letter.'

He unfolded it carefully and read what Caroline Crale had written sixteen years ago.

My darling little Angela,

You will hear bad news and you will grieve, but what I want to impress upon you is that it is all all right. I have never told you lies and I don't now when I say that I am actually happy – that I feel an essential rightness and a peace that I have never known before. It's all right, darling, it's all right. Don't look back and regret and

193

*grieve for me – go on with your life and succeed. You
can, I know. It's all, all right, darling, and I'm going to
Amyas. I haven't the least doubt that we shall be together.
I couldn't have lived without him . . . Do this one thing
for me – be happy. I've told you – I'm happy. One has to
pay one's debts. It's lovely to feel peaceful.*

Your loving sister,

Caro

Hercule Poirot read it through twice. Then he
handed it back. He said:

'That is a very beautiful letter, mademoiselle – and
a very remarkable one. A *very* remarkable one.'

'Caroline,' said Angela Warren, 'was a very remarkable person.'

'Yes, an unusual mind . . . You take it that this letter
indicates innocence?'

'Of course it does!'

'It does not say so explicitly.'

'Because Caro would know that I'd never dream of
her being guilty!'

'Perhaps – perhaps . . . But it might be taken another
way. In the sense that she was guilty and that in
expiating her crime she will find peace.'

It fitted in, he thought, with the description of her
in court. And he experienced in this moment the
strongest doubts he had yet felt of the course to

which he had committed himself. Everything so far had pointed unswervingly to Caroline Crale's guilt. Now, even her own words testified against her.

On the other side was only the unshaken conviction of Angela Warren. Angela had known her well, undoubtedly, but might not her certainty be the fanatical loyalty of an adolescent girl, up in arms for a dearly loved sister?

As though she had read his thoughts Angela Warren said:

'No, M. Poirot – I *know* Caroline wasn't guilty.'

Poirot said briskly:

'The Bon Dieu knows I do not want to shake you on that point. But let us be practical. You say your sister was not guilty. Very well, then, *what really happened*?'

Angela nodded thoughtfully. She said:

'That is difficult, I agree. I suppose that, as Caroline said, Amyas committed suicide.'

'Is that likely from what you know of his character?'

'Very unlikely.'

'But you do not say, as in the first case, that you *know* it is impossible?'

'No, because, as I said just now, most people *do* do impossible things – that is to say things that seem out of character. But I presume, if you know them intimately, it wouldn't be out of character.'

'You knew your brother-in-law well?'

'Yes, but not like I knew Caro. It seems to me quite fantastic that Amyas should have killed himself – but I suppose he *could* have done so. In fact, he *must* have done so.'

'You cannot see any other explanation?'

Angela accepted the suggestion calmly, but not without a certain stirring of interest.

'Oh, I see what you mean . . . I've never really considered that possibility. You mean one of the other people killed him? That it was a deliberate cold-blooded murder . . .'

'It might have been, might it not?'

'Yes, it might have been . . . But it certainly seems very unlikely.'

'More unlikely than suicide?'

'That's difficult to say . . . On the face of it, there was no reason for suspecting anybody else. There isn't now when I look back . . .'

'All the same, let us consider the possibility. Who of those intimately concerned would you say was – shall we say – the most likely person?'

'Let me think. Well, I didn't kill him. And the Elsa creature certainly didn't. She was mad with rage when he died. Who else was there? Meredith Blake? He was always very devoted to Caroline, quite a tame cat about the house. I suppose that *might* give him a motive in a way. In a book he might have wanted to get Amyas out of the way so that he himself could marry Caroline. But he could have achieved that just as well by letting Amyas go off with Elsa and then in due time consoling Caroline. Besides I really can't *see* Meredith as a murderer. Too mild and too cautious. Who else was there?'

Poirot suggested: 'Miss Williams? Philip Blake?'

Angela's grave face relaxed into a smile for a minute.

'Miss Williams? One can't really make oneself believe that one's governess could commit a murder! Miss Williams was always so unyielding and so full of rectitude.'

She paused a minute and then went on:

'She was devoted to Caroline, of course. Would have done anything for her. And she hated Amyas. She was a great feminist and disliked men. Is that enough for murder? Surely not.'

'It would hardly seem so,' agreed Poirot.

Angela went on:

'Philip Blake?' She was silent for some few moments. Then she said quietly: 'I think, you know, if we're just talking of *likelihoods*, *he's* the most likely person.'

Poirot said:

'You interest me very much, Miss Warren. May I ask why you say that?'

'Nothing at all definite. But from what I remember of him, I should say he was a person of rather limited imagination.'

Agatha Christie

'And a limited imagination predisposes you to murder?'

'It might lead you to take a crude way of settling your difficulties. Men of that type get a certain satisfaction from action of some kind or other. Murder is a very crude business, don't you think so?'

'Yes – I think you are right . . . It is definitely a point of view, that. But all the same, Miss Warren, there must be more to it than that. What motive could Philip Blake possibly have had?'

Angela Warren did not answer at once. She stood frowning down at the floor.

Hercule Poirot said:

'He was Amyas Crale's best friend, was he not?'

She nodded.

'But there is something in your mind, Miss Warren. Something that you have not yet told me. Were the two men rivals, perhaps, over the girl – over Elsa?'

Angela Warren shook her head.

'Oh, no, not Philip.'

'What is there then?'

Angela Warren said slowly:

'Do you know the way that things suddenly come back to you – after years perhaps. I'll explain what I mean. Somebody told me a story once, when I was eleven. I saw no point in that story whatsoever. It didn't worry me – it just passed straight over my head. I don't believe I ever, as they say, thought of it again. But about two years ago, sitting in the stalls at a revue, that story came back to me, and I was so surprised that I actually said aloud, "Oh, *now* I see the point of that silly story about the rice pudding." And yet there had been no direct allusion on the same lines – only some fun sailing rather near the wind.'

Poirot said: 'I understand what you mean, mademoiselle.'

'Then you will understand what I am going to tell you. I was once staying at a hotel. As I walked along a passage, one of the bedroom doors opened and a woman I knew came out. It was not her bedroom – and she registered the fact plainly on her face when she saw me.

'*And I knew then the meaning of the expression I had once seen on Caroline's face when at Alderbury she came out of Philip Blake's room one night.*'

She leant forward, stopping Poirot's words.

'I had no idea at the *time*, you understand. I *knew* things – girls of the age I was usually do – but I didn't connect them with reality. Caroline coming out of Philip Blake's bedroom was just Caroline coming out of Philip Blake's bedroom to me. It might have been Miss William's room or my room. But what I *did* notice was the expression on her face – a queer expression that I didn't know and couldn't understand. I didn't understand it until, as I have told you, the night in Paris when I saw that same expression on another woman's face.'

Agatha Christie

Poirot said slowly:

'But what you tell me, Miss Warren, is sufficiently astonishing. From Philip Blake himself I got the impression that he disliked your sister and always had done so.'

Angela said:

'I know. I can't explain it but there it is.'

Poirot nodded slowly. Already, in his interview with Philip Blake, he had felt vaguely that something did not ring true. That overdone animosity against Caroline – it had not, somehow, been natural.

And the words and phrases from his conversation with Meredith Blake came back to him. 'Very upset when Amyas married – did not go near them for over a year . . .'

Had Philip, then, always been in love with Caroline? And had his love, when she chose Amyas, turned to bitterness and hate?

Yes, Philip had been too vehement – too biased. Poirot visualized him thoughtfully – the cheerful prosperous man with his golf and his comfortable house. What had Philip Blake really felt sixteen years ago.

Angela Warren was speaking.

'I don't understand it. You see, I've no experience in love affairs – they haven't come my way. I've told you this for what it's worth in case – in case it might have a bearing on what happened.'

Book II

Narrative of Philip Blake

(Covering letter received with manuscript)

Dear M. Poirot,

I am fulfilling my promise and herewith find enclosed an account of the events relating to the death of Amyas Crale. After such a lapse of time I am bound to point out that my memories may not be strictly accurate, but I have put down what occurred to the best of my recollection.

Yours truly,

Philip Blake

Notes on Progress of Events Leading up to Murder of Amyas Crale on Sept., 19 . . .

My friendship with deceased dates back to a very early period. His home and mine were next door to each other in the country, and our families were friends. Amyas Crale was a little over two years older than I was.

Agatha Christie

We played together as boys, in the holidays, though we were not at the same school.

From the point of view of my long knowledge of the man I feel myself particularly qualified to testify as to his character and general outlook on life. And I will say this straight away – to any one who knew Amyas Crale well – the notion of his committing suicide is quite ridiculous. Crale would *never* have taken his own life. He was far too fond of living! The contention of the defence at the trial that Crale was obsessed by conscience, and took poison in a fit of remorse, is utterly absurd to any one who knew the man. Crale, I should say, had very little conscience, and certainly not a morbid one. Moreover, he and his wife were on bad terms, and I don't think he would have had any scruples about breaking up what was, to him, a very unsatisfactory married life. He was prepared to look after her financial welfare and that of the child of the marriage, and I am sure would have done so generously. He was a very generous man – and altogether a warm-hearted and lovable person. Not only was he a great painter, but he was a man whose friends were devoted to him. As far as I know he had no enemies.

I had also known Caroline Crale for many years. I knew her before her marriage, when she used to come and stay at Alderbury. She was then a somewhat neurotic girl, subject to uncontrollable outbursts of temper, not without attraction, but unquestionably a difficult person to live with.

She showed her devotion to Amyas almost immediately. He, I do not think, was really very much in love with her. But they were frequently thrown together – she was, as I say, attractive, and they eventually became engaged. Amyas Crale's best friends were rather apprehensive about the marriage, as they felt that Caroline was quite unsuited to him.

This caused a certain amount of strain in the first few years between Crale's wife and Crale's friends, but Amyas was a loyal friend and was not disposed to give up his old friends at the bidding of his wife. After a few years, he and I were on the same old terms and I was a frequent visitor at Alderbury. I may add that I stood godfather to the little girl, Carla. This proves, I think, that Amyas considered me his best friend, and it gives me authority to speak for a man who can no longer speak for himself.

To come to the actual events of which I have been asked to write, I arrived down at Alderbury (so I see by an old diary) five days before the crime. That is, on Sept. 13th. I was conscious at once of a certain tension in the atmosphere. There was also staying in the house Miss Elsa Greer whom Amyas was painting at the time.

Agatha Christie

It was the first time I had seen Miss Greer in the flesh, but I had been aware of her existence for some time. Amyas had raved about her to me a month previously. He had met, he said, a marvellous girl. He talked about her so enthusiastically that I said to him jokingly: 'Be careful, old boy, or you'll be losing your head again.' He told me not to be a bloody fool. He was painting the girl; he'd no personal interest in her. I said: 'Tell that to the marines! I've heard you say that before.' He said: 'This time it's different'; to which I answered somewhat cynically: 'It always is!' Amyas then looked quite worried and anxious. He said: 'You don't understand. She's just a girl. Not much more than a child.' He added that she had very modern views and was absolutely free from old-fashioned prejudices. He said: 'She's honest and natural and absolutely fearless!'

I thought to myself, though I didn't say so, that Amyas had certainly got it badly this time. A few weeks later I heard comments from other people. It was said that the 'Greer girl was absolutely infatuated.' Somebody else said that it was a bit thick of Amyas considering how young the girl was, whereupon somebody else sniggered and said that Elsa Greer knew her way about all right. Further remarks were that the girl was rolling in money and had always got everything she wanted, and also that 'she was the one who was making most of the running.' There was a question as to what Crale's wife thought about it – and the significant reply that she must be used to that sort of thing by now, to which someone demurred by saying they'd heard that she was jealous as hell and led Crale such an impossible life that any man would be justified in having a fling from time to time.

I mention all this because I think it is important that the state of affairs before I got down there should be fully realized.

I was interested to see the girl – she was remarkably good-looking and very attractive – and I was, I must admit, maliciously amused to note that Caroline was cutting up very rough indeed.

Amyas Crale himself was less light-hearted than usual. Though to any one who did not know him well, his manner would have appeared much as usual, I who knew him so intimately noted at once various signs of strain, uncertain temper, fits of moody abstraction, general irritability of manner.

Although he was always inclined to be moody when painting, the picture he was at work upon did not account entirely for the strain he showed. He was pleased to see me and said as soon as we were alone: 'Thank goodness you've turned up, Phil. Living in a house with four women is enough to send any man clean off his chump. Between them all they'll send me into a lunatic asylum.'

It was certainly an uncomfortable atmosphere. Caroline, as I said, was obviously cutting up rough about the whole thing. In a polite, well-bred way, she was ruder to Elsa than one would believe possible – without a single actually offensive word. Elsa herself was openly and flagrantly rude to Caroline. She was top dog and she knew it – and no scruples of good breeding restrained her from overt bad manners. The result was that Crale spent most of his time scrapping with the girl Angela when he wasn't painting. They were usually on affectionate terms, though they teased and fought a good deal. But on this occasion there was an edge in everything Amyas said or did, and the two of them really lost their tempers with each other. The fourth member of the party was the governess. 'A sour-faced hag,' Amyas called her. 'She hates me like poison. Sits there with her lips set together, disapproving of me without stopping.'

It was then that he said:

'God damn all women! If a man is to have any peace he must steer clear of women!'

'You oughtn't to have married,' I said. 'You're the sort of man who ought to have kept clear of domestic ties.'

He replied that it was too late to talk about that now.

He added that no doubt Caroline would be only too glad to get rid of him. That was the first indication I had that something unusual was in the wind.

I said: 'What's all this? Is this business with the lovely Elsa serious then?' He said with a sort of groan:

'She *is* lovely, isn't she? Sometimes I wish I'd never seen her.'

I said: 'Look here, old boy, you must take a hold on yourself. You don't want to get tied up with any more women.' He looked at me and laughed. He said: 'It's all very well for you to talk. I can't let women alone – simply can't do it – and if I could, they wouldn't let me alone!' Then he shrugged those great shoulders of his, grinned at me and said: 'Oh well, it will all pan out in the end, I expect. And you must admit the picture is good?'

He was referring to the portrait he was doing of Elsa, and although I had very little technical knowledge of painting, even I could see that it was going to be a work of especial power.

Whilst he was painting, Amyas was a different man. Although he would growl, groan, frown, swear extravagantly, and sometimes hurl his brushes away, he was really intensely happy.

It was only when he came back to the house for meals that the hostile atmosphere between the women got him down. That hostility came to a head on

Sept. 17th. We had had an embarrassing lunch. Elsa had been particularly – really, I think *insolent* is the only word for it! She had ignored Caroline pointedly, persistently addressing the conversation to Amyas as though he and she were alone in the room. Caroline had talked lightly and gaily to the rest of us, cleverly contriving so that several perfectly innocent-sounding remarks should have a sting. She hadn't got Elsa Greer's scornful honesty – with Caroline every thing was oblique, suggested rather than said.

Things came to a head after lunch in the drawing-room just as we were finishing coffee. I had commented on a carved head in highly polished beechwood – a very curious thing, and Caroline said: 'That is the work of a young Norwegian sculptor. Amyas and I admire his work very much. We hope to go and see him next summer.' That calm assumption of possession was too much for Elsa. She was never one to let a challenge pass. She waited a minute or two and then she spoke in her clear, rather over-emphasized voice. She said: 'This would be a lovely room if it was properly fixed. It's got far too much furniture in it. When I'm living here I shall take all the rubbish out and just leave one or two good pieces. And I shall have copper-coloured curtains, I think – so that the setting sun will just catch them through that big western window.' She turned to me and said. 'Don't you think that would be rather lovely?'

I didn't have time to answer. Caroline spoke, and her voice was soft and silky and what I can only describe as dangerous. She said:

'Are you thinking of buying this place, Elsa?'

Elsa said: 'It won't be necessary for me to buy it.'

Caroline said: 'What do you mean?' And there was no softness in her voice now. It was hard and metallic. Elsa laughed. She said: 'Must we pretend? Come now, Caroline, you know very well what I mean!'

Caroline said: 'I've no idea.'

Elsa said to that: 'Don't be such an ostrich. It's no good pretending you don't see and know all about it. Amyas and I care for each other. This isn't your home. It's his. And after we're married I shall live here with him!'

Caroline said: 'I think you're crazy.'

Elsa said: 'Oh no, I'm not, my dear, and you know it. It would be much simpler if we were honest with each other. Amyas and I love each other – you've seen that clearly enough. There's only one decent thing for you to do. You've got to give him his freedom.'

Caroline said: 'I don't believe a word of what you are saying.'

But her voice was unconvincing. Elsa had got under her guard all right.

And at that minute Amyas Crale came into the room and Elsa said with a laugh:

'If you don't believe me, ask him.'

And Caroline said: 'I will.'

She didn't pause at all. She said:

'Amyas, Elsa says you want to marry her. Is this true?'

Poor Amyas. I felt sorry for him. It makes a man feel a fool to have a scene of that kind forced upon him. He went crimson and started blustering. He turned on Elsa and asked her why the devil she couldn't have held her tongue?

Caroline said: 'Then it *is* true?'

He didn't say anything, just stood there passing his finger round inside the neck of his shirt. He used to do that as a kid when he got into a jam of any kind. He said – and he tried to make the words sound dignified and authoritative – and of course couldn't manage it, poor devil:

'I don't want to discuss it.'

Caroline said: 'But we're going to discuss it!'

Elsa chipped in and said:

'I think it's only fair to Caroline that she should be told.'

Caroline said, very quietly:

'Is it true, Amyas?'

He looked a bit ashamed of himself. Men do when women pin them down in a corner.

She said:

'Answer me, please. I've got to know.'

He flung up his head then – rather the way a bull does in the bull-ring. He snapped out:

'It's true enough – but I don't want to discuss it now.'

And he turned and strode out of the room. I went after him. I didn't want to be left with the women. I caught up with him on the terrace. He was swearing. I never knew a man swear more heartily. Then he raved:

'Why couldn't she hold her tongue? Why the devil couldn't she hold her tongue? Now the fat's in the fire. And I've got to finish that picture – do you hear, Phil? It's the best thing I've done. The best thing I've ever done in my *life*. And a couple of damn' fool women want to muck it up between them!'

Then he calmed down a little and said women had no sense of proportion.

I couldn't help smiling a little. I said:

'Well, dash it all, old boy, you have brought this on yourself.'

'Don't I know it,' he said, and groaned. Then he added: 'But you must admit, Phil, that a man couldn't be blamed for losing his head about her. Even Caroline ought to understand that.'

I asked him what would happen if Caroline got her back up and refused to give him a divorce.

But by now he had gone off into a fit of abstraction. I repeated the remark and he said absently:

'Caroline would never be vindictive. You don't understand, old boy.'

'There's the child,' I pointed out.

He took me by the arm.

'Phil, old boy, you mean well – but don't go on croaking like a raven. I can manage my affairs. Everything will turn out all right. You'll see if it doesn't.'

That was Amyas all over – an absolutely unjustified optimist. He said now, cheerfully:

'To hell with the whole pack of them!'

I don't know whether we would have said anything more, but a few minutes later Caroline swept out on the terrace. She'd got a hat on, a queer, flopping, dark-brown hat, rather attractive.

She said in an absolutely ordinary, every-day voice:

'Take off that paint-stained coat, Amyas. We're going over to Meredith's to tea – don't you remember?'

He stared, stammered a bit as he said:

'Oh, I'd forgotten. Yes, of c-c-course we are.'

She said:

'Then go and try and make yourself look less like a rag-and-bone man.'

Although her voice was quite natural, she didn't look at him. She moved over towards a bed of dahlias and began picking off some of the overblown flowers.

Amyas turned round slowly and went into the house.

Caroline talked to me. She talked a good deal. About the chances of the weather lasting. And whether there might be mackerel about, and if so Amyas and Angela and I might like to go fishing. She was really amazing. I've got to hand it to her.

But I think, myself, that that showed the sort of woman she was. She had enormous strength of will and complete command over herself. I don't know whether she'd made up her mind to kill him then – but I shouldn't be surprised. And she was capable of making her plans carefully and unemotionally, with an absolutely clear and ruthless mind.

Caroline Crale was a very dangerous woman. I ought to have realized then that she wasn't prepared to take this thing lying down. But like a fool I thought that she had made up her mind to accept the inevitable – or else possibly she thought that if she carried on exactly as usual Amyas might change his mind.

Presently the others came out. Elsa looking defiant – but at the same time triumphant. Caroline took no notice of her. Angela really saved the situation. She came out arguing with Miss Williams that she wasn't going to change her skirt for any one. It was quite all right – good enough for darling old Meredith anyway – *he* never noticed anything.

We got off at last. Caroline walked with Angela.

And I walked with Amyas. And Elsa walked by herself – smiling.

I didn't admire her myself – too violent a type – but I have to admit that she looked incredibly beautiful that afternoon. Women do when they've got what they want.

I can't remember the events of that afternoon clearly at all. It's all blurred. I remember old Merry coming out to meet us. I think we walked round the garden first. I remember having a long discussion with Angela about the training of terriers for ratting. She ate an incredible lot of apples, and tried to persuade me to do so too.

When we got back to the house, tea was going on under the big cedar tree. Merry, I remember, was looking very upset. I suppose either Caroline or Amyas had told him something. He was looking doubtfully at Caroline, and then he stared at Elsa. The old boy looked thoroughly worried. Of course Caroline liked to have Meredith on a string more or less, the devoted, platonic friend who would never, never go too far. She was that kind of woman.

After tea Meredith had a hurried word with me. He said:

'Look here, Phil, Amyas *can't* do this thing!'

I said:

'Make no mistake, he's going to do it.'

'He can't leave his wife and child and go off with this

girl. He's years older than she is. She can't be more than eighteen.'

I said to him that Miss Greer was a fully sophisticated twenty.

He said: 'Anyway, that's under age. She can't know what she's doing.'

Poor old Meredith. Always the chivalrous pukka sahib. I said:

'Don't worry, old boy. *She* knows what she's doing, *and* she likes it!'

That's all we had the chance of saying. I thought to myself that probably Merry felt disturbed at the thought of Caroline being a deserted wife. Once the divorce was through she might expect her faithful Dobbin to marry her. I had an idea that hopeless devotion was really far more in his line. I must confess that that side of it amused me.

Curiously enough I remember very little about our visit to Meredith's stink room. He enjoyed showing people his hobby. Personally I always found it very boring. I suppose I was in there with the rest of them when he gave a dissertation on the efficacy of coniine, but I don't remember it. And I didn't see Caroline pinch the stuff. As I've said, she was a very adroit woman. I do remember Meredith reading aloud the passage from Plato describing Socrates' death. Very boring I thought it. Classics always did bore me.

Agatha Christie

There's nothing much more I can remember about that day. Amyas and Angela had a first-class row, I know, and the rest of us rather welcomed it. It avoided other difficulties. Angela rushed off to bed with a final vituperative outburst. She said A, she'd pay him out. B, she wished he were dead. C, she hoped he'd die of leprosy, it would serve him right. D, she wished a sausage would stick to his nose, like in the fairy story, and never come off. When she'd gone we all laughed, we couldn't help it, it was such a funny mixture.

Caroline went up to bed immediately afterwards. Miss Williams disappeared after her pupil. Amyas and Elsa went off together into the garden. It was clear that I wasn't wanted. I went for a stroll by myself. It was a lovely night.

I came down late the following morning. There was no one in the dining-room. Funny the things you do remember. I remember the taste of the kidneys and bacon I ate quite well. They were very good kidneys. Devilled.

Afterwards I wandered out looking for everybody. I went outside, didn't see anybody, smoked a cigarette, encountered Miss Williams running about looking for Angela, who had played truant as usual when she ought to have been mending a torn frock. I went back into the hall and realized that Amyas and Caroline were having a set-to in the library. They were talking very loud. I heard her say:

'You and your women! I'd like to kill you. Some day I will kill you.' Amyas said: 'Don't be a fool, Caroline.' And she said: 'I mean it, Amyas.'

Well, I didn't want to overhear any more. I went out again. I wandered along the terrace the other way and came across Elsa.

She was sitting on one of the long seats. The seat was directly under the library window, and the window was open. I should imagine that there wasn't much she had missed of what was going on inside. When she saw me she got up as cool as a cucumber and came towards me. She was smiling. She took my arm and said:

'Isn't it a lovely morning?'

It was a lovely morning for her all right! Rather a cruel girl. No, I think merely honest and lacking in imagination. What she wanted herself was the only thing that she could see.

We'd been standing on the terrace talking for about five minutes, when I heard the library door bang and Amyas Crale came out. He was very red in the face.

He caught hold of Elsa unceremoniously by the shoulder.

He said: 'Come on, time for you to sit. I want to get on with that picture.'

She said: 'All right. I'll just go up and get a pullover. There's a chilly wind.'

She went into the house.

I wondered if Amyas would say anything to me, but he didn't say much. Just: 'These women!'

I said: 'Cheer up, old boy.'

Then we neither of us said anything till Elsa came out of the house again.

They went off together down to the Battery garden. I went into the house. Caroline was standing in the hall. I don't think she even noticed me. It was a way of hers at times. She'd seem to go right away – to get inside herself as it were. She just murmured something. Not to me – to herself. I just caught the words:

'It's too cruel . . .'

That's what she said. Then she walked past me and upstairs, still without seeming to see me – just like a person intent on some inner vision. I think myself (I've no authority for saying this, you understand) that she went up to get the stuff, and that it was then she decided to do what she did do.

And just at that moment the telephone rang. In some houses one would wait for the servants to answer it, but I was so often at Alderbury that I acted more or less as one of the family. I picked up the receiver.

It was my brother Meredith's voice that answered. He was very upset. He explained that he had been into his laboratory and that the coniine bottle was half-empty.

I don't need to go again over all the things I know now I ought to have done. The thing was so startling and I was foolish enough to be taken aback. Meredith was dithering a good bit at the other end. I heard someone on the stairs, and I just told him sharply to come over at once.

I myself went down to meet him. In case you don't know the lay of the land, the shortest way from one estate to the other was by rowing across a small creek. I went down the path to where the boats were kept by a small jetty. To do so I passed under the wall of the Battery garden. I could hear Elsa and Amyas talking as he painted. They sounded very cheerful and carefree. Amyas said it was an amazingly hot day (so it was, very hot for September), and Elsa said that sitting where she was, poised on the battlements, there was a cold wind blowing in from the sea. And then she said: 'I'm horribly stiff from posing. Can't I have a rest, darling?' And I heard Amyas cry out: 'Not on your life. Stick it. You're a tough girl. And this is going good, I tell you.' I heard Elsa say, 'Brute' and laugh, as I went out of earshot.

Meredith was just rowing himself across from the other side. I waited for him. He tied up the boat and came up the steps. He was looking very white and worried. He said to me:

'Your head's better than mine, Philip. What ought I to do? That stuff's dangerous.'

I said: 'Are you absolutely sure about this?' Meredith, you see, was always a rather vague kind of chap. Perhaps that's why I didn't take it as seriously as I ought to have done. And he said he was quite sure. The bottle had been full yesterday afternoon.

I said: 'And you've absolutely *no* idea who pinched it?'

He said none whatever and asked me what *I* thought. Could it have been one of the servants? I said I supposed it might have been, but it seemed unlikely to me. He always kept the door locked, didn't he? Always, he said, and then began a rigmarole about having found the window a few inches open at the bottom. Someone might have got in that way.

'A chance burglar?' I asked sceptically. 'It seems to me, Meredith, that there are some very nasty possibilities.'

He said what did I really think? And I said, if he was sure he wasn't making a mistake, that probably Caroline had taken it to poison Elsa with – or that alternatively Elsa had taken it to get Caroline out of the way and straighten the path of true love.

Meredith twittered a bit. He said it was absurd and melodramatic and couldn't be true. I said: 'Well, the stuff's gone. What's *your* explanation?' He hadn't any, of course. Actually thought just as I did, but didn't want to face the fact.

He said again: 'What are we to do?'

I said, damned fool that I was: 'We must think it over carefully. Either you'd better announce your loss, straight out when everybody's there, or else you'd better get Caroline alone and tax her with it. If you're convinced *she's* nothing to do with it, adopt the same tactics for Elsa.' He said: 'A girl like that! She couldn't have taken it.' I said I wouldn't put it past her.

We were walking up to the house as we talked. After that last remark of mine neither of us spoke for some few seconds. We were rounding the Battery garden again and I heard Caroline's voice.

I thought perhaps a three-handed row was going on, but actually it was Angela that they were discussing. Caroline was protesting. She said: 'It's very hard on the girl.' And Amyas made some impatient rejoinder. Then the door to the garden opened just as we came abreast of it. Amyas looked a little taken aback at seeing us. Caroline was just coming out. She said: 'Hallo, Meredith. We've been discussing the question of Angela's going to school. I'm not at all sure it's the right thing for her.' Amyas said: 'Don't fuss about the girl. She'll be all right. Good riddance.'

Just then Elsa came running down the path from the

house. She had some sort of scarlet jumper in her hand. Amyas growled:

'Come along. Get back into the pose. I don't want to waste time.'

He went back to where his easel was standing. I noticed that he staggered a bit and I wondered if he had been drinking. A man might easily be excused for doing so with all the fuss and the scenes.

He grumbled.

'The beer here is red hot. Why can't we keep some ice down here?'

And Caroline Crale said:

'I'll send you down some beer just off the ice.'

Amyas grunted out:

'Thanks.'

Then Caroline shut the door of the Battery garden and came up with us to the house. We sat down on the terrace and she went into the house. About five minutes later Angela came along with a couple of bottles of beer and some glasses. It was a hot day and we were glad to see it. As we were drinking it Caroline passed us. She was carrying another bottle and said she would take it down to Amyas. Meredith said he'd go, but she was quite firm that she'd go herself. I thought – fool that I was – that it was just her jealousy. She couldn't stand those two being alone down there. That was what had taken her down there once already with the weak pretext of arguing about Angela's departure.

She went off down that zigzag path – and Meredith and I watched her go. We'd still not decided anything, and now Angela clamoured that I should come bathing with her. It seemed impossible to get Meredith alone. I just said to him: 'After lunch.' And he nodded.

Then I went off bathing with Angela. We had a good swim – across the creek and back, and then we lay out on the rocks sunbathing. Angela was a bit taciturn and that suited me. I made up my mind that directly after lunch I'd take Caroline aside and accuse her point-blank of having stolen the stuff. No use letting Meredith do it – he'd be too weak. No, I'd tax her with it outright. After that she'd have to give it back, or even if she didn't she wouldn't dare use it. I was pretty sure it must be her on thinking things over. Elsa was far too sensible and hard-boiled a young woman to risk tampering with poisons. She had a hard head and would take care of her own skin. Caroline was made of more dangerous stuff – unbalanced, carried away by impulses and definitely neurotic. And still, you know, at the back of my mind was the feeling that Meredith *might* have made a mistake. Or some servant might have been poking about in there and split the stuff and then not dared to own up. You see, poison seems such a melodramatic thing – you can't believe in it.

Not till it happens.

It was quite late when I looked at my watch, and Angela and I fairly raced up to lunch. They were just sitting down – all but Amyas, who had remained down in the Battery painting. Quite a normal thing for him to do – and privately I thought him very wise to elect to do it today. Lunch was likely to have been an awkward meal.

We had coffee on the terrace. I wish I could remember better how Caroline looked and acted. She didn't seem excited in any way. Quiet and rather sad is my impression. What a devil that woman was!

For it is a devilish thing to do, to poison a man in cold blood. If there had been a revolver about and she caught it up and shot him – well, that might have been understandable. But this cold, deliberate, vindictive poisoning. . . . And so calm and collected.

She got up and said she'd take his coffee to him in the most natural way possible. And yet she knew – she must have known – that by now she'd find him dead. Miss Williams went with her. I don't remember if that was at Caroline's suggestion or not. I rather think it was.

The two women went off together. Meredith strolled away shortly afterwards. I was just making an excuse to go after him, when he came running up the path again. His face was grey. He gasped out:

'We must get a doctor – quick – Amyas –'

I sprang up.

'Is he ill – dying?'

Meredith said:

'I'm afraid he's dead . . .'

We'd forgotten Elsa for the minute. But she let out a sudden cry. It was like the wail of a banshee.

She cried:

'Dead? Dead? . . .' And then she ran. I didn't know any one could move like that – like a deer – like a stricken thing. And like an avenging Fury, too.

Meredith panted out:

'Go after her. I'll telephone. Go after her. You don't know what she'll do.'

I did go after her – and it's as well I did. She might quite easily have killed Caroline. I've never seen such grief and such frenzied hate. All the veneer of refinement and education was stripped off. You could see her father and her father's mother and father had been millhands. Deprived of her lover, she was just elemental woman. She'd have clawed Caroline's face, torn her hair, hurled her over the parapet if she could. She thought for some reason or other that Caroline had knifed him. She'd got it all wrong – naturally.

I held her off, and then Miss Williams took charge. She was good, I must say. She got Elsa to control herself in under a minute – told her she'd got to be quiet and that we couldn't have this noise and violence going on. She was a tartar, that woman. But she did the trick. Elsa was quiet – just stood there gasping and trembling.

As for Caroline, so far as I am concerned, the mask was right off. She stood there perfectly quiet – you might have said dazed. But she wasn't dazed. It was her eyes gave her away. They were watchful – fully aware and quietly watchful. She'd begun, I suppose, to be afraid . . .

I went up to her and spoke to her. I said it quite low. I don't think either of the two women overheard.

I said:

'You damned murderess, you've killed my best friend.'

She shrank back. She said:

'No – oh no – he – he did it himself . . .'

I looked her full in the eyes. I said:

'You can tell that story – to the police.'

She did – and they didn't believe her.

End of Philip Blake's Statement.

Narrative of Meredith Blake

Dear M. Poirot,

As I promised you, I have set down in writing an account of all I can remember relating to the tragic events that happened sixteen years ago. First of all I would like to say that I have thought over carefully all you said to me at our recent meeting. And on reflection I am more convinced than I was before that it is in the highest degree unlikely that Caroline Crale poisoned her husband. It always seemed incongruous, but the absence of any other explanation and her own attitude led me to follow, sheep-like, the opinion of other people and to say with them – that if she didn't do it, what explanation could there be?

Since seeing you I have reflected very carefully on the alternative solution presented at the time and brought forward by the defence at the trial. That is, that Amyas Crale took his own life. Although from what I knew of him that solution seemed quite fantastic at the time, I now see fit to modify my opinion. To begin with, and highly significant, is the fact that Caroline believed it. If we are now to take it that that charming and gentle lady was unjustly convicted, then her own frequently reiterated belief must carry great weight. She knew Amyas better than anyone else. If *she* thought suicide possible, then suicide *must* have been possible in spite of the scepticism of his friends.

I will advance the theory, therefore, that there was in Amyas Crale some core of conscience, some under-current of remorse and even despair at the excesses to which his temperament led him, of which only his wife was aware. This, I think, is a not impossible supposition. He may have shown that side of himself only to her. Though it is inconsistent with anything I ever heard him say, yet it is nevertheless a truth that in most men there is some unsuspected and inconsistent streak which often comes as a surprise to people who have known them intimately. A respected and austere man is discovered to have had a coarser side to his life hidden. A vulgar money-maker has, perhaps, a secret appreciation of some delicate work of art. Hard and ruthless people have been convicted of unsuspected hidden kindnesses. Generous and jovial men have been shown to have a mean and cruel side to them.

So it may be that in Amyas Crale there ran a strain of

morbid self-accusation, and that the more he blustered out his egoism and his right to do as he pleased, the more strongly that secret conscience of his worked. It is improbable, on the face of it, but I now believe that it must have been so. And I repeat again, Caroline herself held steadfastly to that view. That, I repeat, is significant!

And now to examine *facts*, or rather my memory of facts, in the light of that new belief.

I think that I might with relevance include here a conversation I held with Caroline some weeks before the actual tragedy. It was during Elsa Greer's first visit to Alderbury.

Caroline, as I have told you, was aware of my deep affection and friendship for her. I was, therefore, the person in whom she could most easily confide. She had not been looking very happy. Nevertheless I was surprised when she suddenly asked me one day whether I thought Amyas really cared very much for this girl he had brought down.

I said: 'He's interested in painting her. You know what Amyas is.'

She shook her head and said:

'No, he's in love with her.'

'Well – perhaps a little.'

'A great deal, I think.'

I said: 'She is unusually attractive, I admit. And we

231

both know that Amyas is susceptible. But you must know by now, my dear, that Amyas really only cares for one person – and that is you. He has these infatuations – but they don't last. You are the one person to him, and though he behaves badly, it does not really affect his feeling for you.'

Caroline said: 'That is what I always used to think.'

'Believe me, Caro,' I said. 'It is so.'

She said: 'But this time, Merry, I'm afraid. That girl is so – so terribly sincere. She's so young – and so intense. I've a feeling that this time – it's serious.'

I said: 'But the very fact that she is so young and, as you say, so sincere, will protect her. On the whole, women are fair game to Amyas, but in the case of a girl like this it will be different.'

She said: 'Yes, that's what I'm afraid of – it will be different.'

And she went on. 'I'm thirty-four, you know, Merry. And we've been married ten years. In looks I can't hold a candle to this Elsa child, and I know it.'

I said: 'But you know, Caroline, you *know* – that Amyas is really devoted to you?'

She said to that: 'Does one ever know with men?' And then she laughed a little ruefully and said: 'I'm a very primitive woman, Merry. I'd like to take a hatchet to that girl.'

I told her that the child probably didn't understand

in the least what she was doing. She had a great admiration and hero-worship for Amyas, and she probably didn't realize at all that Amyas was falling in love with her.

Caroline just said to me:

'Dear Merry!' and began to talk about the garden. I hoped that she was not going to worry any more about the matter.

Shortly afterwards, Elsa went back to London. Amyas was away too for several weeks. I had really forgotten all about the business. And then I heard that Elsa was back again at Alderbury in order that Amyas might finish the picture.

I was a little disturbed by the news. But Caroline, when I saw her, was not in a communicative mood. She seemed quite her usual self – not worried or upset in any way. I imagined that everything was all right.

That's why it was such a shock to me to learn how far the thing had gone.

I have told you of my conversations with Crale and with Elsa. I had no opportunity of talking to Caroline. We were only able to exchange those few words about which I have already told you.

I can see her face now, the wide dark eyes and the restrained emotion. I can still hear her voice as she said:

'*Everything's finished . . .*'

I can't describe to you the infinite desolation she conveyed in those words. They were a literal statement of truth. With Amyas's defection, everything was finished for her. That, I am convinced, was why she took the conüne. It was a way out. A way suggested to her by my stupid dissertation on the drug. And the passage I read from the Phædo gives a gracious picture of death.

Here is my present belief. She took the coniine, resolved to end her own life when Amyas left her. He may have seen her take it – or he may have discovered that she had it later.

That discovery acted upon him with terrific force. He was horrified at what his actions had led her to contemplate. But notwithstanding his horror and remorse, he still felt himself incapable of giving up Elsa. I can understand that. Any one who had fallen in love with her would find it almost impossible to tear himself away.

He could not envisage life without Elsa. He realized that Caroline could not live without *him*. He decided there was only one way out – to use the coniine himself.

And the manner in which he did it might be characteristic of the man, I think. His painting was the dearest thing in life to him. He chose to die literally with his brush in his hand. And the last thing his eyes would see was the face of the girl he loved so desperately.

He might have thought, too, that his death would be the best thing for her . . .

I admit that this theory leaves certain curious facts unexplained. Why, for instance, were only Caroline's fingerprints found on the empty coniine bottle. I suggest that after Amyas had handled it, all prints got smudged or rubbed off by the soft piles of stuffs that were lying over the bottle and that, after his death, Caroline handled it to see if any one had touched it. Surely that is possible and plausible? As to the evidence about the fingerprints on the beer bottle, the witnesses for the defence were of opinion that a man's hand *might* be distorted after taking poison and so could manage to grasp a beer bottle in a wholly unnatural way.

One other thing remains to be explained. Caroline's own attitude throughout the trial. But I think I have now seen the cause for that. It was *she who actually took the poison from my laboratory*. It was *her* determination to do away with herself that impelled her husband to take his own life instead. Surely it is not unreasonable to suppose that in a morbid excess of responsibility she considered herself responsible for his death – that she persuaded herself that she *was* guilty of murder – though not the kind of murder of which she was being accused?

I think all that could be so. And if that is the case, then surely it will be easy for you to persuade little Carla of the fact? And she can marry her young man and rest contented that the only thing of which her mother was guilty was an impulse (no more) to take her own life.

All this, alas, is not what you asked me for – which was an account of the happenings as I remember them. Let me now repair that omission. I have already told you fully what happened on the day preceding Amyas's death. We now come to the day itself.

I had slept very badly – worried by the disastrous turn of events for my friends. After a long wakeful period whilst I vainly tried to think of something helpful I could do to avert the catastrophe, I fell into a heavy sleep about six a.m. The bringing of my early tea did not awaken me, and I finally woke up heavy-headed and unrefreshed about half-past nine. It was shortly after that that I thought I heard movements in the room below me, which was the room I used as a laboratory.

I may say here that actually the sounds were probably caused by a cat getting in. I found the window-sash raised a little way as it had carelessly been left from the day before. It was just wide enough to admit the passage of a cat. I merely mention the sounds to explain how I came to enter the laboratory.

I went in there as soon as I had dressed, and looking along the shelves I noticed that the bottle containing the preparation of coniine was slightly out of line with the rest. Having had my eye drawn to it in this way, I was startled to see that a considerable quantity of it had gone. The bottle had been nearly full the day before – now it was nearly empty.

I shut and locked the window and went out, locking the door behind me. I was considerably upset and also bewildered. When startled, my mental processes are, I am afraid, somewhat slow.

I was first disturbed, then apprehensive, and finally definitely alarmed. I questioned the household, and they all denied having entered the laboratory at all. I thought things over a little while longer, and then decided to ring up my brother and get his advice.

Philip was quicker than I was. He saw the seriousness of my discovery, and urged me to come over at once and consult with him.

I went out, encountering Miss Williams, who had come across from the other side to look for a truant pupil. I assured her that I had not seen Angela and that she had not been to the house.

I think that Miss Williams noticed there was something amiss. She looked at me rather curiously. I had no intention, however, of telling her what had happened. I suggested she should try the kitchen garden – Angela had a favourite apple tree there – and I myself hurried down to the shore and rowed myself across to the Alderbury side.

My brother was already there waiting for me.

We walked up to the house together by the way you and I went the other day. Having seen the topography you can understand that in passing underneath the wall of the Battery garden we were bound to overhear anything being said inside it.

Beyond the fact that Caroline and Amyas were engaged in a disagreement of some kind, I did not pay much attention to what was said.

Certainly I overheard no threat of any kind uttered by Caroline. The subject of discussion was Angela, and I presume Caroline was pleading for a respite from the fiat of school. Amyas, however, was adamant, shouting out irritably that it was all settled, he'd see to her packing.

The door of the Battery opened just as we drew abreast of it, and Caroline came out. She looked disturbed – but not unduly so. She smiled rather absently at me, and said they had been discussing Angela. Elsa came down the path at that minute, and as Amyas clearly wanted to get on with the sitting without interruption from us, we went on up the path.

Philip blamed himself severely afterwards for the fact that we did not take immediate action. But I myself cannot see it the same way. We had no earthly right to assume that such a thing as murder was being contemplated. (Moreover I now believe that it was *not* contemplated.) It was clear that we should have to adopt *some* course of action, but I still maintain that we were right to talk the matter over carefully first. It was necessary to find the right thing to do – and once or twice I found myself wondering if I had not after all made a mistake. Had the bottle really been full the day before as I thought? I am not one of those people (like my brother Philip) who can be cock-sure of everything. One's memory does play tricks on one. How often, for instance, one is convinced one has put an article in a certain place, later to find that you have put it somewhere quite different. The more I tried to recall the state of the bottle on the preceding afternoon, the more uncertain and doubtful I became. This was very annoying to Philip, who began completely to lose patience with me.

We were not able to continue our discussion at the time, and tacitly agreed to postpone it until after lunch. (I may say that I was always free to drop in for lunch at Alderbury if I chose.)

Later, Angela and Caroline brought us beer. I asked Angela what she had been up to playing truant, and told her Miss Williams was on the warpath, and she said she had been bathing – and added that she didn't see why she should have to mend her horrible old skirt when she was going to have all new things to go to school with.

Since there seemed no chance of further talk with

Agatha Christie

Philip alone, and since I was really anxious to think things out by myself, I wandered off down the path towards the Battery. Just above the Battery, as I showed you, there is a clearing in the trees where there used to be an old bench. I sat there smoking and thinking, and watching Elsa as she sat posing for Amyas.

I shall always think of her as she was that day. Rigid in the pose, with her yellow shirt and dark-blue trousers and a red pullover slung round her shoulders for warmth.

Her face was so alight with life and health and radiance. And that gay voice of hers reciting plans for the future.

This sounds as though I was eavesdropping, but that is not so. I was perfectly visible to Elsa. Both she and Amyas knew I was there. She waved her hand at me and called up that Amyas was a perfect bear that morning – he wouldn't let her rest. She was stiff and aching all over.

Amyas growled out that she wasn't as stiff as he was. He was stiff all over – muscular rheumatism. Elsa said mockingly: 'Poor old man!' And he said she'd be taking on a creaking invalid.

It shocked me, you know, their lighthearted acquiescence in their future together whilst they were causing so much suffering. And yet I couldn't hold it against her. She was so young, so confident, so very much in love. And she didn't really know what she was doing. She didn't understand suffering. She just assumed with the naïve confidence of a child that Caroline would be 'all right', that 'she'd soon get over it.' She saw nothing, you see, but herself and Amyas – happy together. She'd already told me my point of view was old-fashioned. She had no doubts, no qualms – no pity either. But can one expect pity from radiant youth? It is an older, wiser emotion.

They didn't talk very much, of course. No painter wants to be chattering when he is working. Perhaps every ten minutes or so Elsa would make an observation and Amyas would grunt a reply. Once she said:

'I think you're right about Spain. That's the first place we'll go to. And you must take me to see a bullfight. It must be wonderful. Only I'd like the bull to kill the man – not the other way about. I understand how Roman women felt when they saw a man die. Men aren't much, but animals are splendid.'

I suppose she was rather like an animal herself – young and primitive and with nothing yet of man's sad experience and doubtful wisdom. I don't believe Elsa had begun to *think* – she only *felt*. But she was very much alive – more alive than any person I have ever known . . .

That was the last time I saw her radiant and assured – on top of the world. Fey is the word for it, isn't it?

The bell sounded for lunch, and I got up and went down the path and in at the Battery door, and Elsa joined me. It was dazzlingly bright there coming in out of the shady trees. I could hardly see. Amyas was sprawled back on the seat, his arms flung out. He was staring at the picture. I've so often seen him like that. How was I to know that already the poison was working, stiffening him as he sat?

He so hated and resented illness. He would never own to it. I dare say he thought he had got a touch of the sun – the symptoms are much the same – but he'd be the last person to complain about it.

Elsa said:

'He won't come up to lunch.'

Privately I thought he was wise. I said:

'So long, then.'

He moved his eyes from the picture until they rested on me. There was a queer – how shall I describe it – it looked like malevolence. A kind of malevolent glare.

Naturally I didn't understand it then – if his picture wasn't going as he liked he often looked quite murderous. I thought *that* was what it was. He made a sort of grunting sound.

Neither Elsa nor I saw anything unusual in him – just artistic temperament.

So we left him there and she and I went up to the house laughing and talking. If she'd known, poor child, that she'd never see him alive again ... Oh, well, thank God she didn't. She was able to be happy a little longer.

Caroline was quite normal at lunch – a little preoccupied; nothing more. And doesn't that show that she had nothing to do with it? She *couldn't* have been such an actress.

She and the governess went down afterwards and found him. I met Miss Williams as she came up. She told me to telephone a doctor and went back to Caroline.

That poor child – Elsa, I mean! She had that frantic unrestrained grief that a child has. They can't believe that life can do these things to them. Caroline was quite calm. Yes, she was quite calm. She was able, of course, to control herself better than Elsa. She didn't seem remorseful – then. Just said he must have done it himself. And we couldn't believe that. Elsa burst out and accused her to her face.

Of course she may have realized, already, that she herself would be suspected. Yes, that probably explains her manner.

Philip was quite convinced that she *had* done it.

The governess was a great help and standby. She made Elsa lie down and gave her a sedative, and she kept Angela out of the way when the police came. Yes, she was a tower of strength, that woman.

Agatha Christie

The whole thing became a nightmare. The police searching the house and asking questions, and then the reporters, swarming about the place like flies and clicking cameras and wanting interviews with members of the family.

A nightmare, the whole thing . . .

It's a nightmare, after all these years. Please God, once you've convinced little Carla what really happened, we can forget it all and never remember it again.

Amyas *must* have committed suicide – however unlikely it seems.

End of Meredith Blake's Narrative.

Narrative of Lady Dittisham

I have set down here the full story of my meeting with Amyas Crale, up to the time of his tragic death.

I saw him first at a studio party. He was standing, I remember, by a window, and I saw him as I came in at the door. I asked who he was. Someone said: 'That's Crale, the painter.' I said at once that I'd like to meet him.

We talked on that occasion for perhaps ten minutes. When any one makes the impression on you that Amyas Crale made on me, it's hopeless to attempt to describe them. If I say that when I saw Amyas Crale, everybody else seemed to grow very small and fade away, that expresses it as well as anything can.

Immediately after that meeting I went to look at as many of his pictures as I could. He had a show on in Bond Street at the moment, and there was one of his pictures in Manchester and one in Leeds and two in public galleries in London. I went to see them all. Then I met him again. I said: 'I've been to see all your pictures. I think they're wonderful.'

He just looked amused. He said:

'Who said you were any judge of painting? I don't believe you know anything about it.'

I said: 'Perhaps not. But they are marvellous, all the same.'

He grinned at me and said: 'Don't be a gushing little fool.'

I said: 'I'm not. I want you to paint me.'

Crale said: 'If you've any sense at all, you'll realize that I don't paint portraits of pretty women.'

I said: 'It needn't be a portrait and I'm not a pretty woman.'

He looked at me then as though he'd begun to see me. He said: 'No, perhaps you're not.'

I said: 'Will you paint me then?'

He studied me for some time with his head on one side. Then he said: 'You're a strnage child, aren't you?'

I said: 'I'm quite rich, you know. I can afford to pay well for it.'

He said: 'Why are you so anxious for me to paint you?'

I said: 'Because I want it!'

He said: 'Is that a reason?'

And I said: 'Yes, I always get what I want.'

He said then: 'Oh, my poor child, how young you are!'

I said: 'Will you paint me?'

He took me by the shoulders and turned me towards the light and looked me over. Then he stood away from me a little. I stood quite still, waiting.

He said: 'I've sometimes wanted to paint a flight of impossibly-coloured Australian Maccaws alighting on St Paul's Cathedral. If I painted you against a nice traditional bit of outdoor landscape, I believe I'd get exactly the same result.'

I said: 'Then you will paint me?'

He said: 'You're one of the loveliest, crudest, most flamboyant bits of exotic colouring I've ever seen. I'll paint you!'

I said: 'Then that's settled.'

He went on: 'But I'll warn you, Elsa Greer. If I do paint you, I shall probably make love to you.'

I said: 'I hope you will . . .'

I said it quite steadily and quietly. I heard him catch his breath, and I saw the look that came into his eyes.

You see, it was as sudden as all that.

A day or two later we met again. He told me that he wanted me to come down to Devonshire – he'd got the very place there that he wanted for a background. He said:

'I'm married, you know. And I'm very fond of my wife.'

I said if he was fond of her she must be very nice.

He said she was extremely nice. 'In fact,' he said, 'she's quite adorable – and I adore her. So put that in your pipe, young Elsa, and smoke it.'

I told him that I quite understood.

He began the picture a week later. Caroline Crale welcomed me very pleasantly. She didn't like me much – but, after all, why should she? Amyas was very circumspect. He never said a word to me that his wife couldn't have overheard, and I was quite polite and formal to him. Underneath, though, we both knew.

After ten days he told me I was to go back to London.

I said: 'The picture isn't finished.'

He said: 'It's barely begun. The truth is, I can't paint you, Elsa.'

I said: 'Why?'

He said: 'You know well enough why, Elsa. And that's why you've got to clear out. I can't think about the painting – I can't think about anything but you.'

We were in the Battery garden. It was a hot sunny day. There were birds and humming bees. It ought to have been very happy and peaceful. But it didn't feel like that. It felt – somehow – tragic. As though

– as though what was going to happen was already mirrored there.

I knew it would be no good my going back to London, but I said: 'Very well, I'll go if you say so.'

Amyas said: 'Good girl.'

So I went. I didn't write to him.

He held out for ten days and then he came. He was so thin and haggard and miserable that it shocked me.

He said: 'I warned you, Elsa. Don't say I didn't warn you.'

I said: 'I've been waiting for you. I knew you'd come.'

He gave a sort of groan and said: 'There are things that are too strong for any man. I can't eat or sleep or rest for wanting you.'

I said I knew that and that it was the same with me, and had been from the first moment I'd seen him. It was Fate and it was no use struggling against it.

He said: 'You haven't struggled much, have you, Elsa?' And I said I hadn't struggled at all.

He said he wished I wasn't so young, and I said that didn't matter. I suppose I might say that for the next few weeks we were very happy. But happiness isn't quite the word. It was something deeper and more frightening than that.

We were made for each other and we'd found each

other – and we both knew we'd got to be together always.

But something else happened, too. The unfinished picture began to haunt Amyas. He said to me: 'Damned funny, I couldn't paint you before – you yourself got in the way of it. But I *want* to paint you, Elsa. I want to paint you so that that picture will be the finest thing I've ever done. I'm itching and aching now to get at my brushes to see you sitting there on that hoary old chestnut of a battlement wall with the conventional blue sea and the decorous English trees – and you – you – sitting there like a discordant shriek of triumph.'

He said: 'And I've got to paint you that way! And I can't be fussed and bothered while I'm doing it. When the picture's finished I'll tell Caroline the truth and we'll get the whole messy business cleared up.'

I said: 'Will Caroline make a fuss about divorcing you?'

He said he didn't think so. But you never knew with women.

I said I was sorry if she was going to be upset, but after all, I said, these things did happen.

He said: 'Very nice and reasonable, Elsa. But Caroline isn't reasonable, never has been reasonable, and certainly isn't going to feel reasonable. She loves me, you know.'

I said I understood that, but if she loved him, she'd

put his happiness first, and at any rate she wouldn't want to keep him if he wanted to be free.

He said: 'Life can't really be solved by admirable maxims out of modern literature. Nature's red in tooth and claw, remember.'

I said: 'Surely we are all civilized people nowadays?' and Amyas laughed. He said: 'Civilized people my foot! Caroline would probably like to take a hatchet to you. She might do it too. Don't you realize, Elsa, that she's going to suffer – *suffer*? Don't you know what suffering means?'

I said: 'Then don't tell her.'

He said: 'No. The break's got to come. You've got to belong to me properly, Elsa. Before all the world. Openly mine.'

I said: 'Suppose she won't divorce you?'

He said: 'I'm not afraid of that.'

I said: 'What are you afraid of then?'

And then he said slowly: 'I don't know . . .'

You see, he knew Caroline. I didn't.

If I'd had any idea . . .

We went down again to Alderbury. Things were difficult this time. Caroline had got suspicious. I didn't like it – I didn't like it – I didn't like it a bit. I've always hated deceit and concealment. I thought we ought to tell her. Amyas wouldn't hear of it.

The funny part of it was that he didn't really care at

all. In spite of being fond of Caroline and not wanting to hurt her, he just didn't care about the honesty or dishonesty of it all. He was painting with a kind of frenzy, and nothing else mattered. I hadn't seen him in one of his working spells before. I realized now what a really great genius he was. It was natural for him to be so carried away that all the ordinary decencies didn't matter. But it was different for me. I was in a horrible position. Caroline resented me – and quite rightly. The only thing to put the position quite straight was to be honest and tell her the truth.

But all Amyas would say was that he wasn't going to be bothered with scenes and fusses until he'd finished the picture. I said there probably wouldn't be a scene. Caroline would have too much dignity and pride for that.

I said: 'I want to be honest about it all. We've *got* to be honest!'

Amyas said: 'To hell with honesty. I'm painting a picture, damn it.'

I did see his point of view, but he wouldn't see mine.

And in the end I broke down. Caroline had been talking of some plan she and Amyas were going to carry out next autumn. She talked about it quite confidently. And I suddenly felt it was too abominable, what we were doing – letting her go on like this – and perhaps, too, I was angry, because she was really being very unpleasant to me in a clever sort of way that one couldn't take hold of.

And so I came out with the truth. In a way, I still think I was right. Though, of course, I wouldn't have done it if I'd had the faintest idea what was to come of it.

The clash came right away. Amyas was furious with me, but he had to admit that what I had said was true.

I didn't understand Caroline at all. We all went over to Meredith Blake's to tea, and Caroline played up marvellously – talking and laughing. Like a fool, I thought she was taking it well. It was awkward my not being able to leave the house, but Amyas would have gone up in smoke if I had. I thought perhaps Caroline would go. It would have made it much easier for us if she had.

I didn't see her take the coniine. I want to be honest so I think that it's just possible that she may have taken it as she said she did, with the idea of suicide in her mind.

But I don't *really* think so. I think she was one of those intensely jealous and possessive women who won't let go of anything that they think belongs to them. Amyas was her property. I think she was quite prepared to kill him rather than to let him go – completely and finally – to another woman. I think she

253

made up her mind, right away, to kill him. And I think that Meredith's happening to discuss coniine so freely just gave her the means to do what she'd already made up her mind to do. She was a very bitter and revengeful woman – vindictive. Amyas knew all along that she was dangerous. I didn't.

The next morning she had a final showdown with Amyas. I heard most of it from the outside on the terrace. He was splendid – very patient and calm. He implored her to be reasonable. He said he was very fond of her and the child and always would be. He'd do everything he could do to assure their future. Then he hardened up and said: 'But understand this. I'm damned well going to marry Elsa – and nothing shall stop me. You and I always agreed to leave each other free. These things happen.'

Caroline said to him: 'Do as you please. I've warned you.'

Her voice was very quiet, but there was a queer note in it.

Amyas said: 'What do you mean, Caroline?'

She said: 'You're mine and *I don't mean to let you go.* Sooner than let you go to that girl *I'll kill you . . .*'

Just at that minute, Philip Blake came along the terrace. I got up and went to meet him. I didn't want him to overhear.

Presently Amyas came out and said it was time to

get on with the picture. We went down together to the Battery. He didn't say much. Just said that Caroline was cutting up rough – but for God's sake not to talk about it. He wanted to concentrate on what he was doing. Another day, he said, would about finish the picture.

He said: 'And it'll be the best thing I've ever done, Elsa, even if it is paid for in blood and tears.'

A little later I went up to the house to get a pullover. There was a chilly wind blowing. When I came back again Caroline was there. I suppose she had come down to make one last appeal. Philip and Meredith Blake were there too.

It was then that Amyas said he was thirsty and wanted a drink. He said there was beer but it wasn't iced.

Caroline said she'd send him down some iced beer. She said it quite naturally in an almost friendly tone. She was an actress, that woman. She must have known then what she meant to do.

She brought it down about ten minutes later. Amyas was painting. She poured it out and set the glass down beside him. Neither of us were watching her. Amyas was intent on what he was doing and I had to keep the pose.

Amyas drank it down the way he always drank beer, just pouring it down his throat in one draught. Then he made a face and said it tasted foul – but at any rate it was cold.

And even then, when he said that, no suspicion entered my head, I just laughed and said: 'Liver.'

When she'd seen him drink it Caroline went away.

It must have been about forty minutes later that Amyas complained of stiffness and pains. He said he thought he must have got a touch of muscular rheumatism. Amyas was always intolerant of any ailment and he didn't like being fussed over. After saying that he turned it off with a light: 'Old age, I suppose. You've taken on a creaking old man, Elsa.' I played up to him. But I noticed that his legs moved stiffly and queerly and that he grimaced once or twice. I never dreamt that it wasn't rheumatism. Presently he drew the bench along and sat sprawled on that, occasionally stretching up to put a touch of paint here and there on the canvas. He used to do that sometimes when he was painting. Just sit staring at me and then the canvas. Sometimes he'd do it for half an hour at a time. So I didn't think it specially queer.

We heard the bell go for lunch, and he said he wasn't coming up. He'd stay where he was and he didn't want anything. That wasn't unusual either, and it would be easier for him than facing Caroline at the table.

He was talking in rather a queer way – grunting out

his words. But he sometimes did that when he was dissatisfied with the progress of the picture.

Meredith Blake came in to fetch me. He spoke to Amyas, but Amyas only grunted at him.

We went up to the house together and left him there. We left him there – to die alone. I'd never seen much illness – I didn't know much about it – I thought Amyas was just in a painter's mood. If I'd known – if I'd realized – perhaps a doctor could have saved him . . . Oh God, why didn't I – it's no good thinking of that now. I was a blind fool. A blind, stupid fool.

There isn't much more to tell.

Caroline and the governess went down there after lunch. Meredith followed them. Presently he came running up. He told us Amyas was dead.

Then I knew! Knew, I mean, that it was Caroline. I still didn't think of poison. I thought she'd gone down that minute and either shot him or stabbed him.

I wanted to get at her – to kill her . . .

How *could* she do it? How *could* she? He was so alive, so full of life and vigour. To put all that out – to make him limp and cold. Just so that I shouldn't have him.

Horrible woman . . .

Horrible, scornful, cruel, vindictive woman . . .

I hate her. I still hate her.

They didn't even hang her.

They ought to have hanged her . . .

Agatha Christie

Even hanging was too good for her . . .
I hate her . . . I hate her . . . I hate her . . .

End of Lady Dittisham's Narrative.

Narrative of Cecilia Williams

Dear M. Poirot,

I am sending you an account of those events in September, 19 . . . actually witnessed by myself.

I have been absolutely frank and have kept nothing back. You may show it to Carla Crale. It may pain her, but I have always been a believer in truth. Palliatives are harmful. One must have the courage to face reality. Without that courage, life is meaningless. The people who do us most harm are the people who shield us from reality.

Believe me, yours sincerely,

Cecilia Williams

My name is Cecilia Williams. I was engaged by Mrs Crale as governess to her half-sister Angela Warren, in 19 . . . I was then forty-eight.

I took up my duties at Alderbury, a very beautiful estate in south Devon which had belonged to Mr

Agatha Christie

Crale's family for many generations. I knew that Mr Crale was a well-known painter, but I did not meet him until I took up residence at Alderbury.

The household consisted of Mr and Mrs Crale, Angela Warren (then a girl of thirteen), and three servants, all of whom had been with the family many years.

I found my pupil an interesting and promising character. She had very marked abilities and it was a pleasure to teach her. She was somewhat wild and undisciplined, but these faults arose mainly through high spirits, and I have always preferred my girls to show spirit. An excess of vitality can be trained and guided into paths of real usefulness and achievement.

On the whole, I found Angela amenable to discipline. She had been somewhat spoiled – mainly by Mrs Crale, who was far too indulgent where she was concerned. Mr Crale's influence was, I considered, unwise. He indulged her absurdly one day, and was unnecessarily peremptory on another occasion. He was very much a man of moods – possibly owing to what is styled the artistic temperament.

I have never seen, myself, why the possession of artistic ability should be supposed to excuse a man from a decent exercise of self-control. I did not myself admire Mr Crale's paintings. The drawing seemed to me faulty and the colouring exaggerated, but naturally

I was not called upon to express any opinion on these matters.

I soon formed a deep attachment to Mrs Crale. I admired her character and her fortitude in the difficulties of her life. Mr Crale was not a faithful husband, and I think that that fact was the source of much pain to her. A stronger-minded woman would have left him, but Mrs Crale never seemed to contemplate such a course. She endured his infidelities and forgave him for them – but I may say that she did not take them meekly. She remonstrated – and with spirit!

It was said at the trial that they led a cat and dog life. I would not go as far as that – Mrs Crale had too much dignity for that term to apply, but they *did* have quarrels. And I consider that that was only natural under the circumstances.

I had been with Mrs Crale just over two years when Miss Elsa Greer appeared upon the scene. She arrived down at Alderbury in the summer of 19 . . . Mrs Crale had not met her previously. She was Mr Crale's friend, and she was said to be there for the purpose of having her portrait painted.

It was apparent at once that Mr Crale was infatuated with this girl and that the girl herself was doing nothing to discourage him. She behaved, in my opinion, quite outrageously, being abominably rude to Mrs Crale, and openly flirting with Mr Crale.

Naturally Mrs Crale said nothing to me, but I could see that she was disturbed and unhappy, and I did everything in my power to distract her mind and lighten her burden. Miss Greer sat every day to Mr Crale, but I noticed that the picture was not getting on very fast. They had, no doubt, other things to talk about!

My pupil, I am thankful to say, noticed very little of what was going on. Angela was in some ways young for her age. Though her intellect was well developed, she was not at all what I may term precocious. She seemed to have no wish to read undesirable books, and showed no signs of morbid curiosity such as girls often do at her age.

She, therefore, saw nothing undesirable in the friendship between Mr Crale and Miss Greer. Nevertheless she disliked Miss Greer and thought her stupid. Here she was quite right. Miss Greer had had, I presume, a proper education, but she never opened a book and was quite unfamiliar with current literary allusions. Moreover she could not sustain a discussion on any intellectual subject.

She was entirely taken up with her personal appearance, her clothes, and men.

Angela, I think, did not even realize that her sister was unhappy. She was not at that time a very perceptive person. She spent a lot of time in hoydenish pastimes, such as tree climbing and wild feats of bicycling. She was also a passionate reader and showed excellent taste in what she liked and disliked.

Mrs Crale was always careful to conceal any signs of unhappiness from Angela, and exerted herself to appear bright and cheerful when the girl was about.

Miss Greer went back to London – at which, I can tell you, we were all very pleased! The servants disliked her as much as I did. She was the kind of person who gives a lot of unnecessary trouble and forgets to say thank you.

Mr Crale went away shortly afterwards, and of course I knew that he had gone after the girl. I was very sorry for Mrs Crale. She felt these things very keenly. I felt extremely bitter towards Mr Crale. When a man has a charming, gracious, intelligent wife, he's no business to treat her badly.

However, she and I both hoped the affair would soon be over. Not that we mentioned the subject to each other – we did not – but she knew quite well how I felt about it.

Unfortunately, after some weeks, the pair of them reappeared. It seemed the sittings were to be resumed.

Mr Crale was now painting with absolute frenzy. He seemed less preoccupied with the girl than with his picture of her. Nevertheless I realized that this was not the usual kind of thing we had gone through before.

Agatha Christie

This girl had got her claws into him and she meant business. He was just like wax in her hands.

The thing came to a head on the day before he died – that is on Sept. 17. Miss Greer's manner had been unbearably insolent the last few days. She was feeling sure of herself and she wanted to assert her importance. Mrs Crale behaved like a true gentlewoman. She was icily polite, but she showed the other clearly what she thought of her.

On this day, Sept. 17, as we were sitting in the drawing-room after lunch, Miss Greer came out with an amazing remark as to how she was going to redecorate the room when she was living at Alderbury.

Naturally Mrs Crale couldn't let that pass. She challenged her, and Miss Greer had the impudence to say, before us all, that she was going to marry Mr Crale. She actually talked about marrying a married man – and she said it to his wife!

I was very, very angry with Mr Crale. How dared he let this girl insult his wife in her own drawing-room? If he wanted to run away with the girl, he should have gone off with her, not brought her into his wife's house and backed her up in her insolence.

In spite of what she must have felt, Mrs Crale did not lose her dignity. Her husband came in just then, and she immediately demanded confirmation from him.

He was, not unnaturally, annoyed with Miss Greer

for her unconsidered forcing of the situation. Apart from anything else, it made *him* appear at a disadvantage, and men do not like appearing at a disadvantage. It upsets their vanity.

He stood there, a great giant of a man, looking as sheepish and foolish as a naughty schoolboy. It was his wife who carried off the honours of the situation. He had to mutter foolishly that it was true, but that he hadn't meant her to learn it like this.

I have never seen anything like the look of scorn she gave him. She went out of the room with her head held high. She was a beautiful woman – much more beautiful than that flamboyant girl – and she walked like an Empress.

I hoped, with all my heart, that Amyas Crale would be punished for the cruelty he had displayed and for the indignity he had put upon a long-suffering and noble woman.

For the first time, I tried to say something of what I felt to Mrs Crale, but she stopped me.

She said:

'We must try and behave as usual. It's the best way. We're all going over to Meredith Blake's to tea.'

I said to her then:

'I think you are wonderful, Mrs Crale.'

She said:

'You don't know . . .'

Then, as she was going out of the room, she came back and kissed me. She said:

'You're such a comfort to me.'

She went to her room then and I think she cried. I saw her when they all started off. She was wearing a big-brimmed hat that shaded her face – a hat she very seldom wore.

Mr Crale was uneasy, but was trying to brazen things out. Mr Philip Blake was trying to behave as usual. That Miss Greer was looking like a cat who has got at the cream-jug. All self-satisfaction and purrs!

They all started off. They got back about six. I did not see Mrs Crale again alone that evening. She was very quiet and composed at dinner, and she went to bed early. I don't think that any one knew how she was suffering.

The evening was taken up with a kind of running quarrel between Mr Crale and Angela. They brought up the old school question again. He was irritable and on edge, and she was unusually trying. The whole matter was settled and her outfit had been bought, and there was no sense in starting up an argument again, but she suddenly chose to make a grievance of it. I have no doubt she sensed the tension in the air and that it reacted on her as much as on everybody else. I am afraid I was too preoccupied with my own thoughts to try and check her as I should have done. It all ended with her flinging a paperweight at Mr Crale and dashing out of the room.

I went after her and told her sharply that I was ashamed of her behaving like a baby, but she was still very uncontrolled, and I thought it best to leave her alone.

I hesitated as to whether to go to Mrs Crale's room, but I decided in the end that it would, perhaps, annoy her. I wish since that I had overcome my diffidence and insisted on her talking to me. If she had done so, it might possibly have made a difference. She had no one, you see, in whom she could confide. Although I admire self-control, I must regretfully admit that sometimes it can be carried too far. A natural outlet to the feelings is better.

I met Mr Crale as I went along to my room. He said goodnight, but I did not answer.

The next morning was, I remember, a beautiful day. One felt when waking that surely with such peace all around even a man must come to his senses.

I went into Angela's room before going down to breakfast, but she was already up and out. I picked up a torn skirt which she had left lying on the floor and took it down with me for her to mend after breakfast.

She had, however, obtained bread and marmalade from the kitchen and gone out. After I had had my own breakfast I went in search of her. I mention this to explain why I was not more with Mrs Crale on that morning as perhaps I should have been. At the time, however, I felt it was my duty to look for Angela. She was very naughty and obstinate about mending her clothes, and I had no intention of allowing her to defy me in the matter.

Her bathing-dress was missing and I accordingly went down to the beach. There was no sign of her in the water or on the rocks, so I conceived it possible that she had gone over to Mr Meredith Blake's. She and he were great friends. I accordingly rowed myself across and resumed my search. I did not find her and eventually returned. Mrs Crale, Mr Blake and Mr Philip Blake were on the terrace.

It was very hot that morning if one was out of the wind, and the house and terrace were sheltered. Mrs Crale suggested they might like some iced beer.

There was a little conservatory which had been built on to the house in Victorian days. Mrs Crale disliked it, and it was not used for plants, but it had been made into a kind of bar, with various bottles of gin, vermouth, lemonade, ginger-beer, etc., on shelves, and a small refrigerator which was filled with ice every morning and in which some beer and ginger-beer was always kept.

Mrs Crale went there to get the beer and I went with her. Angela was at the refrigerator and was just taking out a bottle of beer.

Mrs Crale went in ahead of me. She said:

'I want a bottle of beer to take down to Amyas.'

It is so difficult now to know whether I ought to have suspected anything. Her voice, I feel almost convinced, was perfectly normal. But I must admit that at that moment I was intent, not on her, but on Angela. Angela was by the refrigerator and I was glad to see that she looked red and rather guilty.

I was rather sharp with her, and to my surprise she was quite meek. I asked her where she had been, and she said she had been bathing. I said: 'I didn't see you on the beach.' And she laughed. Then I asked her where her jersey was, and she said she must have left it down on the beach.

I mention these details to explain why I let Mrs Crale take the beer down to the Battery garden.

The rest of the morning is quite blank in my mind. Angela fetched her needle-book and mended her skirt without any more fuss. I rather think that I mended some of the household linen. Mr Crale did not come up for lunch. I was glad that he had at least *that* much decency.

After lunch, Mrs Crale said she was going down to the Battery. I wanted to retrieve Angela's jersey from the beach. We started down together. She went into the Battery – I was going on when her cry called me back. As I told you when you came to see me, she asked

269

Agatha Christie

me to go up and telephone. On the way up I met Mr
Meredith Blake and then went back to Mrs Crale.

That was my story as I told it at the inquest and later
at the trial.

What I am about to write down I have never told to
any living soul. I was not asked any question to which
I returned an untrue answer. Nevertheless I *was* guilty
of withholding certain facts – I do not repent of that. I
would do it again. I am fully aware that in revealing this
I may be laying myself open to censure, but I do not
think that after this lapse of time any one will take the
matter very seriously – especially since Caroline Crale
was convicted without my evidence.

This, then, is what happened.

I met Mr Meredith Blake as I said, and I ran down
the path again as quickly as I could. I was wearing sandshoes and I have always been light on my
feet. I came to the open Battery door, and this is
what I saw.

Mrs Crale was busily polishing the beer bottle on
the table with her handkerchief. Having done so, she
took her dead husband's hand and pressed the fingers
of it on the beer bottle. All the time she was listening
and on the alert. It was the fear I saw on her face that
told me the truth.

I knew then, beyond any possible doubt, that Caroline
Crale had poisoned her husband. And I, for one, do

not blame her. He drove her to a point beyond human endurance, and he brought his fate upon himself.

I never mentioned the incident to Mrs Crale and she never knew that I had seen it.

Caroline Crale's daughter must not bolster up her life with a lie. However much it may pain her to know the truth, truth is the only thing that matters.

Tell her, from me, that her mother is not to be judged. She was driven beyond what a loving woman can endure. It is for her daughter to understand and forgive.

End of Cecilia Williams's Narrative.

Narrative of Angela Warren

Dear M. Poirot,

I am keeping my promise to you and have written down all I can remember of that terrible time sixteen years ago. But it was not until I started that I realized how very little I *did* remember. Until the thing actually happened, you see, there is nothing to fix anything by.

I've just a vague memory of summer days – and isolated incidents, but I couldn't say for certain what summer they happened even! Amyas's death was just a thunderclap coming out of the blue. I'd had no warning of it, and I seem to have missed everything that led up to it.

I've been trying to think whether that was to be expected or not. Are most girls of fifteen as blind and deaf and obtuse as I seem to have been? Perhaps they are. I was quick, I think, to gauge people's moods, but

I never bothered my head about what *caused* those moods.

Besides, just at that time, I'd suddenly begun to discover the intoxication of words. Things that I read, straps of poetry – of Shakespeare – would echo in my head. I remember now walking along the kitchen garden path repeating to myself in a kind of ecstatic delirium 'under the glassy green translucent wave' . . . It was just so lovely I had to say it over and over again.

And mixed up with these new discoveries and excitements there were all the things I'd liked doing ever since I could remember. Swimming and climbing trees and eating fruit and playing tricks on the stable boy and feeding the horses.

Caroline and Amyas I took for granted. They were the central figures in my world, but I never *thought* about them or about their affairs or what they thought and felt.

I didn't notice Elsa Greer's coming particularly. I thought she was stupid and I didn't even think she was good-looking. I accepted her as someone rich but tiresome, whom Amyas was painting.

Actually, the very first intimation I had of the whole thing was what I overheard from the terrace where I had escaped after lunch one day – Elsa said she was going to marry Amyas! It struck me as just ridiculous.

I remember tackling Amyas about it. In the garden at Handcross it was. I said to him:

'Why does Elsa say she's going to marry you? She couldn't. People can't have two wives – it's bigamy and they go to prison.'

Amyas got very angry and said: 'How the devil did you hear that?'

I said I'd heard it through the library window.

He was angrier than ever then, and said it was high time I went to school and got out of the habit of eavesdropping.

I still remember the resentment I felt when he said that. Because it was so *unfair*. Absolutely and utterly unfair.

I stammered out angrily that I hadn't been listening – and anyhow, I said, why did Elsa say a silly thing like that?

Amyas said it was just a joke.

That ought to have satisfied me. It did – almost. But not quite.

I said to Elsa when we were on the way back: 'I asked Amyas what you meant when you said you were going to marry him, and he said it was just a joke.'

I felt that ought to snub her. But she only smiled.

I didn't like that smile of hers. I went up to Caroline's room. It was when she was dressing for dinner. I asked her then outright if it were possible for Amyas to marry Elsa.

I remember Caroline's answer as though I heard it now. She must have spoken with great emphasis.

'Amyas will only marry Elsa after I am dead,' she said.

That reassured me completely. Death seemed ages away from us all. Nevertheless, I was still very sore with Amyas about what he had said in the afternoon, and I went for him violently all through dinner, and I remember we had a real flaming row, and I rushed out of the room and went up to bed and howled myself to sleep.

I don't remember much about the afternoon at Meredith Blake's, although I *do* remember his reading aloud the passage from the Phædo describing Socrates' death. I had never heard it before. I thought it was the loveliest, most beautiful thing I had ever heard. I remember that – but I don't remember when it was. As far as I can recall now, it might have been any time that summer.

I don't remember anything that happened the next morning either, though I have thought and thought. I've a vague feeling that I must have bathed, and I think I remember being made to mend something.

But it's all very vague and dim till the time when Meredith came panting up the path from the terrace, and his face was all grey and queer. I remember a coffee cup falling off the table and being broken – Elsa did that. And I remember her running – suddenly running for all she was worth down the path – and the awful look there was on her face.

I kept saying to myself: 'Amyas is dead.' But it just didn't seem real.

I remember Dr Faussett coming and his grave face. Miss Williams was busy looking after Caroline. I wandered about rather forlornly, getting in people's way. I had a nasty sick feeling. They wouldn't let me go down and see Amyas. But by and by the police came and wrote down things in notebooks, and presently they brought his body up on a stretcher covered with a cloth.

Miss Williams took me into Caroline's room later. Caroline was on the sofa. She looked very white and ill.

She kissed me and said she wanted me to go away as soon as I could, and it was all horrible, but I wasn't to worry or think about it any more than I could help. I was to join Carla at Lady Tressillian's because this house was to be kept as empty as possible.

I clung to Caroline and said I didn't want to go away. I wanted to stay with her. She said she knew I did, but it was better for me to go away and would take a lot of worry off her mind. And Miss Williams chipped in and said:

'The best way you can help your sister, Angela, is to do what she wants you to do without making a fuss about it.'

So I said I would do whatever Caroline wished. And Caroline said: 'That's my darling Angela.' And she hugged me and said there was nothing to worry about, and to talk about it and think about it all as little as possible.

I had to go down and talk to a Police Superintendent. He was very kind, asked me when I had last seen Amyas and a lot of other questions which seemed to me quite pointless at the time, but which, of course, I see the point of now. He satisfied himself that there was nothing that I could tell him which he hadn't already heard from the others. So he told Miss Williams that he saw no objection to my going over to Ferriby Grange to Lady Tressillian's.

I went there, and Lady Tressillian was very kind to me. But of course I soon had to know the truth. They arrested Caroline almost at once. I was so horrified and dumb-founded that I became quite ill.

I heard afterwards that Caroline was terribly worried about me. It was at her insistence that I was sent out of England before the trial came on. But that I have told you already.

As you see, what I have to put down is pitiably meagre. Since talking to you I have gone over the little I remember painstakingly, racking my memory for details of this or that person's expression or reaction. I can remember nothing consistent with guilt. Elsa's frenzy. Meredith's grey worried face. Philip's grief and fury – they all seem natural enough. I suppose, though, someone *could* have been playing a part?

I only know this, *Caroline did not do it*.

I am quite certain on this point, and always shall be, but I have no evidence to offer except my own intimate knowledge of her character.

End of Angela Warren's Narrative.

Book III

Chapter 1

Conclusions

Carla Lemarchant looked up. Her eyes were full of fatigue and pain. She pushed back the hair from her forehead in a tired gesture.

She said:

'It's so bewildering all this.' She touched the pile of manuscripts. 'Because the angle's different every time! Everybody sees my mother differently. But the facts are the same. Everyone agrees on the facts.'

'It has discouraged you, reading them?'

'Yes. Hasn't it discouraged you?'

'No, I have found those documents very valuable – very informative.'

Poirot spoke slowly and reflectively.

Carla said:

'I wish I'd never read them!'

Poirot looked across at her.

'Ah – so it makes you feel that way?'

Carla said bitterly:

'They all think she did it – all of them except Aunt Angela and what she thinks doesn't count. She hasn't got any reason for it. She's just one of those loyal people who'll stick to a thing through thick and thin. She just goes on saying: 'Caroline couldn't have done it.'

'It strikes you like that?'

'How else should it strike me? I've realized, you know, that if my mother didn't do it, then one of these five people must have done it. I've even had theories as to why.'

'Ah! That is interesting. Tell me.'

'Oh, they were only theories. Philip Blake, for instance. He's a stockbroker, he was my father's best friend – probably my father trusted him. And artists are usually careless about money matters. Perhaps Philip Blake was in a jam and used my father's money. He may have got my father to sign something. Then the whole thing may have been on the point of coming out – and only my father's death could have saved him. That's one of the things I thought of.'

'Not badly imagined at all. What else?'

'Well, there's Elsa. Philip Blake says here she had her head screwed on too well to meddle with poison, but I don't think that's true at all. Supposing my mother had gone to her and told her that she wouldn't divorce my father – that nothing would induce her to divorce him. You may say what you like, but I think Elsa had a bourgeois mind – she wanted to be respectably married. I think that then Elsa would have been perfectly capable of pinching the stuff – she had just as good a chance that afternoon – and might have tried to get my mother out of the way by poisoning her. I think that would be quite *like* Elsa. And then, possibly, by some awful accident, Amyas got the stuff instead of Caroline.'

'Again it is not badly imagined. What else?'

Carla said slowly:

'Well, I thought – perhaps – *Meredith*!'

'Ah – Meredith Blake?'

'Yes. You see, he sounds to me just the sort of person who would do a murder. I mean, he was the slow dithering one the others laughed at, and underneath, perhaps, he resented that. Then my father married the girl he wanted to marry. And my father was successful and rich. And he did make all those poisons! Perhaps he really made them because he liked the idea of being able to kill someone one day. He had to call attention to the stuff being taken, so as to divert suspicion from himself. But he himself was far the most likely person to have taken it. He might, even, have liked getting Caroline hanged – because she turned him down long ago. I think, you know, it's rather fishy what he says in his account of it all – how people do things that aren't characteristic of them. Supposing he meant *himself* when he wrote that?'

Hercule Poirot said:

'You are at least right in this – not to take what has been written down as necessarily a true narrative. What has been written may have been written deliberately to mislead.'

'Oh, I know. I've kept that in mind.'

'Any other ideas?'

Carla said slowly:

'I wondered – before I'd read this – about Miss Williams. She lost her job, you see, when Angela went to school. And if Amyas had died suddenly, Angela probably wouldn't have gone after all. I mean if it passed off as a natural death – which it easily might have done, I suppose, if Meredith hadn't missed the coniine. I read up coniine, and it hasn't got any distinctive post-mortem appearances. It might have been thought to be sunstroke. I know that just losing a job doesn't sound a very adequate motive for murder. But murders have been committed again and again for what seem ridiculously inadequate motives. Tiny sums of money sometimes. And a middle-aged, perhaps rather incompetent governess might have got the wind up and just seen no future ahead of her.

'As I say, that's what I thought before I read this.

But Miss Williams doesn't sound like that at all. She doesn't sound in the least incompetent –'

'Not at all. She is still a very efficient and intelligent woman.'

'I know. One can see that. And she sounds absolutely trustworthy too. That's what has upset me really. Oh, *you* know – *you* understand. You don't mind, of course. All along you've made it clear it was the truth you wanted. I suppose now we've *got* the truth! Miss Williams is quite right. One must accept truth. It's no good basing your life on a lie because it's what you want to believe. All right then – I can take it! My mother wasn't innocent! She wrote me that letter because she was weak and unhappy and wanted to spare me. I don't judge her. Perhaps I should feel like that too. I don't know what prison does to you. And I don't blame her either – if she felt so desperately about my father, I suppose she couldn't help herself. But I don't blame my father altogether either. I understand – just a little – how *he* felt. So alive – and so full of wanting everything . . . He couldn't help it – he was made that way. And he was a great painter. I think that excuses a lot.'

She turned her flushed excited face to Hecule Poirot with her chin raised defiantly.

Hercule Poirot said:

'So – you are satisfied?'

'Satisfied?' said Carla Lemarchant. Her voice broke on the word.

Poirot leant forward and patted her paternally on the shoulder.

'Listen,' he said. 'You give up the fight at the moment when it is most worth fighting. At the moment when I, Hercule Poirot, have a very good idea of what really happened.'

Carla stared at him. She said:

'Miss Williams loved my mother. She saw her – with her own eyes – faking that suicide evidence. If you believe what she says –'

Hercule Poirot got up. He said:

'Mademoiselle, because Cecilia Williams says she saw your mother faking Amyas Crale's fingerprints on the beer bottle – on the beer *bottle*, mind – that is the only thing I need to tell me definitely, once for all, that your mother did not kill your father.'

He nodded his head several times and went out of the room, leaving Carla staring after him.

Chapter 2

Poirot Asks Five Questions

'Well, M. Poirot?'

Philip Blake's tone was impatient.

Poirot said:

'I have to thank you for your admirable and lucid account of the Crale tragedy.'

Philip Blake looked rather self-conscious.

'Very kind of you,' he murmured. 'Really surprising how much I remembered when I got down to it.'

Poirot said:

'It was an admirably clear narrative, but there were certain omissions, were there not?'

'Omissions?' Philip Blake frowned.

Hercule Poirot said:

'Your narrative, shall we say, was not entirely frank.' His tone hardened. 'I have been informed, Mr Blake, that on at least one night during the summer, Mrs

Crale was seen coming out of your room at a somewhat compromising hour.'

There was a silence broken only by Philip Blake's heavy breathing. He said at last: 'Who told you that?'

Hercule Poirot shook his head.

'It is no matter who told me. That I *know*, that is the point.'

Again there was a silence; then Philip Blake made up his mind. He said:

'By accident, it seems, you have stumbled upon a purely private matter. I admit that it does not square with what I have written down. Nevertheless, it squares better than you might think. I am forced now to tell you the truth.

'I *did* entertain a feeling of animosity towards Caroline Crale. At the same time I was always strongly attracted by her. Perhaps the latter fact induced the former. I resented the power she had over me and tried to stifle the attraction she had for me by constantly dwelling on her worst points. I never *liked* her, if you understand. But it would have been easy at any moment for me to make love to her. I had been in love with her as a boy and she had taken no notice of me. I did not find that easy to forgive.

'My opportunity came when Amyas lost his head so completely over the Greer girl. Quite without meaning to I found myself telling Caroline I loved her. She said quite calmly: 'Yes, I have always known that.' The insolence of the woman!

'Of course I knew that she didn't love me, but I saw that she was disturbed and disillusioned by Amyas's present infatuation. That is a mood when a woman can very easily be won. She agreed to come to me that night. And she came.'

Blake paused. He found now a difficulty in getting the words out.

'She came to my room. And then, with my arms round her, she told me quite coolly that it was no good! After all, she said, she was a one-man woman. She was Amyas Crale's, for better or worse. She agreed that she had treated me very badly, but said she couldn't help it. She asked me to forgive her.

'And she left me. *She left me!* Do you wonder, M. Poirot, that my hatred of her was heightened a hundredfold? Do you wonder that I have never forgiven her? For the insult she did me – as well as for the fact that she killed the friend I loved better than any one in the world!'

Trembling violently, Philip Blake exclaimed:

'*I don't want to speak of it,* do you hear? You've got your answer. Now go! And never mention the matter to me again!'

Agatha Christie

II

'I want to know, Mr Blake, the order in which your guests left the laboratory that day?'

Meredith Blake protested.

'But, my dear M. Poirot. After sixteen years! How can I possibly remember? I've told you that Caroline came out last.'

'You are *sure* of that?'

'Yes – at least – I think so . . .'

'Let us go there now. We must be *quite* sure, you see.'

Still protesting, Meredith Blake led the way. He unlocked the door and swung back the shutters. Poirot spoke to him authoritatively.

'Now then, my friend. You have showed your visitors your interesting preparations of herbs. Shut your eyes now and think –'

Meredith Blake did so obediently. Poirot drew a handkerchief from his pocket and gently passed it to and fro. Blake murmured, his nostrils twitching slightly:

'Yes, yes – extraordinary how things come back to one. Caroline, I remember, had on a pale coffee-coloured dress. Phil was looking bored . . . He always thought my hobby was quite idiotic.'

Poirot said:

'Reflect now, you are about to leave the room. You are going to the library where you are going to read the passage about the death of Socrates. Who leaves the room first – do you?'

'Elsa and I – yes. She passed through the door first. I was close behind her. We were talking. I stood there waiting for the others to come so that I could lock the door again. Philip – yes, Philip came out next. And Angela – she was asking him what bulls and bears were. They went on through the hall. Amyas followed them. I stood there waiting still – for Caroline, of course.'

'So you are quite sure Caroline stayed behind. Did you see what she was doing?'

Blake shook his head.

'No, I had my back to the room, you see. I was talking to Elsa – boring her, I expect – telling her how certain plants must be gathered at the full of the moon according to old superstition. And then Caroline came out – hurrying a little – and I locked the door.'

He stopped and looked at Poirot, who was replacing a handkerchief in his pocket. Meredith Blake sniffled disgustedly and thought: 'Why, the fellow actually uses *scent*!'

Aloud he said:

'I am quite sure of it. That was the order. Elsa,

myself, Philip, Angela and Caroline. Does that help you at all?'

Poirot said:

'It all fits in. Listen. I want to arrange a meeting here. It will not, I think, be difficult . . .'

III

'Well?'

Elsa Dittisham said it almost eagerly – like a child.

'I want to ask you a question, madame.'

'Yes?'

Poirot said:

'After it was all over – the trial, I mean – did Meredith Blake ask you to marry him?'

Elsa stared. She looked contemptuous – almost bored.

'Yes – he did. Why?'

'Were you surprised?'

'Was I? I don't remember.'

'What did you say?'

Elsa laughed. She said:

'What do you think I said? After *Amyas* – Meredith? It would have been ridiculous! It was stupid of him. He always was rather stupid.'

She smiled suddenly.

'He wanted, you know, to protect me – to "look after me" – that's how he put it! He thought like everybody else that the Assizes had been a terrible ordeal for me. And the reporters! And the booing crowds! And all the mud that was slung at me.'

She brooded a minute. Then said:

'Poor old Meredith! Such an ass!' And laughed again.

IV

Once again Hercule Poirot encountered the shrewd penetrating glance of Miss Williams, and once again felt the years falling away and himself a meek and apprehensive little boy.

There was, he explained, a question he wished to ask.

Miss Williams intimated her willingness to hear what the question was.

Poirot said slowly, picking his words carefully:

'Angela Warren was injured as a very young child. In my notes I find two references to that fact. In one of them it is stated that Mrs Crale threw a paperweight at the child. In the other that she attacked the baby with a crowbar. Which of those versions is the right one?'

Miss Williams replied briskly:

'I never heard anything about a crowbar. The paper-weight is the correct story.'

'Who was your own informant?'

'Angela herself. She volunteered the information quite early.'

'What did she say exactly?'

'She touched her cheek and said: "Caroline did this when I was a baby. She threw a paperweight at me. Never refer to it, will you, because it upsets her dreadfully."'

'Did Mrs Crale herself ever mention the matter to you?'

'Only obliquely. She assumed that I knew the story. I remember her saying once: "I know you think I spoil Angela, but you see, I always feel there is nothing I can do to make up to her for what I did." And on another occasion she said: "To know you have permanently injured another human being is the heaviest burden any one could have to bear."'

'Thank you, Miss Williams. That is all I wanted to know.'

Cecilia Williams said sharply:

'I don't understand you, M. Poirot. You showed Carla my account of the tragedy?'

Poirot nodded.

'And yet you are still –' She stopped.

Poirot said:

'Reflect a minute. If you were to pass a fishmonger's and saw twelve fish laid out on his slab, you would think they were all real fish, would you not? But one of them might be stuffed fish.'

Miss Williams replied with spirit:

'Most unlikely and anyway –'

'Ah, unlikely, yes, but not impossible – because a friend of mine once took down a stuffed fish (it was his trade, you comprehend) to compare it with the real thing! And if you saw a bowl of innias in a drawing-room in December you would say that they were false – but they might be real ones flown home from Baghdad.'

'What is the meaning of all this nonsense?' demanded Miss Williams.

'It is to show you that it is the eyes of the mind with which one really sees . . .'

V

Poirot slowed up a little as he approached the big block of flats overlooking Regent's Park.

Really, when he came to think of it, he did not want to ask Angela Warren any questions at all. The only question he did want to ask her could wait . . .

No, it was really only his insatiable passion for

symmetry that was bringing him here. Five people – there should be five questions! It was neater so. It rounded off the thing better.

Ah well – he would think of something.

Angela Warren greeted him with something closely approaching eagerness. She said:

'Have you found out anything? Have you got anywhere?'

Slowly Poirot nodded his head in his best China mandarin manner. He said:

'At last I make progress.'

'Philip Blake?' It was halfway between statement and a question.

'Mademoiselle, I do not wish to say anything at present. The moment has not yet come. What I will ask of you is to be so good as to come down to Handcross Manor. The others have consented.'

She said with a slight frown:

'What do you propose to do? Reconstruct something that happened sixteen years ago?'

'See it, perhaps, from a clearer angle. You will come?'

Angela Warren said slowly:

'Oh, yes, I'll come. It will be interesting to see all those people again. I shall see *them* now, perhaps, from a clearer angle (as you put it) than I did then.'

'And you will bring with you the letter that you showed me?'

Angela Warren frowned.

'That letter is my own. I showed it to you for a good and sufficient reason, but I have no intention of allowing it to be read by strange and unsympathetic persons.'

'But you will allow yourself to be guided by me in this matter?'

'I will do nothing of the kind. I will bring the letter with me, but I shall use my own judgement which I venture to think is quite as good as yours.'

Poirot spread out his hands in a gesture of resignation. He got up to go. He said:

'You permit that I ask one little question?'

'What is it?'

'At the time of the tragedy, you had lately read, had you not, Somerset Maugham's *The Moon and Sixpence*?'

Angela stared at him. Then she said:

'I believe – why, yes, that is quite true.' She looked at him with frank curiosity. 'How did you know?'

'I want to show you, mademoiselle, that even in a small unimportant matter, I am something of a magician. There are things I know without having to be told.'

Chapter 3

Reconstruction

The afternoon sun shone into the laboratory at Handcross
Manor. Some easy chairs and a settee had been brought
into the room, but they served more to emphasize its
forlorn aspect than to furnish it.

Slightly embarrassed, pulling at his moustache,
Meredith Blake talked to Carla in a desultory way.
He broke off once to say: 'My dear, you are very like
your mother – and yet unlike her, too.'

Carla asked: 'How am I like her and how unlike?'

'You have her colouring and her way of moving, but
you are – how shall I put it – more *positive* than she
ever was.'

Philip Blake, a scowl creasing over his forehead,
looked out of the window and drummed impatiently
on the pane. He said:

'What's the sense of all this? A perfectly fine Saturday afternoon –'

Agatha Christie

Hercule Poirot hastened to pour oil on troubled waters.

'Ah, I apologize – it is, I know, unpardonable to disarrange the golf. *Mais voyons*, M. Blake, this is the daughter of your best friend. You will stretch a point for her, will you not?'

The butler announced: 'Miss Warren.'

Meredith went to welcome her. He said: 'It's good of you to spare the time, Angela. You're busy, I know.'

He led her over to the window.

Carla said: 'Hallo, Aunt Angela. I read your article in *The Times* this morning. It's nice to have a distinguished relative.' She indicated the tall, square-jawed young man with the steady grey eyes. 'This is John Rattery. He and I – hope – to be married.'

Angela Warren said: 'Oh! – I didn't know . . .'

Meredith went to greet the next arrival.

'Well, Miss Williams, it's a good many years since we met.'

Thin, frail and indomitable, the elderly governess advanced up the room. Her eyes rested thoughtfully on Poirot for a minute, then they went to the tall, square-shouldered figure in the well-cut tweeds.

Angela Warren came forward to meet her and said with a smile: 'I feel like a schoolgirl again.'

'I'm very proud of you, my dear,' said Miss Williams.

'You've done me credit. This is Carla, I suppose? She won't remember me. She was too young . . .'

Philip Blake said fretfully: 'What *is* all this? Nobody told me –'

Hercule Poirot said: 'I call it – me – an excursion into the past. Shall we not all sit down? Then we shall be ready when the last guest arrives. And when she is here we can proceed to our business – to lay the ghosts.'

Philip Blake exclaimed: 'What tomfoolery is this? You're not going to hold a *séance*, are you?'

'No, no. We are only going to discuss some events that happened long ago – to discuss them and, perhaps, to see more clearly the course of them. As to the ghosts, they will not materialize, but who is to say they are not here, in this room, although we cannot see them. Who is to say that Amyas and Caroline Crale are not here – listening?'

Philip Blake said: 'Absurd nonsense –' and broke off as the door opened again and the butler announced Lady Dittisham.

Elsa Dittisham came in with that faint, bored insolence that was a characteristic of her. She gave Meredith a slight smile, stared coldly at Angela and Philip, and went over to a chair by the window a little apart from the others. She loosened the rich pale furs round her neck and let them fall back. She looked for a minute or two about the room, then at Carla, and the girl stared back, thoughtfully appraising the woman who had wrought the havoc in her parents' lives. There was no animosity in her young earnest face, only curiosity.

Elsa said: 'I am sorry if I am late, M. Poirot.'

'It was very good of you to come, madame.'

Cecilia Williams snorted ever so slightly. Elsa met the animosity in her eyes with a complete lack of interest. She said:

'I wouldn't have known *you*, Angela. How long is it? Sixteen years?'

Hercule Poirot seized his opportunity.

'Yes, it is sixteen years since the events of which we are to speak, but let me first tell you why we are here.'

And in a few simple words he outlined Carla's appeal to him and his acceptance of the task.

He went on quickly, ignoring the gathering storm visible on Philip's face, and the shocked distaste on Meredith's.

'I accepted that commision – I set to work to find out – the truth.'

Carla Lemarchant, in the big grandfather chair, heard Poirot's words dimly, from a distance.

With her hand shielding her eyes she studied five faces, surreptitiously. Could she see any of these people committing murder? The exotic Elsa, the red-faced Philip, dear, nice, kind Mr Meredith Blake, that grim tartar of a governess, the cool, competent Angela Warren?

Could she – if she tried hard – visualize one of them killing someone? Yes, perhaps – but it wouldn't be the right kind of murder. She could picture Philip Blake, in an outburst of fury, strangling some women – yes, she *could* picture that . . . And she could picture Meredith Blake, threatening a burglar with a revolver – and letting it off by accident . . . And she could picture Angela Warren, also firing a revolver, but not by accident. With no personal feeling in the matter – the safety of the expedition depended on it! And Elsa, in some fantastic castle, saying from her couch of oriental silks: 'Throw the wretch over the battlements!' All wild fancies – and not even in the wildest flight of fancy could she imagine little Miss Williams killing anybody at all! Another fantastic picture: 'Did you ever kill anybody, Miss Williams?' 'Go on with your arithmetic, Carla, and don't ask silly questions. To kill anybody is very wicked.'

Carla thought: 'I must be ill – and I must stop this. Listen, you fool, listen to that little man who says he knows.'

Hercule Poirot was talking.

'That was my task – to put myself in reverse gear, as it were, and go back through the years and discover what really happened.'

305

Agatha Christie

Philip Blake said: 'We all know what happened. To pretend anything else is a swindle – that's what it is, a bare-faced swindle. You're getting money out of this girl on false pretences.'

Poirot did not allow himself to be angered. He said: 'You say, *we all know what happened.* You speak without reflection. The accepted version of certain facts is not necessarily the true one. On the face of it, for instance, you, Mr Blake, disliked Caroline Crale. That is the accepted version of your attitude. But anyone with the least flair for psychology can perceive at once that the exact opposite was the truth. You were always violently attracted towards Caroline Crale. You resented the fact, and tried to conquer it by steadfastly telling yourself her defects and reiterating your dislike. In the same way, Mr Meredith Blake had a tradition of devotion to Caroline Crale lasting over many years. In his story of the tragedy he represents himself as resenting Amyas Crale's conduct on *her* account, but you have only to read carefully between the lines and you will see that the devotion of a lifetime had worn itself thin and that it was the young, beautiful Elsa Greer that was occupying *his* mind and thoughts.'

There was a splutter from Meredith, and Lady Dittisham smiled.

Poirot went on.

'I mention these matters only as illustrations, though

they have their bearing on what happened. Very well, then, I start on my backward journey – to learn everything I can about the tragedy. I will tell you how I set about it. I talked to the Counsel who defended Caroline Crale, to the Junior Counsel for the Crown, to the old solicitor who had known the Crale family intimately, to the lawyer's clerk who had been in court during the trial, to the police officer in charge of the case – and I came finally to the five eye-witnesses who had been upon the scene. And from all of these I put together a picture – a composite picture of a woman. And I learned these facts:

'*That at no time did Caroline Crale protest her innocence* (except in that one letter written to her daughter).

'That Caroline Crale showed no fear in the dock, that she showed, in fact, hardly any interest, that she adopted throughout a thoroughly defeatist attitude. That in prison she was quiet and serene. That in a letter she wrote to her sister immediately after the verdict, she expressed herself as acquiescent in the fate that had overtaken her. And in the opinion of everyone I talked to (with one notable exception) *Caroline Crale was guilty.*'

Philip Blake nodded his head. 'Of course she was!'

Hercule Poirot said:

'But it was not my part to accept the verdict of *others*.

I had to examine the evidence for *myself*. To examine the facts and to satisfy myself that the psychology of the case accorded itself with them. To do this I went over the police files carefully, and I also succeeded in getting five people who were on the spot to write me out their own accounts of the tragedy. These accounts were very valuable for they contained certain matter which the police files could not give me – that is to say: A, certain conversations and incidents which, from the police point of view, were not relevant; B, the opinions of the people themselves as to what Caroline Crale was thinking and feeling (not admissible legally as evidence); C, certain facts which had been deliberately withheld from the police.

'I was in a position now to judge the case for *myself*. There seems no doubt whatever that Caroline Crale had ample motive for the crime. She loved her husband, he had publicly admitted that he was about to leave her for another woman, and by her own admission she was a jealous woman.

'To come from motives to means, an empty scent bottle that had contained coniine was found in her bureau drawer. There were no fingerprints upon it but hers. When asked about it by the police, she admitted taking it from this room we are in now. The coniine bottle here also had her fingerprints upon it. I questioned Mr Meredith Blake as to the order in which the five people left this room on that day – for it seemed to me hardly conceivable that *any one* should be able to help themselves to the poison whilst five people were in the room. The people left the room in this order – Elsa Greer, Meredith Blake, Angela Warren and Philip Blake, Amyas Crale, and lastly Caroline Crale. Moreover, Mr Meredith Blake has his back to the room whilst he was waiting for Mrs Crale to come out, so that it was impossible for him to see what she was doing. She had, that is to say, the opportunity. I am therefore satisfied that she did take the coniine. There is indirect confirmation of it. Mr Meredith Blake said to me the other day: 'I can remember standing here and smelling the jasmine through the open window.' But the month was September, and the jasmine creeper outside that window would have finished flowering. It is the ordinary jasmine which blooms in June and July. But the scent bottle found in her room and which contained the dregs of coniine had originally contained jasmine scent. I take it as certain, then, that Mrs Crale decided to steal the coniine, and surreptitiously emptied out the scent from a bottle she had in her bag.

'I tested that a second time the other day when I asked Mr Blake to shut his eyes and try and remember the order of leaving the room. A whiff of jasmine scent stimulated his memory immediately. We are all more influenced by smell than we know.

'So we come to the morning of the fatal day. So far the facts are not in dispute. Miss Greer's sudden revealing of the fact that she and Mr Crale contemplate marriage, Amyas Crale's confirmation of that, and Caroline Crale's deep distress. None of these things depend on the evidence of one witness only.

'On the following morning there is a scene between husband and wife in the library. The first thing that is overheard is Caroline Crale saying: 'You and your women!' in a bitter voice, and finally going on to say, 'Some day I'll kill you.' Philip Blake overheard this from the hall. And Miss Greer overheard it from the terrace outside.

'She then heard Mr Crale ask his wife to be reasonable. And she heard Mrs Crale say: 'Sooner than let you go to that girl – I'll kill you.' Soon after this Amyas Crale comes out and brusquely tells Elsa Greer to come down and pose for him. She gets a pullover and accompanies him.

'There is nothing so far that seems psychologically incorrect. Every one has behaved as they might be expected to behave. But we come now to something that *is* incongruous.

'Meredith Blake discovers his loss, telephones his brother; they meet down at the landing stage and they come up past the Battery garden, where Caroline Crale is having a discussion with her husband on the subject of Angela's going to school. Now that does strike me as very odd. Husband and wife have a terrific scene, ending in a distinct threat on Caroline's part, and yet, twenty minutes or so later, she goes down and starts a trivial domestic argument.'

Poirot turned to Meredith Blake.

'You speak in your narrative of certain words you overheard Crale say. These were: "It's all settled – I'll see to her packing." That is right?'

Meredith Blake said: 'It was something like that – yes.'

Poirot turned to Philip Blake.

'Is your recollection the same?'

The latter frowned.

'I didn't remember it till you say so – but I do remember now. Something *was* said about packing!'

'Said by Mr Crale – not Mrs Crale?'

'Amyas said it. All I heard Caroline say was something about its being very hard on the girl. Anyway, what does all this matter? We all know Angela was off to school in a day or two.'

Poirot said: 'You do not see the force of my objection. Why should *Amyas Crale* pack for the girl? It is absurd, that! There was Mrs Crale, there was Miss Williams, there was a housemaid. It is a woman's job to pack – not a man's.'

Philip Blake said impatiently:

311

'What does it matter? It's nothing to do with the crime.'

'You think not? For me, it was the first point that struck me as suggestive. And it is immediately followed by another. Mrs Crale, a desperate woman, broken-hearted, who has threatened her husband a short while before and who is certainly contemplating either suicide or murder, now offers in the most amicable manner to bring her husband down some iced beer.'

Meredith Blake said slowly: 'That isn't odd if she was contemplating murder. Then, surely, it is just what she *would* do. Dissimulate!'

'You think so? She has decided to poison her husband, she has already got the poison. Her husband keeps a supply of beer down in the Battery garden. Surely if she has any intelligence at all, she will put the poison in one of *those* bottles at a moment when there is no one about.'

Meredith Blake objected.

'She couldn't have done that. Somebody else might have drunk it.'

'Yes, Elsa Greer. Do you tell me that having made up her mind to murder her husband, Caroline Crale would have scruples against killing the girl too?

'But let us not argue the point. Let us confine ourselves to facts. Caroline Crale says she will send her husband down some iced beer. She goes up to the house, fetches a bottle from the conservatory where it was kept and takes it down to him. She pours it out and gives it to him.

'Amyas Crale drinks it off and says: "Everything tastes foul today."

'Mrs Crale goes up again to the house. She has lunch and appears much as usual. It has been said of her that she looks a little worried and preoccupied. That does not help us – for there is no criterion of behaviour for a murderer. There are calm murderers and excited murderers.

'After lunch she goes down again to the Battery. She discovers her husband dead and does, shall we say, the obviously expected things. She registers emotion and she sends the governess to telephone for a doctor. We now come to a fact which has previously not been known.' He looked at Miss Williams. 'You do not object?'

Miss Williams was rather pale. She said: 'I did not pledge you to secrecy.'

Quietly, but with telling effect, Poirot recounted what the governess had seen.

Elsa Dittisham moved her position. She stared at the drab little woman in the big chair. She said incredibly:

'You actually saw her do *that*?'

Philip Blake sprang up.

'But that settles it!' he shouted. 'That settles it once and for all.'

Hercule Poirot looked at him mildly. He said: 'Not necessarily.'

Angela Warren said sharply: 'I don't believe it.' There was a quick hostile glint in the glance she shot at the little governess.

Meredith Blake was pulling at his moustache, his face dismayed. Alone, Miss Williams remained undisturbed. She sat very upright and there was a spot of colour in each cheek.

She said: 'That is what I saw.'

Poirot said slowly: 'There is, of course, only your word for it . . .'

'There is only my word for it.' The indomitable grey eyes met his. 'I am not accustomed, M. Poirot, to having my word doubted.'

Hercule Poirot bowed his head. He said:

'I do not doubt your word, Miss Williams. What you saw took place exactly as you say it did – and because of what you saw I realized that Caroline Crale was not guilty – could not possibly be guilty.'

For the first time, that tall, anxious-faced young man, John Rattery, spoke. He said: 'I'd be interested to know *why* you say that, M. Poirot.'

Poirot turned to him.

'Certainly. I will tell you. What did Miss Williams see

– she saw Caroline Crale very carefully and anxiously wiping off fingerprints and subsequently imposing her dead husband's fingerprints on the beer bottle. On the beer *bottle*, mark. But the coniine was in the glass – not in the bottle. The police found no traces of coniine in the bottle. There had never been any coniine in the bottle. *And Caroline Crale didn't know that.*

'She who is supposed to have poisoned her husband didn't know *how* he had been poisoned. She thought the poison was in the bottle.'

Meredith objected: 'But why –'

Poirot interrupted him in a flash.

'Yes – *why*? Why did Caroline Crale try so desperately to establish the theory of suicide? The answer is – must be – quite simple. Because she knew who *had* poisoned him and she was willing to do anything – endure anything – rather than let that person be suspected.

'There is not far to go now. Who could that person be? Would she have shielded Philip Blake? Or Meredith? Or Elsa Greer? Or Cecilia Williams? No, there is only one person whom she would be willing to protect at all costs.'

He paused: 'Miss Warren, if you have brought your sister's last letter with you, I should like to read it aloud.'

Angela Warren said: 'No.'

'But, Miss Warren –'

Angela got up. Her voice rang out, cold as steel.

'I realize very well what you are suggesting. You are saying, are you not, that I killed Amyas Crale and that my sister knew it. I deny that allegation utterly.'

Poirot said: 'The letter . . .'

'That letter was meant for my eyes alone.'

Poirot looked to where the two youngest people in the room stood together.

Carla Lemarchant said: 'Please, Aunt Angela, won't you do as M. Poirot asks?'

Angela Warren said bitterly: 'Really, Carla! Have you no sense of decency? She was your mother – you –'

Carla's voice rang out clear and fierce.

'Yes, she was my mother. That's why I've a right to ask you. I'm speaking for *her*. I *want* that letter read.'

Slowly, Angela Warren took out the letter from her bag and handed it to Poirot. She said bitterly:

'I wish I had never shown it to you.'

Turning away from them she stood looking out of the window.

As Hercule Poirot read aloud Caroline Crale's last letter, the shadows were deepening in the corners of the room. Carla had a sudden feeling of someone in the room, gathering shape, listening, breathing, waiting.

She thought: '*She's* here – my mother's here. Caroline – Caroline Crale is *here* in this room!'

Hercule Poirot's voice ceased. He said:

'You will all agree, I think, that that is a very remarkable letter. A beautiful letter, too, but certainly remarkable. For there is one striking omission in it – it contains no protestation of innocence.'

Angela Warren said without turning her head: 'That was unnecessary.'

'Yes, Miss Warren, it was unnecessary. Caroline Crale had no need to tell her sister that she was innocent – because she thought her sister knew that fact already – knew it for the best of all reasons. All Caroline Crale was concerned about was to comfort and reassure and to avert the possibility of a confession from Angela. She reiterates again and again – *It's all right, darling, it's all right.*'

Angela Warren said: 'Can't you understand? She wanted me to be happy, that's all.'

'Yes, she wanted you to be happy, that is abundantly clear. It is her one preoccupation. She has a child, but it is not that child of whom she is thinking – that is to come later. No, it is her sister who occupies her mind to the exclusion of everything else. Her sister must be reassured, must be encouraged to live her life, to be happy and successful. And so that the burden of acceptance may not be too great, Caroline includes that one very significant phrase: "*One must pay one's debts.*"

'That one phrase explains everything. It refers explicitly to the burden that Caroline has carried for so many years ever since, in a fit of uncontrolled adolescent rage, she hurled a paperweight at her baby sister and injured that sister for life. Now, at last, she has the opportunity to pay the debt she owes. And if it is any consolation, I will say to you all that I earnestly believe that in the payment of that debt, Caroline Crale did achieve a peace and serenity greater than any she had ever known. Because of her belief that she was paying that debt, the ordeal of trial and condemnation could not touch her. It is a strange thing to say of a condemned murderess – but she had everything to make her happy. Yes, more than you imagine, as I will show you presently.

'See how, by this explanation, everything falls into its place where Caroline's own reactions are concerned. Look at the series of events from her point of view. To begin with, on the preceding evening, an event occurs which reminds her forcibly of her own undisciplined girlhood. Angela throws a *paperweight* at Amyas Crale. That, remember, is what she herself did many years ago. Angela shouts out that she wishes Amyas was dead. Then, on the next morning, Caroline comes into the little conservatory and finds Angela tampering with the beer. Remember Miss Williams's words: "Angela was there. She looked guilty . . ." Guilty of playing truant, was what Miss Williams meant, but to Caroline, Angela's guilty face, as she was caught unawares, would have a different meaning. Remember that on at least one occasion before Angela had put things in Amyas's drink. It was an idea which might readily occur to her.

'Caroline takes the bottle *that Angela gives her* and goes down with it to the Battery. And there she pours it out and gives it to Amyas, and he makes a face as he tosses it off and utters those significant words: "Everything tastes foul today."

'Caroline has no suspicions then – but after lunch she goes down to the Battery and finds her husband dead – and she has no doubt at all but that he has been poisoned. *She* had not done it? Who, then, has? And the whole thing comes over her with a rush – Angela's threats, Angela's face stooping over the beer and caught unawares – guilty – guilty – guilty. Why has the child done it? As a revenge on Amyas, perhaps not meaning to kill, just to make him ill or sick? Or has she done it for her, Caroline's sake? Has she realized and resented Amyas's desertion of her sister? Caroline remembers – oh, so well – her own undisciplined violent emotions at Angela's age. And only one thought springs to her mind. How can she protect Angela? Angela handled that bottle – Angela's fingerprints will be on it. She quickly wipes it and polishes it. If only everybody can be got to believe it is suicide. If Amyas's fingerprints are the only ones found. She tries to fit his dead fingers round the bottle – working desperately – listening for someone to come . . .

'Once take that assumption as true, and everything from then on fits in. Her anxiety about Angela all along, her insistence on getting her away, keeping her out of touch with what was going on. Her fear of Angela's being questioned unduly by the police. Finally, her overwhelming anxiety to get Angela out of England before the trial comes on. Because she is always terrified that Angela might break down and confess.'

Chapter 4
Truth

Slowly, Angela Warren swung round. Her eyes, hard and contemptuous, ranged over the faces turned towards her.

She said:

'You're blind fools – all of you. Don't you know that if I had done it I *would* have confessed! I'd never have let Caroline suffer for what I'd done. Never!'

Poirot said:

'But you did tamper with the beer.'

'I? Tamper with the beer?'

Poirot turned to Meredith Blake.

'Listen, monsieur. In your account here of what happened, you describe having heard sounds in this room, which is below your bedroom, on the morning of the crime.'

Blake nodded.

'But it was only a cat.'

'How do you know it was a cat?'

'I – I can't remember. But it was a cat. I am quite sure it was a cat. The window was open just wide enough for a cat to get through.'

'But it was not fixed in that position. The sash moves freely. It could have been pushed up and a human being could have got in and out.'

'Yes, but I know it was a cat.'

'You did not *see* a cat?'

Blake said perplexedly and slowly:

'No, I did not see it –' He paused, frowning. 'And yet I know.'

'I will tell you *why* you know presently. In the meantime I put this point to you. Someone could have come up to the house that morning, have got into your laboratory, taken something from the shelf and gone again without your seeing them. Now if that someone had come over from Alderbury it could not have been Philip Blake, nor Elsa Greer, nor Amyas Crale nor Caroline Crale. We know quite well what all those four were doing. That leaves Angela Warren and Miss Williams. Miss Williams was over here – you actually met her as you went out. She told you then that she was looking for Angela. Angela had gone bathing early, but Miss Williams did not see her in the water, nor anywhere on the rocks. She could swim across to this side easily – in fact she did so later in the morning when she was bathing with Philip Blake. I suggest that she swam across here, came up to the house, got in through the window, and took something from the shelf.'

Angela Warren said: 'I did nothing of the kind – not – at least –'

'Ah!' Poirot gave a yelp of triumph. '*You have remembered*. You told me, did you not, that to play a malicious joke on Amyas Crale you pinched some of what you called "the cat stuff" – that is how you put it –'

Meredith Blake said sharply:

'Valerian! Of course.'

'Exactly. *That* is what made you sure in your mind that it was a cat who had been in the room. Your nose is very sensitive. You smelled the faint, unpleasant odour of valerian without knowing, perhaps, that you did so – but it suggested to your subconscious mind "Cat". Cats love valerian and will go anywhere for it. Valerian is particularly nasty to taste, and it was your account of it the day before which made mischievous Miss Angela plan to put some in her brother-in-law's beer, which she knew he always tossed down his throat in a draught.'

Angela Warren said wonderingly: 'Was it really that day? I remember taking it perfectly. Yes, and I remember getting out the beer and Caroline coming in and nearly catching me! Of course I remember . . . But I've never connected it with that particular day.'

'Of course not – because there was no connection *in your mind*. The two events were entirely dissimilar to you. One was on a par with other mischievous pranks – the other was a bombshell of tragedy arriving without warning and succeeding in banishing all lesser incidents from your mind. But me, I noticed when you spoke of it that you said: "I pinched, etc., etc., *to put it* in Amyas's drink." You did not say you had actually *done* so.'

'No, because I never did. Caroline came in just when I was unscrewing the bottle. Oh!' It was a cry. 'And Caroline thought – she thought it was *me* –!'

She stopped. She looked round. She said quietly in her usual cool tones: 'I suppose you all think so, too.'

She paused and then said: '*I didn't kill Amyas*. Not as the result of a malicious joke nor in any other way. If I had I would never have kept silence.'

Miss Williams said sharply:

'Of course you wouldn't, my dear.' She looked at Hercule Poirot. 'Nobody but a *fool* would think so.'

Hercule Poirot said mildly:

'I am not a fool and I do not think so. *I know quite well who killed Amyas Crale*.'

He paused.

'There is always a danger of accepting facts as proved which are really nothing of the kind. Let us take the situation at Alderbury. A very old situation. Two women and one man. We have taken it for granted that Amyas Crale proposed to leave his wife for the other woman. But I suggest to you now *that he never intended to do anything of the kind.*

'He had had infatuations for women before. They obsessed him while they lasted, but they were soon over. The women he had fallen in love with were usually women of a certain experience – they did not expect too much of him. But this time the woman did. She was not, you see, a woman at all. She was a girl, and in Caroline Crale's words, she was terribly sincere . . . She may have been hard-boiled and sophisticated in speech, but in love she was frighteningly single-minded. *Because* she herself had a deep and overmastering passion for Amyas Crale she assumed that he had the same for her. She assumed without any question that their passion was for life. She assumed without asking him that he was going to leave his wife.

'But why, you will say, did Amyas Crale not undeceive her? And my answer is – the picture. He wanted to finish his picture.

'To some people that sounds incredible – but not to anybody who knows about artists. And we have already accepted that explanation in principle. That conversation between Crale and Meredith Blake is more intelligible now. Crale is embarrassed – pats Blake on the back, assures him optimistically the whole thing is going to pan out all right. To Amyas Crale, you see, everything is simple. He is painting a picture, slightly encumbered by what he describes as a couple of jealous, neurotic women – but neither of them is going to be allowed to interfere with what to him is the most important thing in life.

'If he were to tell Elsa the truth it would be all up with the picture. Perhaps in the first flush of his feelings for her he did talk about leaving Caroline. Men do say these things when they are in love. Perhaps he merely let it be assumed, as he is letting it be assumed now. He doesn't care what Elsa assumes. Let her think what she likes. Anything to keep her quiet for another day or two.

'Then – he will tell her the truth – that things between them are over. He has never been a man to be troubled with scruples.

'He did, I think, make an effort not to get embroiled with Elsa to begin with. He warned her what kind of a man he was – but she would not take warning. She rushed on her Fate. And to a man like Crale women were fair game. If you had asked him he would have said easily that Elsa was young – she'd soon get over it. That was the way Amyas Crale's mind worked.

'His wife was actually the only person he cared about

at all. He wasn't worrying much about her. She'd only got to put up with things for a few days longer. He was furious with Elsa for blurting out things to Caroline, but he still optimistically thought it would be "all right". Caroline would forgive him as she had done so often before, and Elsa – Elsa would just have to "lump it". So simple are the problems of life to a man like Amyas Crale.

'But I think that that last evening he became really worried. About Caroline, not about Elsa. Perhaps he went to her room and she refused to speak with him. At any rate, after a restless night, he took her aside after breakfast and blurted out the truth. He had been infatuated with Elsa, but it was all over. Once he'd finished the picture he'd never see her again.

'And it was in answer to that that Caroline Crale cried out indignantly: "You and your women!" That phrase, you see, put Elsa in a class with others – those others who had gone their way. And she added indignantly: "Some day I'll kill you."

'She was angry, revolted by his callousness and by his cruelty to the girl. When Philip Blake saw her in the hall and heard her murmur to herself, "It's too cruel!" it was of Elsa she was thinking.

'As for Crale, he came out of the library, found Elsa with Philip Blake, and brusquely ordered her down to go on with the sitting. What he did not know was that Elsa Greer had been sitting just outside the library window and had overheard everything. And the account she gave later of that conversation was not the true one. There is only her word for it, remember.

'Imagine the shock it must have been to her to hear the truth, brutally spoken!

'On the previous afternoon Meredith Blake has told us that whilst he was waiting for Caroline to leave this room he was standing in the doorway with his back to the room. He was talking to Elsa Greer. That means that she would have been *facing* him and that *she* could see exactly what Caroline was doing over his shoulder – and that she *was the only person who could do so*.

'She saw Caroline take that poison. She said nothing, but she remembered it as she sat outside the library window.

'When Amyas Crale came out she made the excuse of wanting a pullover, and went up to Caroline Crale's room to look for that poison. Women know where other women are likely to hide things. She found it, and being careful not to obliterate any fingerprints or to leave her own, she drew off the fluid into a fountain-pen filler.

'Then she came down again and went off with Crale to the Battery garden. And presently, no doubt, she poured him out some beer and he tossed it down in his usual way.

'Meanwhile, Caroline Crale was seriously disturbed. When she saw Elsa come up to the house (this time really to fetch a pullover), Caroline slipped quickly down to the Battery garden and tackled her husband. What he is doing is shameful! She won't stand for it! It's unbelievably cruel and hard on the girl! Amyas, irritable at being interrupted, says it's all settled – when the picture is done he'll send the girl packing! "*It's all settled – I'll send her packing. I tell you.*"

'And then they hear the footsteps of the two Blakes, and Caroline comes out and, slightly embarrassed, murmurs something about Angela and school and having a lot to do, and by a natural association of ideas the two men judge the conversation they have overheard refers to *Angela*, and "I'll send her packing" becomes "I'll see to her packing."

'And Elsa, pullover in hand, comes down the path, cool and smiling, and takes up the pose once more.

'She has counted, no doubt, upon Caroline's being suspected and the coniine bottle being found in her room. But Caroline now plays into her hands completely. She brings down some iced beer and pours it out for her husband.

'Amyas tosses it off, making a face and says: "Everything tastes foul today."

'Do you not see how significant that remark is? *Everything* tastes foul? Then there has been something else *before* that beer that has tasted unpleasant and the taste of which is *still in his mouth*. And one other point. Philip Blake speaks of Crale's staggering a little and wonders "if he has been drinking." But that slight stagger was the *first sign of the coniine working*, and that means *that it had already been administered to him some time before Caroline brought him the iced bottle of beer*.

'And so Elsa Greer sat on the grey wall and posed and, since she must keep him from suspecting until it was too late, she talked to Amyas Crale brightly and naturally. Presently she saw Meredith on the bench above and waved her hand to him and acted her part even more thoroughly for his behalf.

'And Amyas Crale, a man who detested illness and refused to give in to it, painted doggedly on till his limbs failed and his speech thickened, and he sprawled there on that bench, helpless, but with his mind still clear.

'The bell sounded from the house and Meredith left the bench to come down to the Battery. I think in that brief moment Elsa left her place and ran across to the table and dropped the last few drops of the poison into the beer glass that held that last innocent drink. (She got rid of the dropper on the path up to the house – crushing it to powder.) Then she met Meredith in the doorway.

'There is a glare there coming in out of the shadows. Meredith did not see very clearly – only his friend sprawled in a familiar position and saw his eyes turn from the picture in what he described as a malevolent glare.

'How much did Amyas know or guess? How much his conscious mind knew we cannot tell, but his hand and his eye were faithful.'

Hercule Poirot gestured towards the picture on the wall.

'I should have known when I first saw that picture. For it is a very remarkable picture. It is the picture of a murderess painted by her victim – it is the picture of a girl watching her lover die . . .'

Chapter 5

Aftermath

In the silence that followed – a horrified, appalled silence, the sunset slowly flickered away, the last gleam left the window where it had rested on the dark head and pale furs of the woman sitting there.

Elsa Dittisham moved and spoke. She said:

'Take them away, Meredith. Leave me with M. Poirot.'

She sat there motionless until the door shut behind them. Then she said: 'You are very clever, aren't you?'

Poirot did not answer.

She said: 'What do you expect me to do? Confess?'

He shook his head.

Elsa said:

'Because I shall do nothing of the kind! And I shall admit nothing. But what we say here, together, does not matter. Because it is only a question of your word against mine.'

'Exactly.'

'I want to know what you are going to do?'

Hercule Poirot said:

'I shall do everything I can to induce the authorities to grant a posthumous free pardon to Caroline Crale.'

Elsa laughed. She said: 'How absurd! To be given a free pardon for something you didn't do.' Then she said: 'What about me?'

'I shall lay my conclusion before the necessary people. If they decide there is the possibility of making out a case against you then they may act. I will tell you in my opinion there is not sufficient evidence – there are only inferences, not facts. Moreover, they will not be anxious to proceed against any one in your position unless there is ample justification for such a course.'

Elsa said:

'I shouldn't care. If I were standing in the dock, fighting for my life – there might be something in that – something alive – exciting. I might – enjoy it.'

'Your husband would not.'

She stared at him.

'Do you think I care in the least what my husband would feel?'

'No, I do not. I do not think you have ever in your

life cared about what any other person would feel. If
you had, you might be happier.'

She said sharply:

'Why are you sorry for me?'

'Because, my child, you have so much to learn.'

'What have I got to learn?'

'All the grown-up emotions – pity, sympathy, understanding. The only things you know – have ever known
– are love and hate.'

Elsa said:

'I saw Caroline take the coniine. I thought she meant
to kill herself. That would have simplified things. And
then, the next morning, I found out. He told her that
he didn't care a button about me – he *had* cared, but it
was all over. Once he'd finished the picture he'd send
me packing. She'd nothing to worry about, he said.

'And she – was sorry for me . . . Do you understand
what that did to me? I found the stuff and I gave it to
him and I sat there watching him die. I've never felt
so alive, so exultant, so full of power. I watched him
die . . .'

She flung out her hands.

'I didn't understand that I was killing *myself* – not
him. Afterwards I saw her caught in a trap – and that
was no good either. I couldn't hurt her – she didn't
care – she escaped from it all – half the time she
wasn't there. She and Amyas both escaped – they

went somewhere where I couldn't get at them. But they didn't die. *I* died.'

Elsa Dittisham got up. She went across to the door. She said again:

'I died . . .'

In the hall she passed two young people whose life together was just beginning.

The chauffeur held open the door of the car. Lady Dittisham got in and the chauffeur wrapped the fur rug round her knees.